TOOTH AND BLADE

JULIAN BARR

Published by Julian Barr in 2019.

www.jbarrauthor.com

ISBN: 978-0-6487310-0-9 (pbk)
ISBN: 978-0-6487310-1-6 (ebook)

PRAISE FOR JULIAN BARR'S WRITING

"Get lost in a world of magic, myth and monsters... Barr has deftly woven a story featuring gods, magic and Nordic myth." – Tracy M. Joyce

"Beautifully set in a Viking style fantasy world, Julian's done his research and it shows." – Chelle Vess, Amazon Reviewer

"This is a great read for anyone who loves seeing the misty times of legend turned into a driving adventure." – Mawson, Amazon Reviewer

"It was easy to feel the glory and the awe of the gods." – Eleni, Goodreads Reviewer

ALSO BY JULIAN BARR

Ashes of Olympus Trilogy

The Way Home

The Ivory Gate

The Seven Hills (Coming 2020)

Tooth And Blade

Previously published in three parts:

Foundling

Between Worlds

Well of Fate

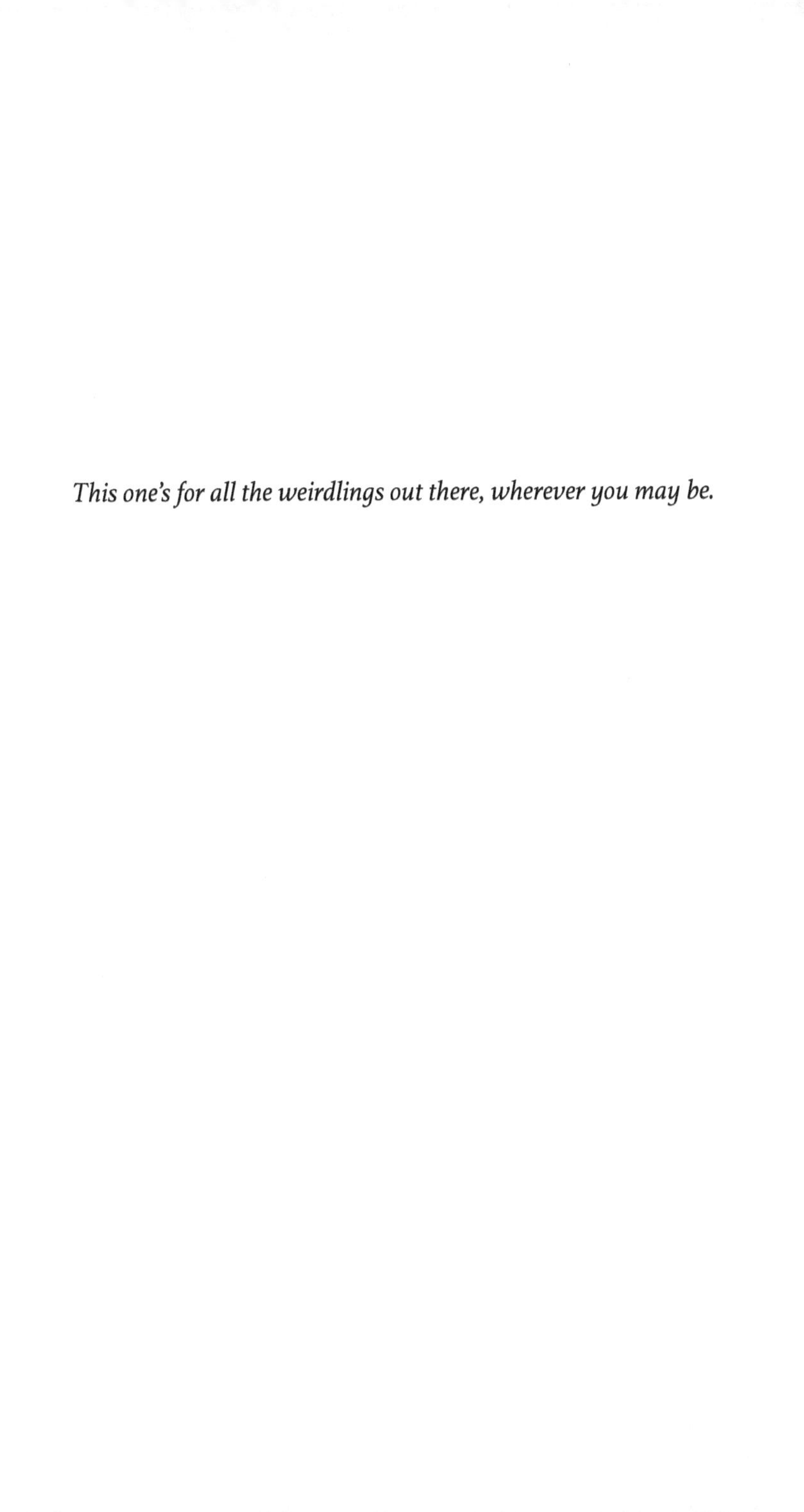

This one's for all the weirdlings out there, wherever you may be.

PART I

FOUNDLING

Brothers shall fight
And slay each other
Sister's children
Shall ruin kinship...
Age of the axe, age of the sword
Shields broken
Age of the winds, age of the wolf
Ere the world falls
No man shall
Spare another.
– Völuspá

TEETH

"They aren't like our kind, Dóta. They are beasts."

My mother's warning echoed through my head, but it would not stop me. I tiptoed through our cave, my path lit by glowing mushrooms which clung to the walls. Módor's wrath would be great if she caught me near her treasure hoard. She was afraid of what I would find there, the truth of what I was. I pressed my lips together and shook off my fear. No matter the risk, I had to know.

Points of rock jutted from the floor like razors as I edged along the passage. Icy droplets fell from the ceiling and ran down the back of my neck. I shuddered as they crawled down my spine and pulled my sheepskin tighter.

I'm not sure how old I was when I figured out I wasn't like Módor. Perhaps it was the day I stumbled and cut my palm on a rock. My blood had run hot and dripped to the ground. Módor had stroked my face to comfort me and for the first time I realized her touch gave me shivers. Then she traced her long nail over the wound and licked it. For an instant her eyes glowed like coals. "There now," she had said. "Nothing to fear, my girl." And Módor had smiled with pointed teeth.

I pressed my way through the jagged gap in the wall which led to Módor's treasure chamber. Módor had chosen a special chamber for her spoils, lit by a spear-shaft of sunlight from a hole in the ceiling far overhead. The light stabbed at my eyes and I squeezed them shut for a moment. When they had grown used to the light, I blinked and looked about. The piled gold shone bright and the gems winked like stars. I ignored the silver cauldrons, coins and fire-stones, for glittering trinkets could tell me nothing. In the corner of the chamber I spied what I was after. A pile of tarnished chain mail and bones, all that was left of the man foolish enough to challenge my mother. Time had picked the skeleton clean long ago; only a few slivers of decayed flesh remained. The dead warrior still clutched a great sword. A rusted helm protected his skull.

Hands trembling, I picked up the skull and held it up to the light. Flakes of rust fell away from the helmet to show boar-shapes etched into the metal. The head. It was the head I needed to see, not some rusted bit of iron. I pulled the helmet off and threw it aside. A thrill of fear passed through me as it clanked to the ground. My brother's ears were delicate. Even the smallest noise would make Grethor bawl for Módor.

Moments passed, but nothing happened. Telling myself it was safe, I peered closer at the skull. The empty sockets stared back at me. I traced my thumb over the teeth and ran my tongue over my own. The warrior's teeth were rounded.

Like mine.

My fears became truth. A beast, that's what I was. A child of men.

I set the skull down upon the floor, bent to study the

body. To judge by the length of the man's leg-bones, he was taller than most, though he was a dwarf compared to Módor and Grethor. Would I grow to that height? At sixteen, I sensed my growing was done but couldn't be sure. Another reason to learn more about my kind. The warrior's mail was crusted with brown and rotted tatters of linen still clung to the skeleton. Clothing, I knew. Grethor had told me once how the creatures of the world above wore a kind of second hide as I wore my sheepskin.

The sunlight caught on something shiny beside the corpse. Without thinking I reached for it and held it up to the light. It was a small disc of polished amber hanging from a rotted leather cord, some kind of amulet. No mere trinket, this. Men must have crafted it in another age, so the gods would protect them. Some of the grime fell away as I rubbed the amulet between my fingers and light shot through veins of yellow in the amber. It was as though the amulet held the sun, waiting to escape. A pretty thing. Perhaps I should put it back? Some instinct told me no; it belonged to me. I slipped it inside my sheepskin. The amulet lay warm against my chest. The feeling was delicious in the coldness of the cave. It had lain hidden under the corpse so long, nobody would miss it. I hoped.

"Well. Hello, Dóta."

I whirled to find Grethor's yellow-green eyes staring down at me. His mottled skin flushed dark and his bitter smell filled the cavern. Under his arm Grethor carried his old leather sack. He hissed. "What are you up to?"

"Nothing." The guilt pressed down upon my shoulders, but I forced myself to stand tall. Had he seen me take the amulet?

"Nothing, eh?" Big Brother's forked tongue flicked from the corner of his mouth. "Thought you'd peek at Módor's hoard, I guess. Ought to be more careful. You know how fiercely Módor guards her gold." He pointed at the scars on his cheek and smirked.

My eyes flicked to the skeleton. "Humans like it too." The words spilled from my mouth without thought.

His pointed ears pricked up. "And what do you know of humans?"

I tried not to cringe and held my shoulders square. My brother could be cruel as Loki and rough as Thor when the mood took him, but I would not quake. "Nothing," I said.

Smugness filled his face. "Tell Módor, I should. Not right to go poking through her things. One shout from me and she'll peel the hide from your bones." Grethor rasped with laughter. "She could sew me a new bag from it." He thrust the sack at me.

I caught it. "No. Don't tell her."

"And what'll you give me if I keep my tongue still?"

My hands curled into fists. "What do I have to give, Grethor?" The only thing I owned was my sheepskin—and now the amulet. And my brother wasn't getting them.

He scratched his chin with one of his claws. "A song, sweet sister."

I released a slow breath. "A song."

"Just like when we were little."

"You were never little."

He shrugged. "Young, then. The bad dreams plague me now as they did then."

I blinked. "Still?"

Grethor flinched. "Dreams of fire and flashing swords and the man who grips like iron. He comes to rip and tear. One of his kind." He glanced at the warrior's skeleton and shuddered. "Every night he comes, since you stopped singing me to sleep. Remember how we'd cuddle?"

I did remember. The earliest thing I could recall was Grethor curled up next to me in the night. It had been nice, when we were children. But as he grew and his muscles thickened, Grethor would squeeze me like a toy until my bones would crack. I would wake to find bruises and that was not so nice. "I can't, Grethor. Not anymore. You need to learn to sleep on your own."

Grethor lowered his head. "Such a pretty voice you have. Soft. And I don't want you to get into trouble with Módor..."

Breath caught in my chest. It was hard to say no to Grethor. "All right. If you want."

Grethor's face split into a grin and his teeth were like needles. "Good. Walk with me, Dóta. My belly's gurgling. I'm going above to get me some meat." He pulled the sack from my hands. As we left the chamber, I glanced at the corpse one last time. The dead man's smile was not so fearsome now.

In silence we wound through the passageways. Grethor twisted left and right to squeeze through the narrow gaps in the rock. He was massive as a frost giant, but could press himself through fine cracks. We made our way down to the chamber where he could enter the underground river. Big Brother leapt over the rocks while I stumbled. His eyes were made for the gloom.

The sound of rushing water filled my ears and the rock floor grew slick under my feet. Beneath the river's surface I could just see the entrance to the underwater tunnel which would take Grethor to the world above.

He laid his clawed hands on my shoulders and they were clammy. "Be good to old Módor and I might bring you back a nice new hide to warm you. And more than that. I'll bring you back more tales of the world above. Of the sky, trees, animals." He leaned close and murmured in my ear. "Of humans, even."

My heartbeat grew faster. "When will you be back?"

He shrugged. "When I'm back." Grethor drew me to him and sniffed my hair. It was something he'd done ever since he was a child, though I'd never felt the urge to mimic him. Was it because we were not the same kind? Grethor slid into the river, treaded water for a moment. He opened his eyes wide and green fire kindled in them. The light on the water cast shimmers upon the roof of the hollow and then he dived and took the light with him.

KIN

I STARED at the ripples Grethor left behind as my eyes read-justed. Talking to Grethor always wearied me, made me feel... wrong, somehow. I had to get clean, so I loosened my sheepskin and let it drop. I pulled off the amulet and tucked it away beneath the hide. If Módor caught me with it, there was no guessing how she would respond. I made sure it was hidden and then stepped into the pool. Icy water flowed over my body. The chill was sharp, but I embraced it. The waters would cleanse me of Grethor's stench, for a time. As soon as the thought passed through my mind, guilt gnawed at me. He was my brother. Grethor kept my secrets and gave me hides from the world above. And he brought me tales. Without him I'd be cold and exposed and I would know nothing. So why did he make me feel as though adders slithered on my skin? I stepped dripping from the water, crouched and hugged myself. My teeth clacked together, I was trembling so hard. Bathing in frigid water was a foolish thing to do. Still, I felt better for it.

Perhaps the sacred amulet would share some of its warmth with me. I was about to pull it from beneath my sheepskin when I heard Módor's footsteps coming up the passageway. I froze. She was coming, of course she was.

Módor stepped into the chamber and fixed a cool stare upon me. "Dóta."

"Módor." I did my best not to look guilty.

"Where is Grethor?"

"Hunting."

"Good." She ran a hand through her long curls. "I'd speak with you alone." Módor sat down by the river. She held her long knife. The blade was carved from bone and gleamed white in the shadows.

I bit the inside of my cheek. "What did I do?"

She cocked her head. A jagged fang was just visible behind her smile. "Why don't you tell me?"

"I..." A lump grew in my throat. Every part of me wanted to dive beneath my sheepskin and hide, but if I lifted it Módor would see I had stolen the amulet. "How did you know?"

"Your smell, child. Your scent is all over my treasure chamber."

"Oh."

Her eyes narrowed. "My gold, is that what you were after?"

I shook my head. Módor would be angry that I had gone to peek at the body, but would erupt in fury if she thought I touched her gold. "You told me once of the man who came to slay you, that his bones still lay there. I wanted to see."

Módor hissed—in anger or triumph, I could not be sure. "What is there to see? He came for my gold and gems. Found them, too. And then I found him." She tensed and stared at the river for a moment. I turned and glimpsed a ripple of movement on the surface. Her hand darted out and snatched a fish from beneath the water. The creature thrashed, fighting to get free of Módor's grip. She raised the fish over her head and slapped it three times against the rocky floor. The crack of bones shattering filled the chamber and the fish struggled no more. Módor stuck her finger into the fish's gill. With her long claw she opened it from the top of the head to the mouth. She passed me her knife and I knew my task. I pressed the blade into the fish's belly, slit it open and prized out the entrails.

Módor cut away a strip of bloody flesh, sniffed it and popped it in her mouth. "Mm. Good. Have some."

The fish's eye stared up at me, empty of life. My stomach grumbled. I hadn't realized how hungry I was. Knife in hand, I cut myself a slice smaller than Módor's and held it up to my nostrils. It was important to sniff your food before you ate it, Módor had taught me. It still smelled of life, promised to make a good meal. I bit into the flesh and crunched the bones. Módor swallowed her portions whole; I had to chew mine with my round teeth or I'd choke. The juices ran down my chin and I licked my lips.

"So tell me, child," said Módor. "What did you want with the dead?"

No point hiding what I knew. Not anymore. "The truth. I'm one of them, aren't I?" I looked down, shoulders hunched. "A human."

Módor put down her morsel of fish and studied my face. "Look into the pool."

That wasn't what I'd expected. I paused for a moment at the water's edge before I looked. Módor leaned over behind me. In the mirror of the waters, I compared our faces. My snub nose poked out of my face, nothing like the slits of her nostrils. My hair was muddy and tangled like tree roots, while hers was a cascade of emerald. My ears like round shells, hers pointed. Where Módor's face was lean and hard, mine was round and soft. A beast's face, with the stain of blood on my chin.

"Do you know what I see?" said Módor.

"What?"

"Eyes for spying and teeth to devour and no matter if mine are pointed. I come from somewhere else, yes. But we're the same."

If only that were true. "Módor, where did I come from, if you didn't birth me?"

Módor was silent for a long moment. "The shivering woods. Near the man-village. I found you there sixteen winters ago. Out hunting, I was. Chasing a hare through the mist. Your brother, he was a bit over a year old then, still clinging to my back like a newborn. That's when I heard you. A squalling babe, left in the woods. I couldn't see you, the fog was so heavy, but it wasn't hard to trace your scent. You stank like a midden. Your swaddling was soaked when I found you. A little thing, face all squashed. Your hide so thin and pale I could see through it. Blood still pulsed through your veins. And it shouldn't have."

"Huh?"

"You'd been left alone in the dark of winter, Dóta—must have been lying there for a day or more. A human babe should have perished and fed the ravens. Not you, though. Not you. The gods spared you for a reason."

I didn't know what to make of that, so I left it aside. "What happened next?"

"Little Grethor slid off my back for a closer look, started poking and prodding you with his stubby little claws. He sniffed those soft hairs on the top of your head. And you showed not a bit of fear. Your hollering stopped and with those tiny fingers you reached for him. And you smiled. Like attracts like. That's how I knew what you were."

My next words came out as a whisper. "And what am I?"

Módor smiled. "Mine. My little Dóta, now and always. It was fate."

I blinked back tears. "But... Who left me there? Why?"

Módor growled, low and soft. "I've told you before. Humans aren't like our kind. They have no love for anybody, not even their own. So I took you in. Raised you as my child with dear Grethor. We are kin, you and I. What does it matter if we are not of the same flesh? Our little clan is perfect, just the way it is."

"Kin." The word felt strange on my tongue. I had expected Módor to cuff me, at least, if she found out what I knew. Perhaps I could risk another question. "But my birth parents. Who were they—who are they?"

"Enough!" Módor's eyes flashed. "I've told you all I can. No more questions about those creatures, I can't bear it."

"But—"

"Enough, I said." Menace filled her voice and I knew I'd gone too far. "They left you behind, went on with their days —why should you care who they were? Humans are beasts, Dóta, destroyers and usurpers. They hunt down our kind. If they had their way, they'd slay us all. Don't you see? I rescued you." She fell silent for a moment. "Hold up your hand."

"What?"

"Do as I say."

I obeyed. She held up her hand and pressed it against mine. Her palm was scaly and rough. My nails were ragged and chewed, while hers tapered into elegant points. "I have no claws," I said.

Módor picked up her knife and stared at the blade, still wet. I tensed, but then she pressed the handle of the knife into my hand. "This will be your claw."

My hoard of words ran empty. That morning I had owned nothing but my sheepskin. Now I had a weapon and an amulet.

"Promise me, Dóta. Ask no more questions and stay away from them. Let me and your brother keep you safe."

"I promise, Módor." I ground my teeth. Even then, I knew it wasn't a promise I could keep.

Módor's eyes shone. "My child." She put her arms around me and pulled me into a cold embrace.

In the days to come, I would look back on that moment and see my mother's lies. Módor could make her eyes shine like Grethor's, but a monster sheds no tears.

WHISPERS

ONCE I WATCHED a spider toying with a beetle caught in its web. The spider was in no hurry to devour its prey. It was content to hang on a thread and watch through cold black eyes, savoring the terror of its next meal. Why should it hurry? The beetle's hard shell would crack between the spider's jaws soon enough. For what seemed an age the beetle struggled against its fetters. If it had a voice, it might have screamed or begged for mercy, but a spider has none. When the beetle grew still, the hunter wearied of the game at last and feasted upon its prize. I might have saved the beetle. All I needed to do was break the spider's web. But who was I to change destiny? Someday it would have ended up in another creature's belly. The weak live to feed the strong and that is the way of things. All of us are bound by fate and nobody has the power to escape. Or so I was taught; I stopped believing it after I stepped out of the dark.

Sleep did not come after my talk with Módor. I rolled onto my side. Too hot to lay wrapped in pelts, too cold without them. Mine was the smoothest patch of earth in our cave, yet I could find no comfort. My mind was a wagon of thoughts jostling against one another. Módor had warned me against voicing questions, but in my head I could ask what I wished. Who were my birth parents? Did I cause them such dismay that they left me behind? What were humans really like? Did they eat as other creatures ate? And why were they so cruel to Módor's kind? If I was a beast like them, would I become as wicked? What if I was wicked already? I was a thief, after all, for I had stolen Módor's amulet. The gods spared me for a reason, my mother had said. But what could it be? My own blood-kin had found no reason to keep me. Why would the gods of Asgard care whether I lived or died?

As soon as I asked myself the question, the amulet grew warm against my chest. It was as though the amulet had heard me. How absurd—I might have laughed at myself. Still, I couldn't resist looking at it once more. I glanced about, squinting in the dark. Grethor hadn't yet returned. Far off, Módor shuffled around the treasure chamber at the opposite end of the cave. She murmured loving words to the gold. I pulled the amulet out and stared at it. It swung gently from the leather cord and I could just make out the amber in the dim light. The back of my neck prickled. The disc was like an eye in the dark. I was staring at the amulet and some instinct told me it was staring back.

"Hello?" I whispered, feeling like a fool.

A golden light flickered within the heart of the amber.

My breath quickened. "Can you... hear me?"

The light pulsed like a heartbeat.

I should have been afraid. This amulet held powerful magics and beasts had made it. No good could come of this and yet I could not look away. "What are you?" That wasn't the right question. I took a breath. "Who are you?"

Are you sure you want to know?

The whisper came from the amulet. It echoed inside me, like a voice in a dream. If I were deaf I still would have heard it. Not a harsh rasp like Grethor's, nor did it have Módor's coolness. A flowing voice, dark and sweet as honeyed mead.

"Y-yes."

You are certain? A word can change all.

"A change... I hope so."

Hope. I see precious little of it inside you, dear one. The fire is all but spent.

My words stuck in my throat. I lowered my eyes.

And yet I can breathe upon an ember.

Then the amulet blazed bright. Motes of dust danced in the air. My skin tingled and my hair rippled.

"Tell me your name."

I must know yours first.

"It's Dóta."

The amulet gave what might have been a chuckle. *Is it?*

I frowned. "Your name, now. I gave you mine."

Closer...

After a moment's pause I cupped the amulet against my ear. The light shone through the flesh of my hand, danced upon the walls of the chamber and from the light there came a word. Some tongue beyond my ken and I knew the meaning. It was a word of power. A name, a true name. The name of a goddess. The knowledge gave me shivers. Not the chills I felt at Módor's touch. Hot shivers, like a delicious fever. It blazed in my chest.

The light went out. Only darkness remained.

Remember my name, even if you don't know yours. Remember the fire.

"I shall."

Too late I realized I had spoken aloud. I strained my ears for any sign of Módor. Surely she had seen the light, heard my voice? But no, there was nothing to fear. She continued to croon at her gold as though it were a babe, seeing nothing, hearing nothing. The amulet lay cold in my hand. I bit my lip, tried to steady my breathing. One of the undying ones had spoken to me, had invited me to call upon her.

The splash of water against stone echoed from the other end of the cave. Grethor had returned. I stuffed the amulet under my sheepskin again and lay as still as I could. Perhaps if I pretended to snore, he might leave me alone. But no, he could always sense a lie, could taste it on the air with that forked tongue of his. Silence was my only friend. My brother's toenails clicked against the rocky floor, growing nearer and nearer. He was still dripping from the underground river. I tensed as Grethor approached. He stood over me, so close that I could smell the blood on his breath—he had feasted. His claw brushed against the layers of pelts, ready to rip them back...

"No, Grethor. Let her rest." Módor's voice was hardly more than a murmur. When had she slipped into the chamber?

Grethor snorted. "This one owes me a song."

"Oh? What for?"

Grethor grunted. "Nothing."

"For every giving there is a taking. How can she owe something for nothing?"

Big Brother growled a warning. "Módor, you can't tell me—"

"You are my son," she snarled. "I will tell you what I want, now and always."

Grethor was silent for a moment and I could almost smell the rage smoldering inside him. I quivered, expecting him to strike. But he answered with a sullen, "Yes, Módor."

I swallowed a sigh of relief.

"Come with me. We have much to speak of."

Grethor yawned, his jaws wide. "I've a full belly and I'm bone-weary. Those farmers gave me more fun than I expected." He belched. "We'll talk on the morrow."

"Now," Módor snapped. "Come."

Grethor's teeth ground together as he stomped after her. I waited for three heartbeats, then got up and tiptoed after them to the treasure chamber. I pressed my ear against the rock wall just outside the entrance. They were too busy hissing at one another to hear me.

"She knows, then?" said Grethor. "You're sure?"

"I told her."

"How much?"

"Enough."

"Why would you do a fool thing like that?"

"You left me little choice. You catch her gawking at the bones and what do you do? You go off *hunting*."

"Can't keep my eyes on her all day, can I? And I need to crunch a bit of sinew now and then. What good are fishies? A decent haunch of meat, that's what I need, else my teeth will go dull." He laughed.

"There will always be prey, Grethor, but there's only one Dóta. And now she..."

"What?"

Módor hissed. "She's started asking questions."

Grethor spat. "What of it?"

"You were meant to guide her. Be her big brother."

"So? I will."

Módor paused. "Go on."

"Girl's clever. Too clever, you ask me. No way we could have kept it from her forever. I reckon she half-knew already. Better this way, isn't it?"

"How?"

"She's one of us? Fine. Let her be one of us. I'll teach her to hunt. No tricks. No lies."

"She does have her claw…" said Módor.

"You wait. Knife in hand, her blood screaming for the kill? She'll care nothing for humans. Not when she knows how to live."

"She is young. And her hide won't turn iron like yours."

"We'll start small. A stag, maybe."

"The stag becomes deadly when fear takes it."

"Good. First kill ought to mean something."

Módor growled a warning. "I've not given her sixteen years to have her gored and trampled."

"Fine. Rabbits, then. Couple of tasty mouthfuls for supper. Don't fear. Little Sister is safe with me, long as she minds what I say."

Módor considered for a moment. "Yes. It is fated. Watch her. No drifting off this time, understand?"

"Yes, Módor." Grethor paused. "There's a shaft under the water which will take us above ground. She is allowed to get her feet wet, yes?"

I'd heard enough. I padded back to my spot on the floor, closed my eyes and willed sleep to come for me, but of course it wouldn't. When morning came, I was going to the surface.

A smile bloomed upon my lips. I feared, of course, for I knew little of the world above and yet my joy was greater. Come the morrow, I'd feel the wind on my face.

KNIFE

"Dóta? Dóta, awaken." Módor's sharp claw prodded me through the pelts.

I struggled to force my eyes open. They were crusted and my limbs felt as though they were made of lead. It seemed I'd only just gone to sleep and then a night-spirit had tormented my slumber. The dream was full of whispered names and skull-faced warriors. There was something I had to discover, something important...

Módor grabbed me by the shoulder and I jerked awake. "Today is the day, child. Your first kill. You're going above with Grethor."

I tried to look surprised. "Oh. Why?"

Módor cocked her head. "To get supper, of course." She laughed. "It's all part of growing, of living in the world. You'll let another creature nourish you, fill you up. Make its strength your own, make its blood run into yours."

I frowned. "Why can't you take me?"

"Because..." Módor licked her hand and smoothed back my hair. "The test isn't just for you, child."

I sat up. "What do you—"

"Questions, questions. Here. Eat. You'll have need of strength." She thrust a hunk of fish at me. I tore a strip of it away with my teeth. The fish was chewy and full of tiny bones, not juicy like yesterday's meal. "You'll taste better fare. Tonight you will tell me of what you see up there. But stay away from the man-village." She gave me a weak smile. "Come back to me." Módor gave me one last look, then turned and stalked off to her treasure chamber. No farewells.

I went to the furthest corner of our cave to squat and then to the chamber with the river.

There I found Grethor already waiting for me. He scratched at the patch of dry scales on his upper chest. "You're here, then. About time. Got your claw?"

I held up the knife.

"Good. I go first," said Grethor. "I'll light the way."

"All right," I said and hoped my fear didn't show.

"Stay close." He stepped into the water and his eyes blazed with greenish light. "Come on, what's keeping you?"

For a moment I paused, icy water flowing over my toes and then I chided myself. No way would Grethor have a reason to call me coward. I shed my sheepskin and it crumpled to the floor.

How little I knew in that moment. Nowadays I can name many things I would find in the world above. Yet much lay beyond my ken in the years before my awakening.

Taking a deep breath, I dived.

The chill bit at my flesh. I kicked and held my arms before me, my dagger clenched between my teeth. We aimed toward a dark fissure in the rock which sucked in water like a mouth. The current drew me to the bottom. Ahead, Grethor pulled himself through the water, sleek and graceful as a seal. The light of his eyes was like a beacon in the black water.

As we swam deeper, red shapes poked their heads from holes in the rock. Adders. They bared their needle-like fangs, but recoiled when they saw it was Grethor swimming toward them, perhaps sensing he was the deadlier hunter.

Deeper we swam until the rocky maw swallowed us. Grethor kicked hard, finding fierce joy in the waters. He surged forward, leaving me behind. Then he rounded a bend in the tunnel ahead and his light vanished. I kicked to catch up, but Grethor was the stronger swimmer by far. My elbow slammed against the wall and anguish pierced my arm. Panic rose within and my lungs started to smolder. I beat down the fear, kicked with all my strength.

The tunnel belched me out and then there was light all around me. The sun shone like a silver penny through the eddies. The waters of the world above were warmer than those of the cave. I swam for the air.

Grethor was nowhere. He must have already gotten out of the water.

I was near the surface when a flash of crimson streaked past. Something slimy seized my leg, clung like iron fetters. A blood-red adder had coiled around my calf. The adder opened its mouth wide, ready to plunge its dagger-teeth into me.

My amulet floated free, the leather thong hanging in the water.

I grabbed the knife in my hand and struck at the adder, my hand clumsy and useless in the water. The blade didn't pierce its hide. The adder's teeth flashed and it bit down upon my leg. Pain tore through my calf. Without thinking, I opened my mouth to scream. Nothing came out but bubbles curling to the surface. The creature clamped its jaws upon the meat of my calf and held tight. My vision blurred. The adder stared up at me with a yellow eye, the black pupil wide with pleasure.

Rage filled me. I would not fill the belly of some lowly creature. With the last of my strength I pushed my blade into the adder's eye. Dark blood clouded the water. The pressure on my leg vanished. I kicked free.

As soon as my head broke the surface I gulped air. A rotting log bobbed past and it saved my life. Every part of me was spent. If I had nothing to cling to, the waters would have taken me.

I retched. Bitter water spewed from my mouth until I was left weak and shaking. My arms remained wrapped around the log. I blinked rapidly, trying to get my eyes to adjust to the light. Gods, it was blinding. The knife remained in my hand, ready for another attack. One heart-beat passed, then two. The dark waters of the lake were smooth as jet. No bubbles disturbed the surface, nor was there any sign of movement beneath.

It took a little time for my breaths to become less ragged. I peered to the lake's edge, judged it wasn't too far. Just a few kicks later, I let go of the log and fell onto the muddy shore. No point trying to get up until I had recovered my strength. Blood dribbled from the wound on my leg. My elbow throbbed, already turning purple where I had smashed it against the tunnel wall. Helpless as a beached whale, I stared upward.

Blue. Endless blue. I shielded my eyes against the glare, my breakfast lurching in my belly. Módor had spoken of the sky, but nothing could have prepared me for the openness, the emptiness. No roof over my head, just the sun staring down. The feeling of exposure rankled me. The wind made my skin tingle. After so long in the darkness of Módor's cave, it would take little for me to burn. Time to move. I needed a safe place to lick my wounds.

I groaned, tried to push myself upright with my arm. Pain spiked from my elbow, but it could take my weight. It was bruised, I decided, but not broken. I stood slowly, tested my ability to stand. My calf gave a twinge of protest and blood leaked, but the leg didn't give out. I limped to the edge of the forest. The darkness of the wood promised shelter, so I pressed my way between the trees. The branches scraped against my skin and my bare feet slipped on the wet leaves, but I savored the coolness of the air. In the heart of a clearing I saw a great pine tree and its shade beckoned me. I leaned against it, the bark rough against my soft hide. I was a mess of cuts and bruises, but it felt safer in the trees.

I pinched the wound on my leg and after a few moments the blood ceased to ooze. Turning at an awkward angle, I inspected the bite. From what I could tell, the adder's tooth hadn't sunk as deep as I'd thought. No puckering around the wound and the flesh showed no sign of corruption.

Perhaps the adder's tooth held no poison. I wondered at the creature's fate, decided it must have slunk back to its hole to die. Satisfaction filled me at the knowledge. My first kill. The wretched creature had thought me a weakling, but I had proven myself. I'd emerged from my first battle battered and bruised, but not broken. Perhaps I would make a hunter yet.

I breathed deep, savoring a strange scent on the wind. In time, I would realize it was not one scent but many: the smells of alder wood and pine, of juniper and lingonberry. At the time, though, all I knew was that the scent was wild and dangerous and free. Trees loomed taller than giants, waving their limbs as though in greeting. The coolness of the breeze was sharp, like my knife.

Over my head small birds flitted about from bough to bough and their warbling filled the wood. I blinked: strange to think of it, but I'd never seen a flying creature before. To me it seemed like the dark sorcery of the hanged god. My belly grumbled and I decided the birds looked tasty. Barely any meat on them, but together they would be more than a mouthful. I crouched, ready to pounce, but they flew beyond my grasp in a flutter of wings. Perhaps there would be eggs to snatch if I climbed a tree. The throbbing of my leg warned me that was a bad notion.

The wind picked up and moaned through the trees like a wraith. Left and right I peered. It was all so much greater than I'd thought it would be. A chill touched me. I was alone in a world that had no end. My blood pounded through my ears and I swallowed my dread. Wasn't this what I'd wanted so long? To see raw sunlight, feel the air on my skin? No rocky walls to protect or hold me. No Módor waiting to snap at me if I breathed wrong, no Grethor sneering at me. I flushed with annoyance. Whatever else I might have felt, Módor had told him to stay with me.

"Grethor?" I called. My voice echoed through the woods, mocking me. No answer came. I gnawed my lip and reached for the amulet against my chest, only to find it gone. My eyes widened. For the first time, I felt truly naked. "Grethor?"

A low, gurgling laugh came from behind. "Wondered how long it would take." Grethor stood from the brush that had concealed him. He held up his hand. The amulet dangled from his claws. It flashed in the sun. Grethor's face twisted into a cruel smile which stretched the scars on his cheek. "Looking for this, thief?"

THIEF

In the shadow of the pine, Grethor and I glared at each other, our hands curled into fists. Grethor still held the amulet by its cord. A hush fell upon the wood. I could hear the drip of water on leaves. The forest was holding its breath, waiting.

"Where did you get that, Grethor?"

"Found it, I did."

"Where?"

"On the shore. Not too far from your footprints. You'll have to learn to cover your tracks if you're going to live, sweet sister. Those soft little soles will lead all sorts of nasties right to you." He snorted. "How'd this pretty little amulet get up here, I wonder?"

"I—I don't—"

"Liar." His eyes flashed. "You stole it from Módor's hoard, didn't you? I saw you in there, crouching over the bones."

"It's mine. It... I can't explain it. Soon as I saw it, I knew the amulet belonged with me. Módor said the gods chose—"

"Hah!" Grethor laughed. "So now the truth comes out—you think you're better than me. Módor reckons you're one of us. Dunno why. You're nothing but a thief. You know it, I know it."

I made a swipe for it and he dodged away with a mocking laugh. "Give it back, Grethor," I said. "It's mine."

"Is it? I don't think so... Poor Módor will be so upset when she finds out. Her precious little Dóta..."

"No. You can't tell her. Please."

"Should have sung me a song, shouldn't you?" He sniggered. "You had your chance."

"That's not fair. Módor told you not to wake me, it's not my fault."

Grethor's eyes narrowed. "So you were awake. How much did you hear?"

"Not a lot, I swear." I did my best not to tremble.

He stared at me through narrowed eyes. His tongue flicked out, tasting the air for a lie. Then he shrugged. "Doesn't matter what you heard. We both know you're not one of us. Always asking questions about humans, aren't you?" He sniffed the amulet. "Thing reeks of man-flesh. It reeks of you."

"Probably it does." I folded my arms and willed my heart to slow down. "It's true, Grethor. I am one of them. But that doesn't mean we aren't kin... Does it? Módor said."

Grethor released a slow breath, but said nothing.

"Besides," I said, "I'm a hunter, good as you. See this?" I pointed to the bite on my leg. "An adder attacked me in the water. It's dead now."

"So?" He guffawed.

"What do you mean, so?"

"Doesn't mean much, does it? Even a rat will bite when you've got it cornered. You were just saving your own worthless life." He toyed with the amulet and anger rose within me. "You've not stalked your prey, not peeled back the hide and sunk your teeth in. Hot blood down your gullet— that's what hunting is all about. That's what it means to be one of us. You're not there, not yet."

I crossed my arms. "You say so."

Grethor stepped forward and laid a scaly hand under my jaw. "Look up, sweet sister." He tilted my head upward so I had no choice but to look him in the eye: yellow, flecked with green. "There's time for you to prove yourself. Day's not over yet. I've already chosen your first."

I blinked. "My first."

"You can be one of us still." He sniffed the air and I did the same. I smelled nothing but the woods, but his senses were always keener than mine. He found the scent he was looking for and his eyes darkened with pleasure. "Come. Follow me and hush your mouth. Do as I do. Don't want to startle it."

We bent low and scrambled through the underbrush. I did my best to mimic Grethor, who slithered across the ground, hardly making a noise. Every step made me wince. He didn't let go of the amulet and I didn't let go of my knife.

The sun hadn't moved far when we halted at the edge of a clearing. Grethor dropped onto his belly and crept over to a holly bush. I followed and crouched down next to him, pulled the leaves aside and peered into the clearing. There stood... What was it? Some kind of spirit? It glowed orange and yellow, swayed left tond right in the wind. It rippled like water—but waves of heat came from it. The spirit rested atop a pile of fallen sticks, whispered to itself in hisses and crackles. A bitter mist rose from its heart, curled into the air. Then I raised my brows in realization. This was no spirit, this was—

"Fire. Wood's bane," murmured Grethor. "Yeah, that's what it looks like. But that's not why I brought you here." He pointed with a hooked claw. "Look. Sitting by the fire."

I squinted. Through the fire I could just pick out two creatures resting nearby. The first was a four-legged animal tethered to an oak. It was long-eared, shaggy and grey and it chewed upon something. The other creature... I smothered a gasp.

Two round eyes. A snub nose. Golden hairs bristling on its scalp and chin. A beast. Different from me, but just as human as I was. She... No. Something told me this one was a man. He sat on a fallen log, stared into the fire with his eyes half-closed. The human shape was almost like Grethor's, but smaller, weaker, not a scale on him. The stranger wore a kind of second skin, a coarse grey layer of wool. Clothing. I cocked my head, for I'd never seen a clothed body before. It seemed almost absurd. Even from our hiding spot the stench of dried sweat trapped beneath the woolens wafted over us. Around his upper arm the man wore a band of iron.

"Take a good look, thief. One of your kind," said Grethor.

I shook my head. "In flesh only."

"Prove it."

"Huh?"

"Módor wanted you hunting little rabbits, but I've found you something better for your first kill." He jabbed a finger toward the man. "Slay it. Then I'll know you're one of us. Time to choose. The beast's world or ours."

SEETHE

THE MAN STOOD and pulled an axe from his belt. I froze, still hidden behind the bush, but he only held the axe up to the firelight to inspect it. Perhaps he was looking for notches? The blade looked wickedly sharp. On his hip the man carried a dagger with an antler handle. No doubting it, this was a warrior, like the man who had come to slay my mother.

Grethor stared at me, eagerness written across his face.

"He'll cut me in two," I said.

"You've got your knife—or your claw, is it? Doubt this beast will give you much of a fight if you sneak up on it."

The man slipped the axe back into his belt and sat down again. He stretched and yawned.

"Do it," said Grethor in my ear.

Unaware he was being watched, the warrior picked at his teeth with his fingernail. His teeth were yellowish, not pointed like Grethor's. They were like mine.

Sweat pooled on my forehead. My hand was clenched so tightly upon the handle of my knife that my fingers cramped. I bit the inside of my cheek until I tasted blood.

"I can't," I whispered.

"What was that?" said Grethor.

"No!"

The man stood, his ice-blue eyes narrow. He made no move to flee, but his hand fell upon the handle of the axe. "Who's there? Show yourself, outlaw. Face a worthy foe."

"Do it," hissed Grethor, his eyes aflame with wrath. He leapt to his feet and grabbed me by the wrist, wrenched my bruised elbow.

The tethered animal whinnied and the warrior blanched at the sight of Grethor. Then the man glanced back to me. Confusion filled his eyes for a moment and then he turned back to Grethor. He squared his stance, ready to battle.

"Let me go. You're hurting me!" I struggled, but Grethor dragged me into the clearing and advanced upon the man.

"You won't finish it? Fine. Watch." Big Brother gripped my wrist in one hand and reached for the stranger with the other.

The man should have run. Instead he pulled out his axe and the iron glinted in the sun. His eyes remained fixed on Grethor. "Back, troll. Let go of the girl, unless you want a taste of this." He raised the blade, hefted the axe in both hands.

Grethor hissed and made to tear out the warrior's throat. The axe came down upon Grethor's wrist. With a clang that echoed between the pines, the axe-head shattered. The warrior sprang back from Grethor's reach, his lips parted in disbelief. Then he snatched out his dagger from its sheath, snarled at Grethor. "Come on then, you fatherless bastard."

My brother roared and threw me to the ground. I lay winded, too stunned to move.

"Run, girl," said the warrior, his gaze still fixed on Grethor. "I'll hold the beast."

Grethor's laugh was like poison. He swiped at the warrior's arm with his claws. Just a lazy attack; Grethor was playing with him. The man was caught in a snare.

I lay sprawled on the pine needles, my entire body throbbing. A sob shook me. Everything had gone wrong, it was all my fault.

Then I heard the whisper in my mind.

Remember my name. Remember the fire.

I blinked, stunned. The amulet. Lying on the ground before me. Grethor must have dropped it.

I belly-crawled over to the amulet and grabbed it. The amulet grew hot in my fist and calm filled me.

Grethor aimed a savage kick at the warrior's ankle and the man sprawled. His bronze dagger fell point-first into the sod. Shrieking in triumph, Grethor raised his fist, ready to bring it down on the warrior's skull.

And I spoke the name of the goddess.

The flames of the campfire turned yellow, blazed bright as the sun. Hot winds streamed from the fire, made the boughs of the trees quiver.

Grethor still leaned over the warrior, one hand around the man's throat and the other poised to strike.

"Stop him," I whispered to the goddess. "Do whatever you wish, just don't let him do this."

Embers rose from the fire and the wind held no sway over them. They twisted through the air, guided by an unseen hand and they spiraled around Grethor. He released the man and tried to bat them away like fireflies.

The man took advantage of the distraction and crawled backward, panting and rubbing his throat. He plucked up his knife as he went.

Then the embers of the fire gathered around Grethor's head. Through them I could just see his eyes rolling, mad with fear.

"That's enough," I said.

Is it? The voice came from the amulet.

"He's learned his lesson."

I think not.

The lights circling Grethor's head were blinding now. "Help me," he said, real terror in his voice. "Make it stop!"

"Stop it," I said.

Did you not say to do as I wish?

"Yes, but I didn't think—I know he's a brute, but... Just stop this. Now."

I told you my name, dear one. That doesn't make me your thrall.

"But—"

I shall make him hear the suffering of the world—the suffering he has caused.

The embers converged upon Grethor's ears and they swarmed through his earholes into his skull. The power of the gods seethed through Grethor. He clapped his hands to the sides of his head and howled. "No—I'll be good! I can be good." He looked at me, glowing eyes filled with desperation. "Please, Dóta. Make it stop."

"Please—didn't you hear him? He'll change."

Grethor moaned, reeling back from me. It was as though my very words scalded him.

The goddess of the amulet gave no reply. The fire sputtered and died.

The man still lay upon the ground, watching everything.

The tethered animal strained against its rope and brayed with fear. Grethor recoiled from the noise, hands still pressed against his ears. His lips were pulled back, a vision of agony.

With a shrewd look on his face, the man tapped his bronze knife on a rock.

I could barely hear the clink, but Grethor cringed. His eyes shone as though with tears. "What have you done to me?"

"It wasn't me. I swear it wasn't."

Grethor shook his head from side to side and moaned.

"Grethor..." I raised my hand, meant to lay it on his shoulder.

He tore himself from my side. "Don't touch me. You'll never be one of us." His voice ran thick with venom. My brother pointed at the warrior. "And his kind will never accept you. Monster."

His curse pierced me. A chill spread through my heart.

The warrior started to clang the bronze against the rock, louder every time.

Grethor made a feeble effort to reach for him.

The man raised himself to his full height and roared. "Away with you, troll. You've no right to walk my lands."

Grethor turned away from me and loped off through the wood. He vanished between the trees. Only when he was out of sight did I hear him weep. The sound faded to silence.

I turned my head sideways and looked up at the man. He stood still as a runestone, made no move to chase Grethor.

And neither did I.

TRUST

THE WARRIOR and I stared after Grethor for a moment and
then turned to one another. He was tall, so much taller than
me. Up close, his skin wasn't as smooth as it had seemed.
The man kept his eyes on my face, did not look anywhere
else. "Are you hurt?"

I had no response but a hiss. It was a wonder that he did
not bark like a hound, but spoke a tongue within my
knowing.

"Who are you? I thought I knew all the youths around
these parts."

I bared my teeth at him and growled. I had let him live,
but didn't want him near.

The man retreated half a step and sheathed his dagger.
"I mean no harm." He pointed. "But your leg, your arm. Did
the troll do that?"

I grunted and jerked my head to the left. A beast, I told
myself. That's all he was. No need to fear him. Or trust him.

"Let me take a closer look. We don't want the bite to
turn nasty." He bent down in front of me and reached for
my leg.

My wrath was swift as Grethor's. As soon as I saw his hand moving toward my calf, I kneed him in the belly.

The warrior grunted and doubled over with his hands around his middle. He breathed hard for a moment through clenched teeth.

I held my dagger in one hand and the amulet in the other, ready for him to return the blow. I'd rip him with my teeth if he tried to touch me again.

His gaze flicked warily from the bone knife to the amulet. He swallowed as he straightened and then put his hands up as though in surrender. "You're no feckless waif, girl. I'll give you that." He looked me in the eye once more. "I wasn't going to hurt you, honest. But I probably would have done the same if I were you." He held out a hand. "Name's Anskar Aralson. I'm the earl of this shire. Folks call me Wind-Rime. Dóta, that's what it called you, wasn't it?"

I didn't lower the dagger. "Go."

His brow creased. "Eh? Don't fear, Dóta. I'll take you home, get you cleaned up. I'd like to talk to your parents."

"Leave me." I tried to sound dauntless, but still my voice quavered. I backed away, not taking my eyes off the man.

"Where is your father, girl? Your mother?"

I chewed my lip and glared at him. Módor would never take me back, not after what I did to Grethor. The knowledge struck me like a blow to the head. Tears leaked from my eyes and I tried to blink them back. "Gone."

The warrior was silent for a moment. "Another attack—the troll slew them?"

Not knowing what else to do, I nodded.

"And made you its thrall."

I drew in a breath, but it caught in my chest—I'd only heard that word once before, from the goddess. What did it mean? Nothing good, I was certain.

A strange look crossed Anskar's face. It was as though he was in anguish, but I saw nothing to pain him. "I grieve with you. You hear such things in tales, but I never would have believed... That monster will know vengeance." He glanced over to the spot where we had last seen Grethor, then turned back to me. "Let me help, Dóta."

I lowered my knife, just a little.

"Please," he said. "I just need to check your wound. Won't touch you, I promise."

I relaxed my arm, let the blade fall to my side. But I was not such a fool as to let it go.

Anskar bent and examined the puncture on my calf. His mouth hardened in a grim line as he took in the sight. After a heartbeat, he stood. "You were lucky—blood's already thickened. I've seen worse bites. Much worse. Now, some clothes for you."

"Clothes?"

"In my saddlebag, on the donkey." He strode over to the four-legged animal, which brayed in distress. It tried to pull away as he approached, strained upon the rope which tethered it to the tree. Anskar patted the animal, ran his fingers through its mane. "Easy, silly creature, easy. Quite a day we're having, eh? I'll give you a nice rub down tonight. Just calm yourself, all right?" As he spoke the soft words into the donkey's ear, its breathing slowed and its ears no longer stood rigid. "That's it." He reached into the pack strapped on the donkey's back, pulled out the clothes. Anskar held them up and gazed at them for a moment. A smaller version of his own garb, dyed a rich green. Then he sighed and pressed the clothes into my hands. "Here. Just a boy's tunic and breeches, but they'll serve."

I looked down at the bundle of clothing and wrinkled my nose. "Why do I need clothes?"

He rolled his eyes. "Because otherwise you'll be blue as Death herself by nightfall. And gods know I'd feel better if you were dressed."

"Why?"

Anskar's cheeks reddened. "There's a time for walking about with no clothes on and this isn't it. Go on, put them on."

The clothes would protect my pale flesh from the sun, at least. Then I blinked, feeling like a fool. Now it was my turn to blush. "I don't know how."

He scratched his chin. "What, nobody ever taught you to dress yourself?"

"No."

"Oh. Well, then." Anskar cleared his throat. "If I give you a hand, you won't lop it off or seethe a spell over me, will you?"

I took a few breaths, measuring him. The man kept his distance, waiting for my word. No danger in him, I decided. If he was a beast, he was a dumb beast, no more harmful than the donkey. I gave a curt nod, set my amulet and the knife on the ground.

He took the bundle of clothing off my hands. "I, eh, I've never done this before. Arms up?" With some difficulty, he tugged the tunic over my head and pulled my arms through the sleeves. Then he crouched down and held out the breeches, raised his eyebrows.

I raised mine back at him, not sure what he wanted me to do.

"Step into them—there, like that."

He pulled them up and tied a length of cord around my waste. "There. You'll have to learn how to do that yourself." A sudden fear came over him. "You do know how to squat, don't you?"

"I'm not an animal."

"Had to ask. Forgive me." He stood back and looked me up and down, more relaxed now. "Not a bad fit. Odd, they look good on you."

Every part of me felt restricted, too hot. It was almost like wearing my sheepskin in the cave, but it clung to me no matter how I squirmed. I reached for the thing choking my throat and stretched it out, trying to get some air on my skin. "I hate it. It itches."

Anskar shrugged. "I'll see if I can get you a nice kirtle."

"Kirtle?"

"You know, girl's clothes. A dress."

My eyes narrowed in suspicion at his offer.

He cocked his head to the side. "What's the matter?"

"For every giving there is a taking. What do you want from me?"

"Oh!" He gave a bark of laughter. "No need to worry about that. You owe me nothing. Other way around, if anything. You saved my life back there with your magic. Trust me, I've not begun to pay my debt."

If not for me, Grethor would never have stalked the man. But I didn't think this was the time to say so. "Why do you carry boy's clothes?"

Anskar lowered his head. "They were for my son."

"Will he not need them?"

He acted as though he hadn't heard me. "I've no boots for you. But you can ride the donkey, if you want." He strode over to the donkey, unstrapped the load from its back.

"Ride?"

"I want to take you to see a friend of mine. He's wise. Strong. A much greater man than I am. I think he'll know what to do with you—he was a foundling too." He hesitated.

"I'd be your travelling companion, not your master. You need not come, if you choose."

I turned over the offer in my mind. The gloom of Módor's cave seemed far behind me now. And I would find no welcome there. Of that, I was sure. What choice was there? It was not as though I could stay in the woods forever. And something else tugged at me. The yearning to learn more about humans. *Like attracts like.* Grethor had called me a monster, said they would never accept me. What did that make me? A monster among monsters. A spike of anger dug into my heart at the thought, a need to prove Grethor wrong.

I picked up my knife and the amulet. "Very well."

"You need a hand getting on?"

I nodded.

With a grunt, Anskar plucked me up and set me in the saddle. He showed me how to sit on it so I wouldn't slide off like a sack of grain. "Ready, Dóta?"

"I think so." I slipped the amulet over my neck.

He eyed the amulet until I tucked it under my tunic and then he untied the donkey.

"Where are we going?" I said.

Anskar laughed and led the donkey by the hand. "To Valdskali, of course. The Hall of the Wolf. We're going to see the king."

MAGIC

"Do you want to see?"

Little Dóta's eyes grow large. "Really, Módor?"

Módor pauses. "Yes. It is time you learned a few things."

Dóta's heart flails in confusion. The treasure chamber is forbidden. Whenever she looks toward the entrance, Módor growls at her.

"It's all right," says Módor. "You may enter, so long as I say so. You're old enough now that I can trust you. Grethor?" Her voice echoes through the cave. "Where are you?"

Young Grethor stomps into the chamber. "What?" He is already taller than Módor and still growing.

The girl claps her hands. "Módor wants to show us her gold."

"Gold?" Greed flares in Grethor's eyes.

"My gold," says Módor.

"Yeah, yeah. I know."

"Hm. Show me your hands."

Grethor holds up his hands. "Clean." He is just shy of ten and his claws are little more than stubs. Still, they will draw blood when he is riled.

*Módor inspects his hands, frowning. "Come along, then."
Módor holds her hands out to her children. Dóta takes the right.*

*Grethor doesn't take Módor's left. He flicks his tongue out and
then turns away and bounds ahead.*

Módor sighs. "Just like his father. Come along, Dóta."

*The girl tries not to tremble as they approach the entrance to
the chamber. She has wanted to see inside for an age, yet terror
holds her back. How can she want something and be scared of it
at the same time? They step through the gap in the wall and Dóta
gasps. She has never seen sunlight before. This is her first inkling
of the world above. The beam falls upon the mounds of gold and
fills the room with gilded light.*

*Grethor already rolls around in the coins. He grabs handfuls
of gold and casts them into the air. They jingle as they hit the
rocky floor.*

"Grethor." Módor's voice is full of ire.

He ignores her, giggles like a maddened dwarf.

*Dóta glances up at her mother's face. Módor's face is drawn,
like she is about to bare her fangs. "No, Grethor," says Dóta.
"Stop. Módor says no."*

Big Brother glares, then lowers his eyes. "Fine."

*Módor relaxes a little, yet the scent of violence still lingers on
the air. The little girl tries to distract herself, make the moment
pass. Her gaze is drawn to the pile of bones in the corner. "What
is that?"*

*"I'll tell you when you're older. Over here." Módor beckons
Dóta and Grethor over to the opposite side of the chamber. She
picks up two coins, rubs them between her fingers and then
presses one into Dóta's soft palm. "Do you feel it? This came from
Midgard—this middle earth. Gold is the blood of this world."*

*Dóta climbs into Módor's lap and squeezes the coin as hard as
she can. It is dull and cold as stone.*

"Dead now," Módor says, still looking at the gold. "Dried up."

She is far away, lost in memory. "Midgard is a cold place. But where I'm from, living gold flows through the veins of the world."

Dóta places a hand on Módor's shoulder. "Was it warm there?"

Sadness taints Módor's smile. "The summer never ended. Every night the stars would shine."

"What are stars like?"

"Their light is cool, near and far as memory. It doesn't burn like the sun."

Dóta thinks over her mother's words. "Why would you leave such a world?"

Módor stares at Grethor, then shakes herself as she realizes he's biting down on the coin with a pointed tooth. "Grethor? Enough."

"What?" Grethor snorts. "I was just testing if it's real gold. Men do it all the time."

Módor's nostrils flare. Her voice fills with malice. "What men do doesn't matter. That belongs to me."

"So?"

"So I'll never bring you back here if you don't stop."

Grethor rolls his eyes. "I'm sure."

Módor hisses and Grethor laughs.

Módor rises to her feet, sends Dóta tumbling to the floor and Grethor only laughs harder.

Dóta cradles a skinned knee, then realizes what is about to happen. "Módor, please—"

Módor takes no notice. With a snarl, she rakes her claws across Grethor's face.

He holds his hand up to his slashed cheek. Dark blood drips between his fingers. He looks up at Módor, his green eyes filled with shock and he keens with distress.

"Oh, stop your sniveling, child. It'll heal." Then Módor sweeps

out of the room and Dóta is certain she sees shame on her mother's face.

The girl's knee throbs, but she swallows the pain and puts her arms around her brother as he wails.

"Wake up, girl. A night-spirit has you." Anskar tapped my shoulder until my eyelids slid open. By the light of the fire, I could see a concerned look on his face. The sun was asleep and the shadows were awake. Nearby, the donkey nibbled at the long grass. We had travelled along the forest path for most of the day before Anskar decided to halt for the night. By the time we'd stopped, I was nearly sleep in the saddle and Anskar had bidden me to rest while he made camp. I lay wrapped in his fur sleeping bag. He was still watching me. "You all right, Dóta? Do you have a fever?"

"Just a bad dream."

He nodded and performed a warding gesture over me. "Good, I was worried. Night-spirits I can deal with, but I've no charms for an elf-fever. That's what you Seethers are for."

"Seether?"

His lean face crinkled in a smile. "You know, folks who can seethe real spells—not just simple hearth stuff like this." He performed the gesture again.

"Oh." I sat up and rubbed my eyes.

"I've made us dinner. Just a bit of porridge, but it'll fill our bellies all the same. No, don't get up. Rest." He ambled over to the fire, over which he had set up a cauldron on a metal frame.

I lay back down, breathed in the musky scent of the fur sleeping bag. It reminded me of my sheepskin. The boughs of the trees shivered in the cool breeze. The darkness was close, threatening to choke the joy out of the world. The thought made me shudder. Not once had I spent the night without the comfort of glowing mushrooms. A low, mournful voice pierced the quiet of the evening. I sat up, knife in hand.

Anskar barked with laughter. "Just an owl. Here, take this." He passed me a shallow wooden bowl and some kind of tool carved from antler.

Unsure what to do with the tool, I set it aside and stared into the bowl. Nothing but a kind of mush. I sniffed it and made a face. "What kind of meat is this?"

Anskar raised a brow as he sat down opposite me. "No meat—just oats. Don't worry. At Valdskali there'll be haunches of fresh venison. Boar, even, if we're lucky."

I dipped my knife into the glop and scooped some out. The sticky stuff clung to the blade and I tried to lick it off. Half the porridge wound up slathered on my chin. The other half made me want to retch. It was hot like blood, but tasted like bad breath. That's the only way to describe it.

"It's not that awful, is it?" said Anskar. He blew on his and dipped into it with a tool like the one he had given me. "You'll find it easier with the scoop. See?" The warrior pulled the scoop out from the bowl, put it in his mouth with exaggerated care. "Mm. Good." He swallowed and rubbed his belly. "Give it a try."

I picked up the scoop and did my best to mimic him. A few tries later I decided it was better to suck the oats off my fingers.

He stared at me for a few moments and then shrugged. "You'll learn."

The rest of the meal passed in silence until my bowl was empty. My belly gave a quiver and then a lurch. I wasn't made for porridge. I kicked off the sleeping bag and jumped to my feet. "I need to squat."

"Don't forget to dig a hole for it."

Módor had taught me that much. I grabbed my knife and hurried as far into the wood as I dared, but made sure to keep the fire in sight. My breeches were loosened just in time before relief came. When I was done, I wiped myself with a leaf. It wasn't soft as the moss in the cave, but it served. The noise of a running stream filled my ears and I realized how dry my mouth was. I stumbled toward the sound, tripped on a pine cone in the dark. On the bank of the river I kneeled and lapped up water. After that, I plunged my knife into the running stream, desperate to clean off the dried-up oats.

To this day, I've never been able to touch porridge again.

Anskar looked up as I returned to camp and chortled when he saw me holding up my breeches. I was glad he couldn't see the sickened look on my face by the light of the dying fire. "You were gone awhile." He scraped the edge of his bronze knife on a rock, sharpening it.

I held up my own blade and it gleamed in the red light of the flame. "Needed to clean my knife."

"Yes, your knife." He sheathed his own blade. "I meant to talk to you about that."

"What of it?"

He frowned, unsure how to start. "What kind of bone is it?"

"Not sure."

"You didn't make it, then?"

"What? No. My mother gave it to me."

"Before the troll slew her."

My eyes flicked to the left. "Yes."

He nodded and ran his hand through his beard. "Does it have powers?"

"Eh?"

"You are a Seether, after all. Could the blade pierce Grethor's hide?" He fixed his blue eyes on me.

I froze. "How do you know that name?"

"Forgive me. You talk in your sleep—you were thrashing and called out over and over. "No, Grethor!" That is the beast's name, yes?"

I said nothing.

"You must understand, Dóta," said Anskar. "That hell-fiend has harassed my people for a long time. Any scrap of knowledge will help me."

"With what?"

He blinked. "To slay the beast, of course."

I stiffened. "No. You can't."

"Not with iron, I can't. That was my best axe and it shattered like ice. But a Seether, with the power of the gods on her side? That'd be different."

I lowered my eyes and pressed my teeth into my lower lip. "I've done enough."

Anskar's face darkened. "What do you fear, girl? One word, you set him to flight."

What was I meant to say? That Grethor was cruel and crude, but he would never stop being my brother? "I fear nothing," I said. "But I can't do it. I won't. I'm not a—"

Kin-slayer. I caught myself before I said the word.

Anskar's lip curled. "You don't know what he's done, do you? If you knew the lives that monster has taken—" He took a steadying breath and then another. "Enough, then. It's better to speak of such things by the light of morning. You can have my sleeping bag. I'll keep watch." He turned away from me, wrapped himself in his cloak and strode over to the donkey. "Come on, silly. Time for that rub-down, eh?"

The donkey snorted in contentment as Anskar pulled a brush through its shaggy hair.

I glared at Anskar's back for a moment. Then I rolled over onto my side and hugged myself. Anskar was a fool—why was he so surprised that I didn't want to help kill my brother? But that was foolish too. Anskar didn't know about me and Grethor—he didn't know anything. I crossed my arms inside the sleeping bag. This whole thing was stupid and I knew it and I didn't care. The man was just a dumb beast and I didn't even know why I had agreed to travel with him. A tree root was digging into my back, so I rolled onto my other side. Anskar threw more wood onto the fire, then sat upright with his hood up. I lay on my back and turned my eyes skyward, not wanting to look at him. The sky above was like a rock wall worn smooth by running water.

Almost without thinking I reached for the amulet which lay snug against my chest. I glanced over to Anskar. Speaking to the gods aloud would only invite questions. But earlier the amulet had responded to my thoughts. *What am I supposed to do?*

Silence.

Should I continue on?

The amulet remained cold.

In my head I called the goddess by name, but she did not heed me.

I gnashed my teeth in silence. It seemed the goddess's words were spent. What good was the power of Asgard if it would abandon me when I really needed it?

Then through the treetops I saw a light peeking down at me. First one and then a dozen. The stars, coming out from behind a cloud. Módor had spoken of them and I had always wondered what they were like. Their light was as cold and distant as my mother had said. And yet they twinkled pale blue, like Anskar's gaze. A strange notion, I thought.

The last thing I saw before I closed my eyes was Anskar performing his warding gesture over me again. No spirit tormented me further that night. Sometimes simple magic is all you need.

RAVENS

I'm NOT sure whether the emptiness of my stomach or the fullness of my bladder woke me. The woods were clad in a chilly grey light and thin trailers of mist clung to the pines. Anskar snored by the smoking pile of ash which had been our fire. So much for keeping watch. I yelped as I stretched muscles unused to riding, then tiptoed into the woods to relieve myself. A quick check of the wound on my leg showed it was healing. Afterward it took eight attempts to tie the cord around my waist properly, but I managed.

The rumble of my belly was like the clash of frost giants. It needed some real food, not that horrid mush Anskar had made. Just the thought of him was enough to make me prickle with irritation. No way was I ready to speak to him again. I bent low to the ground and kept my eyes open for any sign of a rabbit or vole, anything to fill me. And then perhaps I would just keep walking, let Anskar find his own answers.

As I searched through the woods for prints, I relived last night's argument with Anskar. He hadn't asked me what I wanted to do, just assumed. And he'd given me a fight when

I said I didn't want to kill Grethor and that wasn't fair. But was it a fight, really? It wasn't as though he'd struck me. When the anger filled him, Anskar hadn't let it spill over. More than that, though. He'd promised that we'd talk more in the morning. He was softer than Módor or Grethor and that's what humans were like.

No, Anskar wasn't softer. He was gentler.

I shook off the notion and went on with my search. Something big had passed by this way not too long ago, to judge from the broken stalks of grass here and there. I spied a footprint in the soft earth up ahead. My quarry walked on two feet and had five toes like a man, but the print was bigger than that of any human, or so I gathered from the humans I'd seen. Only one creature was so massive.

Grethor.

Could he be watching me even now? I peered closer at the footprint, decided it was unlikely. The footprint was half-full of water and it hadn't rained yesterday. Grethor had come here perhaps the day before, the same day I'd found my amulet. That made sense, he'd gone above to hunt. What had he said? That the farmers had given him more fun than he expected. I knew Grethor came above to raid the farms and steal livestock. That's where he got my sheepskin. But yesterday he had wanted to slay Anskar and not just to prove something. Dread surged through me. What lay at the end of the trail?

Then I took a breath to gird my strength and stepped forward. Fate had led me this far. Only a craven would turn from the path now. The signs of Grethor's passage grew clearer as the trail extended. Broken branches lay strewn everywhere and the footprints grew deeper. My brother hadn't bothered to conceal his trail. He must have run faster and faster as he neared his prey and so did I.

I burst from the woods and stumbled into the sunshine. Grethor's trail led to an empty, treeless place. Not even stumps, just soft grass. I stopped a moment to catch my breath with my hands on my knees. Then I looked up. Ahead there was a row of wooden spikes, planted so close together in the ground that a dormouse couldn't squeeze between the gaps. A fence, that's what this was called. My brother had told me humans kept animals penned inside fences. But part of it had been smashed away, leaving a jagged gap like a mouth filled with teeth. From the other side of the fence came the shriek of ravens. They were arguing, snapping at one another.

I started toward the gap and then felt a pulse of heat against my chest.

No, dear one, said the amulet. *There's nothing in there for you.*

"Go back to sleep," I said aloud. "I have to see."

The amulet went cold. I tiptoed through the break in the fence. On the other side was a vast, empty field, no animals in sight. At the center of the field stood something hewn of wood. It loomed taller than me. It was all straight lines, like the edge of Anskar's axe. A human thing. Was this one of their shelters? They had given it a roof like a cave, but it pointed into the sky. What looked like a hundred ravens perched atop the roof, chattering at one other in harsh voices. The black birds stared at me with grey eyes as I took a few steps toward the shelter. Then they lifted from the ground and wheeled through the air. They howled in outrage at my intrusion. A flurry of glistening black wings surrounded me, a dark mist. I fumbled with my knife, ready to fend off an attack. After a few breaths, the ravens decided I was neither threat nor prey and settled atop the house again.

Something lay on the ground nearby. I bent and examined it. Just a few rags, sewn into the rough likeness of a human wearing boy's clothes like mine. A smile had been etched on the face. Months would pass before I recognized it as a doll, a child's toy. It had been ripped open at the seams and the woolen stuffing spilled to the ground.

And Grethor's footprints were everywhere.

"Dóta?" I spun around to find Anskar behind me, knife in hand. My heart flooded with relief at the sight of him. "This place is cursed, girl. You can see Odin's ravens. You must not linger."

I ran to Anskar and thrust the remains of the doll into his face. "Grethor's been here. He did this."

Anskar took the doll and his eyes filled with sorrow. "I know. This farmstead belongs to Garmund and Gerlaug—friends of mine. They have a daughter."

"A child."

He swallowed. "Go back to the woods and wait for me there. I'm going to check inside the house."

I sprinted back to the gap in the fence until I reached the tree line. The sun crawled across the sky and burned away the mist as I waited.

After a time, Anskar emerged from the break in the fence. His face was set in a grim line.

"Are they—" I started.

Anskar shook his head. "I found Garmund with a blade in his hand. Valhalla shall welcome him."

"And the girl? Her mother?"

He bowed his head. "The fiend leaves nothing alive."

Tears stung my eyes. Stupid, really. Módor would have slapped me for showing such weakness. I didn't even know why I was crying. The weak lived to feed the strong, that's what I had been taught. But it wasn't right, wasn't fair. The girl would have been about my age and Grethor... I had smelled the blood on him. "What can we do?"

Anskar laughed without humor. "For them? Nothing. For the living? Everything." He swallowed. "The king must know of this. Will you walk with me, Dóta?"

I said nothing, just gnawed on my lip. The tears spilled at last and ran down my cheeks. And then I nodded.

HUNGER

THE SUN CREPT across the sky as we walked away from the ruined farmstead and it was near the zenith by the time we made it back to the campsite. Anskar muttered a word in the donkey's ear and it blinked at him. I was about to ask whether the animal could understand him when the world suddenly tilted. My knees buckled and I threw out a hand against a tree to save myself from falling. I sank to the ground, sat hunched forward.

Anskar ran up. "What's wrong?"

"I feel..." I swallowed. Words didn't want to come out. "My head doesn't feel right. Or my belly. And my legs are empty of strength."

Anskar stared at me for a moment. "You're hungry. And small wonder, we've not broken our fast." He dashed to the saddle bag, pulled something out and held it to me. "Just hardtack," he said. "You know, flour and salt baked crisp. But it'll fill your belly until we reach the king's hall."

The hardtack was like a disc hewn of stone. I took it and sniffed, found hardly any scent. "This is food? Are you sure?"

He shrugged. "Or what passes for it on the road. Sorry I don't have any more oats."

"I'm not." I nibbled at the hardtack, tried not to remember what happened last time I ate human food. The feeling of something solid crunching between my jaws was comforting, at least, but it was so dry that swallowing made me splutter.

Anskar tipped his water skin into my mouth and thumped me on the back until my coughing ceased. "I would have brought better provisions, if I'd known I'd have a companion for my journey. I go alone, normally." He himself ate and drank nothing, but paced around the edge of the campsite. After a few moments my stomach settled—the hardtack sat better than wet mush and I felt almost normal again.

Hunger was a terrible thing, I decided. In the cave Módor had always given us plenty of roots and mushrooms and fish. They had been enough for me, though Grethor always whined that our fare was tasteless. I winced at the thought. After seeing the kind of food Grethor preferred, the idea of meat made my stomach turn. I cast the thought away, didn't want to ponder what Grethor had done to that little girl and her kin.

Anskar gestured toward the donkey as I popped the last of the hardtack into my mouth. "Ready?" he said. "If we press on we'll be at Valdskali by dark."

"Mmhh!" I nodded and tried to say yes, but found my mouth stuffed too full.

He laughed. "Need a hand mounting up?"

I took a swig of water and swallowed. "I can do it."

"Aye. That you can." He took the water skin and watched me put my feet in the stirrups and pull myself up. When I sat astride the donkey, his eyes shone with something I had never seen before. Was it pride? Then he took the reins and led the donkey onward. "We should pick up the pace," he said over his shoulder.

"Why?"

"There's an Althing at the hall tonight. Don't want to be late."

"A what?"

"A meeting of earls—shire chiefs. It happens every year. That's where I was headed when our paths met."

"So there will be many humans there." I adjusted my knife in my hand.

Anskar stopped and gave me a strange look, then shrugged. "Yes. Many humans—warriors and their sons." He walked on, tugging gently on the reins. After that Anskar said little and kept his eyes fixed on the path ahead. The sound of his teeth grinding together set me on edge. My hand began to ache, I had been holding the knife so long. I leaned over and slipped it into the saddle bag.

The shadows lengthened as the day waned. The light of early evening burnished the oak-leaves before twilight came. The wind cut deeper than a blade. I shuddered in the saddle and hugged myself; clothing did little to keep the chill away. My breath rose before me and I puffed vapors like a dragon. A sharp tang filled the air.

Anskar halted and sniffed. "The whale road—the sea. We're close now." He pointed. "There, up the hill. See that light? That's Valdskali."

I squinted between the trees. An orange flame flickered at the top of a far-off hill. It was impossible to see more from this distance. "Is it far?"

"Not far. But soon it'll be too dark to travel. We'd best hurry."

We trotted on in the gathering darkness for a little time and then Anskar broke the silence. "Your knife."

I rolled my eyes. "I already told you—"

"No, not that. You'll need to hand it over to the guardsmen of the hall."

"Huh?"

"No blades at the Althing, no weapons of any kind. Put too many warriors in one place with barrels of mead? There's bound to be a few scuffles. It's the nature of men, especially the young. Normally they just knuckle each other up good and find themselves friends by sunrise, but—"

"They? Not we?"

Anskar stopped walking and turned to me. "I'm too old for that nonsense and I know who my friends are. But if the youths were using knives and axes instead of words and fists... Well, that's when scuffles become blood-feuds."

I frowned. "Nobody takes my knife. My mother gave it to me."

Anskar grunted. "A strange gift, some might say."

I bared my teeth. "Some would be stupid."

His face darkened. "By the gods..." Anskar took a breath. "Did your parents teach you nothing of the world? I thought you'd understand the need to keep the peace."

"Eh?"

"Well, you're a woman-child. A peace-weaver."

My laugh was so loud that a nearby bird fluttered from the oaks in alarm. "A peace-weaver!" Ask the adder that attacked me if I was a peace-weaver.

"Girls are peace-weavers," he insisted. "Boys are war-makers. Girls give life, boys take it. Boys win glory with their weapons and girls... Well, girls are won. Don't you see?"

I wrinkled my nose. "No."

"That is the balance of the world, has been since the first humans were carved from the elm."

"Can girls not be warriors?"

Anskar paused a moment. "In the sagas, maybe. And I've heard of such things in other lands." Then he shook himself. "But this isn't a saga. It's here, now."

I jutted my jaw. "Boy, girl, what's the difference?"

Anskar raised his hands as though he was trying to grasp air. "You don't understand what it is to be a man. Nine tenths of the year it's working the soil until your nails are ragged and bleeding. Then, when summer comes, you have to go out on raids and then it's blood and fury and not knowing if you'll be coming home. Knowing at least one of your companions won't be. And for what? Gold? A king's love?" He swallowed hard.

"So why go raiding?"

"Cattle sicken and die. Lands may be taken. But gold? Gold is forever. You can bury it, take it with you—that's what you want to leave your kin. And I'll not tarry while my friends stand in the shield wall." His voice took on a hard edge. "Better to stay home with the children, safe. Loved. Why make war when you can make peace? Trust me, you don't want to be a man."

I studied his face. "You don't."

Anskar scowled and said a harsh word under his breath. Then he steadied himself. "I know my place, girl. Maybe you should learn yours." His mouth said the words, but his eyes said something else. He looked away. "I'm not asking you to throw away your knife. Just let the guardsmen keep it during the Althing and I'll do the same with mine."

I crossed my arms and spat. "Fine."

"And after the Althing, I'll see about getting you some

proper clothes. That's the problem here, I think. Girls can't wear breeches."

I looked down. "But I'm wearing them. So I'm a boy?" For the first time since I left the cave, I smiled.

Anskar laughed, not unkindly. "No, you're not."

"Well then, I'm different."

He combed his fingers through his beard and his brows drew together. "Aye. That much I'll grant you." Anskar pondered for a moment with a scheming look in his eye, then shrugged. "Perhaps it works differently for Seethers. I don't know. What I do know is that we've lost enough time already." He turned away and patted the donkey on the back of the head.

The donkey lurched forward and I held tight to its bristling mane. A few more moments passed as I debated whether or not to tell him. Honesty beat cunning, in the end. "I'm not really a Seether."

"Oh?"

"What happened with Grethor and the amulet—I can't explain, it just sort of happened." My eyes dropped; I hated letting him down, though I couldn't say why. "I'm sorry."

Anskar didn't check his steps. "No. Only a Seether could have done that. So you must be—you just don't know it yet. Maybe with a bit of teaching..." He trailed off.

The amulet lay cold against my chest, gave no answers.

Night came as we went further up the slope and we walked beneath the meagre light of the moon. The path wound around the hillside, spiraling to the top. At last the ground we walked upon levelled out and gravel crunched underfoot. A great fence loomed at the highest point of the hill, lit by torches planted around the outside. It wasn't made of wood but grey stone, as high as three men. Even Grethor would struggle to rip his way through this.

"The walls of Valdskali," said Anskar.

"Wall." I knew the word, but had never seen anything like this. Módor's cave had walls, but they were small compared to those of Valdskali. "It's huge."

"The king has many enemies."

"Grethor."

"And others—though walls may not be enough to keep them out."

A voice came from the wall. "Who comes creeping to the king's hall? Name yourself, else I'll put an arrow in you."

Anskar stepped into the pool of torchlight, his hands raised. "You've no need of weapons with me, friend."

"Oh, frosty blue hell. It's you."

My mouth fell open as the wall parted and swung forward, for I could never have imagined such a thing—a gateway, I'd call it now. The creak made my bones rattle. A round figure stepped through the gate. He was cladded all in leather and wore a silver arm ring like Anskar's. An axe hung from his hip and the torchlight flickered on his bald pate. He hurried forward, a little bow-legged. "Anskar Wind-Rime." He reached for Anskar and my hand darted into the saddle-bag for my knife. I relaxed when Anskar grabbed the other warrior by the shoulders and pulled him into an embrace.

"It's been too long, Boli Butterworth," said Anskar.

The other warrior grinned, revealing a gap in his teeth. "Blood-axe. It's Boli Blood-axe. How many times must I tell you?"

"Who calls you that?"

"Ah, just folks. You're late."

Anskar nodded. "Delays. Has it started yet?"

Boli shook his head. "He's been waiting. You don't think Hrut would start without you?"

"King Hrut," Anskar corrected him.

Boli shrugged. "He wasn't king when we were young—just a farmer like the rest of us. You too."

Anskar smiled. "I'm still a farmer, Boli."

Boli rolled his eyes. "Yeah. That's why they call you Wind-rime. For your farming. Your raids got Hrut where he is, Anskar. Why do you—" He caught sight of me lurking on the edge of the shadows. "And who's this, then? Get off the donkey and step into the light."

I pulled my feet out of the stirrups and slid off the donkey, stiff and sore from having been in the saddle so long.

Boli's eyes widened as he took a good look at me and then he turned to Anskar. "Your son, Anskar? Where have you been hiding him all these years?"

I frowned, confused.

Anskar's smile froze on his face and his eyes hardened like ice. "This is not my son. As you know well."

"Oh, I—" Boli cleared his throat. "Forgive me, Anskar. I forgot."

"How good that must be."

The moment stretched until Boli turned back to me. "Well then, boy. Who are you? Speak up."

I looked at my bare feet. "I—um, I'm not—"

Anskar laid a hand on my shoulder. "This is Boia. He is my companion on the road."

THRESHOLD

Boia.

The amulet against my chest pulsed hot with satisfaction. *Your true name at last.*

My heart beat against the amulet, full of confusion. My true name—what was that supposed to mean?

"All right, Boia," said Boli with a nod. "You've not earned your arm ring yet, I see. And your hair..." He glanced at my tangles and left the thought unspoken. "But any friend of Anskar is a friend of the kingdom, so you're welcome at the Althing. You'd best make haste, though. Your weapons, Anskar." He held out his hand.

Anskar unsheathed his dagger and passed it to Boli by the handle.

Boli took it and raised his eyebrows. "Axe?"

"Gone. Long story."

"A regular saga, I'm sure. And you, Boia?"

It took me a heartbeat to respond. "My knife. In the saddlebag."

"That it?"

I nodded.

"Off with you then. Think of me out here in the cold while you enjoy your mead, Anskar. Harald, you sluggard!" he called over his shoulder. "Where are you? Take the donkey to the stable while I stow this gear."

"Come, Boia." Anskar grabbed my arm and led me up the road.

The reek of the town threatened to overwhelm me. The acrid stench of burning dung, the dizzying fumes rising from the ale-house. I gaped left and right as we passed between shelters arranged in crooked rows. The air was thick with the sounds of animals braying and mewling. And voices. Chattering, laughing, singing songs of gods and heroes. The shadowy outlines of humans dashed from house to house, lanterns in their hands. They moved too fast for me to get a proper look. What seemed like a hundred pairs of eyes watched us from doorways.

"What's the matter?" said Anskar. "Never seen a town before?"

"It's so..." I trailed off, for I didn't have the words.

"Do you like it?"

A group of small humans ran past and splattered mud on my breeches. I craned my neck, trying to get a closer glimpse at them, for I was curious to know what humans closer to my own age looked like. One of them—a pale-eyed imp—turned around and poked its tongue at me, then ran on giggling.

"No," I said.

He chortled. "Nor me. But don't fear, we won't be here long." Anskar lengthened his stride.

I hurried along behind him. "Why did you call me that? Boia?"

He shrugged. "Didn't think they'd accept a strange girl at the Althing, least of all one who comes in looking like a goblin out of the wild. I figured you're skinny enough to pass for a boy. Besides," he said with a smile, "who ever heard of a girl who wore breeches and carried a knife?"

"Boia, though."

"A good strong name. Youthful." Anskar was silent a moment and then he pointed. "We're here. The hall of the wolf."

The road turned from mud to cobblestones as it wound uphill. At the end of the road, overlooking the town, was a massive wooden shelter. It was bigger than others I'd seen. The walls were long and curved, with none of the harsh lines I'd seen on other things crafted by men.

Anskar caught sight of me staring. "Long ago, the ancestors came to this land on long ships. When they arrived, they turned their boats over and huddled beneath them. And so we still use the shape of the longboat when we build our halls. To honor those who came before." Anskar led me up the stone steps to an oaken door.

From inside the hall came the sound of boisterous laughter, unmistakably male, followed by the sound of something breaking.

"Ready?" said Anskar.

"No."

Anskar gave a gruff laugh. "You'll be fine." He knocked three times against the door.

Silence fell inside. The door creaked open and a grizzled face peaked out. The man's moustache was shaggy and spattered with grey, like the wolf's pelt he wore over his shoulders. I caught a golden flash of a torque around his neck and from an arm ring like Anskar's. He held a golden horn in his hand, full of some amber liquid which dripped to the floor. His eyes were bleary and unfocused. "Anskar!"

Anskar nodded in respect. "Hrut, my king."

"Eh? None of that, brother." Hrut pulled Anskar into a rough hug, squeezed him tight.

My eyes widened. Anskar had a brother. Was he like mine?

Anskar returned the hug, then glanced at the horn in the king's hand. "You started early."

Hrut shook his head, a dazed smile on his face. "No, you got here late."

Anskar raised his eyebrows. "And what kind of king answers his own door?"

"The impatient kind. Where have you been? And who is this?" Hrut jerked his thumb in my direction and I shuffled my feet.

Anskar hesitated. "A friend I can vouch for. Saved my life on the road. We have much to speak of, my lord." He lowered his voice. "It's been hunting again."

The king stared at Anskar and all cheer retreated from his face. He blinked, trying to gather himself. "Well, the Althing's waited this long. It won't hurt them to wait another hour." He sighed and offered his horn to me. "You may as well drink this, boy. Go in, warm up. Come on, Anskar."

"Watch yourself," said Anskar over his shoulder as they walked off into the town. "Don't do anything foolish. I'll be back soon."

I hesitated a moment and then stepped over the threshold and into the hall, slopping a little of the yellow liquid on the hard earth floor. It took my eyes a few moments to adjust to the light. A great fire blazed in a pit at the center of the hall, casting shadows which danced upon the walls. An empty chair hewn of wood stood at the end of the hall, carved with shapes of humans and animals and leaves. Dozens of warriors sat at long benches, horns in their hands like the one the king had given me. The humans' skin was soft and their cheeks ruddy, but their eyes were hard and cold enough to make Grethor seem gentle.

"Come on, come on," called a man from inside. "You're letting the bloody cold air in."

I froze, not sure what to do.

"Fine, I'll do it." Somebody jumped up and slammed the door shut.

My damp woolen clothing steamed in the warmth of so many hot-blooded humans pressed close together. The air smelled of charcoal mingled with bad breath and fumes like those I had smelled from the ale-house. My eyes stung and I blinked tears away.

A warrior on the bench closest to me chuckled and slicked back his red hair with a brawny hand. "Well, look at that. Anskar's brought us a weeper." He turned his face toward me and revealed an empty socket where his left eye should have been.

"Eh?" said the man at his elbow. "I've never seen a scarecrow cry."

The one-eyed man guffawed.

I ground my teeth, tried to swallow the gourd lodged in my throat. "I'm not crying," I said, wiping away the tears. "It's the smoke."

When he smirked, the one-eyed man looked like the skull I'd found in Módor's treasure chamber. "Ah, of course. No need to start a feud, lad. Was just having a laugh, is all. Here, come drink with us." He put the horn to his lips.

Determined not to shame myself again, I tilted the yellow liquid into my mouth. Half of it dribbled down my front. The sweetness was so thick that I gagged, then doubled over coughing and choking. The horn clattered to the floor. The hall exploded with laughter and my cheeks burned.

The one-eyed man sat back on his bench, a satisfied smirk on his face. "The Althing's for free men, boy, not beardless thralls out of the hill-country."

On the other side of the hall, an old man with leathery skin and milky eyes stood. "That's enough out of you, Ulf Redmane. Don't go insulting a companion of Wind-rime."

"Anskar?" Ulf spat. "A swineherd who can barely hold his shield up. I hear from the peddlers that half his shire's been eaten. Why should I respect a man who can't keep his affairs in order?"

The men surrounding Ulf nodded and grunted. All except one—a boy, just a little older than me, I think, whose hair was red like Ulf's. He stared into his mead, a glum look on his face. "Father, please..." Ulf ignored him.

On the other side of the hall, the knot of youths on either side of the old man rose from their bench. The old man crossed his arms and narrowed his blank eyes. "You've had too much of the king's mead, I think."

Ulf lowered his horn. "And what's that supposed to mean?"

"The king ought never have invited you or your pack of horse-thieves."

"That right?" Ulf lurched to his feet and the knot of men around him did the same. "And why should I follow a petty king who surrounds himself with doddering old fools and milksop boys?"

Ulf's son tugged on his father's tunic, tried to pull him back down into his seat. "Peace, Father," he said. "We came here to discuss the summer raids, not to feud."

Ulf shrugged off his son's hand, didn't take his eye off the old man. Two groups of warriors were now on their feet. Their fists were raised. It didn't matter that they had no weapons. Blood would spill. I could almost taste it on the air.

SONG

THE HALL FILLED with the growls of beasts. The two groups of men stared at each other with murder in their eyes. A pair of youths with spotted faces stepped in front of the elder. They reeked of violence. Ulf cracked his knuckles and his men tensed. Hearth smoke curled from their nostrils. Only Ulf's son remained seated on the bench, staring into his cup.

I hunched my shoulders and raised my fists. Every sinew in my body was raw. Any who came near me would suffer, though I had no blade but my nails.

And then the men froze and a shiver ran through me as a new magic filled the air. That is the only name for it. To call it sound would be an insult. I could not see or smell it. If it had a taste, it would have been sweet as strawberries. Yet this power was only for the ears, a quivering of the air. My heart rose as it did when the goddess whispered to me. By all Midgard, could humans have crafted this? In time I would know the power as lyre music. A common charm, though I had no inkling then.

I craned my neck to find the source. The men parted as a

new figure glided into their midst, plucking a wooden lyre.
A human whose form was like none I had ever seen, her
long white kirtle flowing like ocean waves. A girl. Her hair
was golden as that of Sif. With an elfin grace she swayed to
her own tune between the two knots of men. She opened
her mouth to sing. I recall few of the song's words, but her
voice gave strength to its charm.

> *The hero stalks the night,*
> *Slaking the raven's thirst,*
> *Monster unto monsters,*
> *Blade light in weary hand,*
> *Great in word, more so deed,*
> *He seldom boasts, no need.*
> *Shining sword-sweat tells all—*
> *Slayer of worm, orc, elf.*
> *True foes of men, takers*
> *Of youth, bearers of blight.*
> *Yet his friends he loves more*
> *Than black wings; raven's eyes*
> *Are cold. And so he slakes*
> *His friends' thirst before all.*
> *The wine, the ale, the mead—*
> *Cheer and warmth fill the hall.*

Every man stopped to heed the song. The youths on
both sides of the hall clapped in time. One of Ulf's men
pulled a set of pan pipes from his tunic and played along.
Ulf himself sank down onto his bench and reached for a cup
of ale, a sullen look on his face. The quarrel was forgotten,
the feud never begun.

And that's when I saw the singer for what she was.

A true peace-weaver.

All that I would never be.

The song ceased. She turned her grey-blue eyes toward me and my breath caught in my throat. I had never dreamed a face like this. She was the sun upon azaleas, a dizzying brightness for one raised in the dark. "Welcome to my father's hall, stranger," she said. "I am Princess Arína." And then her lips curled and she showed me her teeth: ivory and unjagged.

I stepped back, my muscles taut. A smile could mean anything.

Her brow furrowed. "Fear not. You are a guest at Vald-skali. No harm may befall you here." She turned to Ulf and his companions. "This youth walks with Anskar Aralson. All men know Anskar is wise in his choice of friends. And so he is under my clan's protection. Do you heed me?"

Ulf drained his cup and muttered something.

Arína arched her brow. "Speak if you will."

Ulf glared at her with one eye. "I've naught to say. Only that we didn't come here to taste your clan's bread and salt. The hour is late for an Althing. Where is our king?"

The princess lifted her chin. "The king comes and goes by his own will, Ulf Redmane. For now, friends, enjoy the sweet wine from my father's last raid." She clapped her hands and a few girls scurried into the hall with jugs in their hands. They kept their eyes to the floor as they poured. The men cheered and toasted the princess. She turned to me once more. "Will you not sit?" She reached and touched my upper arm.

I recoiled at the touch and shook it off.

She frowned. "What troubles you?"

I ground my teeth and looked away, sure my face was glowing like iron from the forge. "Don't grab me."

The princess stared. "Very well." She pointed me toward

the bench next to the old man with the whitish eyes. "Sit with Rokia. A place of honor. I'll have the girls bring you some food."

My stomach growled at her words and I perched at the end of the bench. She strode off and within a few heartbeats one of the serving girls laid out a bowl made of dry stuff that crumbled when I touched it. Within the bowl lay hunks of meat.

Rokia beside me leaned over and smacked his lips. "Ah, roasted boar. I'd know that smell anywhere. Cooked rare, I'd say."

I reached into the bowl and picked up a chunk of meat between my fingers. It steamed hot as though it still held life. The warriors around the table glutted themselves on flesh, worked their jaws and ground it with their teeth.

I sniffed the meat and the scent of fresh blood made bile crawl up my gullet. I dropped the meat and pressed my hand against my mouth. "Do you have any hardtack?" I said.

Rokia snorted. "Hardtack? You've some gall, boy."

A straw-haired warrior overheard me. "You don't want it? Can I have it?"

I shrugged and held the bowl out to him. He plucked out the meat and snaffled it, though I was left holding the bowl.

The elder sighed. "Eat the trencher, if you must."

"Trencher?"

He fumbled for the bowl and crumbled off a piece. "Bread. Hard and stale, but still bread. Do your kinsmen not eat such fare?"

"They don't." I broke off a smaller piece and sniffed. Deciding it was harmless, I put it in my mouth and chewed. Dry and hard, but I could stomach it.

The warriors took up a bawdy song, stamping their feet and clapping so loud it filled my skull. Sweat trickled down my brow; it was too hot in here, not enough air. The flickering light made me giddy. The smell of char and blood caused my belly to curdle. I pulled at my collar once more, trying to get some air on my hide. The woolens rankled, made me feel as though spiders had bitten me all over. Two men at the next table roared and butted heads like stags in the meadow. Drops of mead flew from their horns and soaked the back of my tunic and that only made the men laugh harder.

Humans, too many humans, all of them laughing and drinking foul stuff, all in one place.

Had to get out. The dark, that's what I needed, to go where even the gods could not see me. I lurched to my feet and bolted for the door.

I pushed at the door, but it stood firm. Panic welled up within me. Trapped, no way out. The corner of the hall offered a haven from the crowd. I made myself small as I could until a warrior ran to the door, clutching his belly. He grabbed a metal ring built into the wood and pulled. The door swung open. I swept past the man and ran from the light.

I crouched upon the stair, my hands on my knees. The night was comfort. The town was all but silent now and at last there was space to breathe. I rubbed the weariness from my eyes.

The warrior ran past me, retched and emptied his stomach onto the stairs. The rancid stink of his puke filled my nostrils. After a few dry heaves he wiped his mouth with the back of his hand. Then he turned back to me with a toothy grin. "Great night, eh?" Without waiting for an answer, he ran back up the stairs to join the revels once more.

A lead weight settled in my gut. Módor was right.

Humans were wicked and craven as she said. They cared for nothing, not even themselves and were as crude as Grethor. A vile thought, but truth. And if that's all there was to humans, I had no yearning to join them.

Damn my flesh.

I faced the darkness. I belonged nowhere. No going back, no going forward. I was nobody, nothing, a misfit. The woods were made for lonely creatures like me. I laid my foot upon the stair, ready to slip away.

"Why do you offer insult?"

The voice of Princess Arína made me turn. "Eh?"

She stood on the stair above me, her arms folded. "You tread barefoot into my father's hall and start a feud with your ill manners. I offer you the protection of my clan and not a word of thanks. Then you scorn our meat and board. Now you mean to slink off without farewell?"

"Why would I say farewell?"

She stared hard at me. "Most boys show proper respect for their host."

I shrugged. "I'm not a boy."

She shook her head and laughed. "So you'd call yourself a man."

"No."

"What, then?"

"A beast... a monster."

She laughed again and rolled her eyes. "Monster unto monsters." My well of words ran dry, for she spoke truth. "Are you truly a friend of the Wind-rime?"

"Anskar? Dunno. We met on the road. I was alone."

"Who are your kin?"

I swallowed. "I have none."

Her face softened. She sat down beside me. "Then he brought you out of the greatness of his heart."

"He wanted me to meet the king."

She nodded. "I'm sure."

I sat down on the hard stair. "Anskar is your kinsman?"

She turned her head to one side and toyed with her hair. Most distracting. "Not quite. He and my father are milk brothers."

"Milk?"

"Not kin by birth, but reared together. Anskar's clan took my father in when he was but a babe. They found him in the bottom of a longboat, adrift on the sea." I wanted to ask what a longboat was—Anskar had used this word earlier— but she spoke on. "Even now, Anskar is like kin to me."

I frowned at her words. "Not like kin. He is kin."

"Perhaps." The princess raised a brow. "You are not of this land, are you?"

It was impossible to meet her eye. "No."

"Where do you hail from? Why do you not tell me your name? Are you one of the hill folk? Some outlaw? Or are you truly a monster unto monsters?" She leaned close. Too close. "Who are you, stranger?"

I looked up to find her staring into my eyes. A light filled her gaze and only now do I see it for what it was. "I'm nobody," I said.

"Nobody's nobody." She reached to stroke my cheek and I did not shy away. The warmth and softness of her touch made my heart quicken. I knew naught of who she was, but I knew the rightness of her, sure as hunger was bad and fullness good.

A dry cough made us both turn. The blind man stood behind us, his arms crossed. "Princess Arína."

"Yes, Rokia?"

"You must not be caught alone with a boy, Princess. Especially an outsider."

"Is talk forbidden?"

Rokia huffed. "My eyes are misted, but I'm not blind yet. Inside now, you pair. The king will return soon."

"I suppose." Princess Arína stood. "Are you coming?" She offered me her hand.

I took it.

RAGNARÖK

As soon as we were back in the hall, Rokia hailed one of the serving girls for more mead. When she didn't answer, he trailed after her and tried to draw her notice. The princess led me back to the bench. She patted the spot next to her and raised her brows at me.

"Huh?"

A smile lurked upon her lips. "Just sit down, will you? I don't bite. Much."

Hoping she was jesting, I did as she asked. The princess leaned over to me and opened her mouth to speak. Then the hearth fire guttered as the door flew open. When her father entered the hall, Arína closed her mouth and stood.

The king's footsteps echoed through the hall as he strode up to the empty throne and sat. His moustache did not twitch, his face grim. The golden torque weighed upon him. Anskar walked behind, his face bluff as a cliffside. He took his place at the king's side and crossed his arms. Whispers skittered through the hall, but Anskar gave no sign that he noticed.

King Hrut raised his hand for silence. "Brothers, free

men, loyal companions. I bring ill tidings. We gathered here this night to talk of plunder and the axe. Yet a greater need presses us."

Ulf sneered. "Greater than the summer raids?"

The king nodded. "Evil roams our lands."

Rokia's hand froze as he reached for a cup. "What evil, mighty king?"

"A shadow-fiend born of the darkness. Its hide like scale armor, eyes of a devil. It breathes death and hears all things. Blood is its mead. A motherless demon."

I squirmed in my seat. Grethor was not motherless. Nor was I.

Ulf snorted. "Skald spit, a worthless fable."

Anskar shook his head. "I faced it myself."

"And what is the name of this woe? Or does it have none?"

Anskar's blue eyes flashed toward me. "Tell them."

Every warrior stared at me. My mouth became dry as sandstone. Then Arína gave me a nod and my courage rose. "Grethor. His name is Grethor. And I know him for all he is."

Ulf chortled. "Ah. Anskar's pet. Such a witness. And has anyone else seen it?"

Silence.

"Anskar tells the truth," I said.

Ulf spat on the floor. "Anskar has found another excuse to shirk the raid. He was a great man in his younger days, no doubt. But he has suffered much. Too grief-shattered to stand in the shield wall."

Anskar's lip twitched. "Words are air."

"You see?" Ulf wheezed with laughter. "Why should I yield my honor to a coward who won't defend his own?"

The king glared at Ulf. "Enough. We shall hunt the beast, or it will surely hunt us. The raids shall wait until the creature is slain." Howls of rage echoed through the hall and I fought the urge to cover my ears. "Enough!" King Hrut's voice rang like Thor's hammer, but that only made the men shout louder. The elders cried that they had bride-prices to pay, the youths that they had glory to win.

"My king," said Anskar. His soft voice sliced through the din. A hush fell upon the crowd when he spoke. "There is another way—one which will allow our brothers to raid. I have found a Seether. One whose power is greater than any. Even the beast would quail before him."

"Him?" Ulf chortled. "Seething is for women and weaklings."

The king stroked his moustache. "Who is this Seether?"

"You've met him. Stand, Boia. Let King Hrut look upon you properly."

It took me a moment to realize he was talking to me. I got to my feet and shuffled up to the throne. The floor held my gaze as I stood before Anskar and the king.

"The weeper?" Ulf's words were like darts in my back.

For the first time Anskar's voice sharpened. "A man can wield many weapons. Boia's is the power of Asgard. Though if you'd prefer to forsake the summer raids and stand with me against Grethor..." When Ulf said nothing, Anskar spoke on. "Thought not. Take Boia as your champion, friends. He will slay our monster."

The king beckoned. "Come closer, Boia." He pulled off his golden arm ring and presented it to me. "You know what this is? The token of manhood. If you wear it, you will be one of us." I looked into his face. His eyes were grave. "Know that if you accept this ring, you must swear fealty to me. Do you understand?"

I glanced over my shoulder. A hundred grizzled faces glared at me.

I reached for the arm ring and held up one finger to touch it. Just to sense it was real and not some dream. As soon as the gold brushed my skin, the amulet grew warm.

Sparks rise from the hearth, hiss through the air. The wooden beams of the roof glow, erupt in flame. The heat sears, leaps across the walls.

I cry out and point. Nobody heeds. Men remain on their benches, drunken grins on their faces even as flames rush across their hides. Greasy smoke. The reek of burnt flesh.

Ulf's sneer crisps and blackens and he collapses into ashes. His son falls with him, crying for his mother.

Tears spill from Anskar's eyes, but cannot quench the agony of flames. Skin blisters. Ragged sinews are devoured. Flesh sloughs from his bones, leaving only the grinning skull.

Princess Arína's eyes lock on me. Reproach for my failure. Flame-fingers stroke her hair, rip her kirtle, snatch her from me.

Walls shudder and groan beneath wood's bane. The world comes crashing down.

None hear me scream.

When I opened my eyes, I stood beneath a leaden sky. Flakes of white fell, cold enough to burn. The chill of the rocky ground nipped at my bare feet. The north wind raised shudders of gooseflesh. No amulet to warm me. Where was I? Some empty land where nothing grew. The sweet tang of death on the air. Trees twisted and broken, their corpses cast upon the ground. The wind keened between great mounds upon the earth. Houses for the dead. A wolf howled nearby.

"Anskar? Princess?" I called. The wind smothered my voice. Despair crawled over me like a night-spirit. "Módor? Anybody?"

A low, gurgling laugh echoed. "I hear you…"

"Grethor." My fists clenched. "Where are you?"

"Poor darling Dóta. All alone. No place for you in this world or any other."

I bared my teeth and tracked his laughter between the mounds. Something snapped beneath my foot. An arrow-shaft. Broken spears and cloven shields lay strewn upon the frost. A field long ago ploughed by war.

Ravens circled over my brother. His eyes shone with triumph. Between his claws he twirled a golden coin.

"Where is Módor?"

"Should have been nicer to poor Grethor."

"What have you done?"

Grethor sniggered. "Nothing yet, sweet sister. Nothing yet." Without warning he dropped the coin and ran at me, a blur of malice.

My knife. I needed my knife. Hands empty.

Clawed hands already on my throat. Grip like steel, his eyes green fire. My tears flowed as he lifted me from the ground. A sniff of my hair. His face cracked to reveal teeth shining red. Tongue lolling as he leaned into me. Raw hunger on his face. I could smell the decay in his throat...

Then the weight of the amulet lay against my chest once more. It pulsed with heat beneath my tunic. I was under the roof of the hall, standing before the throne. The fire was penned in its hearth. The people were safe and whole, jesting and laughing. Brothers among brothers. As though no time at all had passed.

What was that? I thought.

The voice of the goddess sounded in my skull. *Call it Ragnarök, dear one. The world's ending. Doom for all your kin.*

I bit the inside of my cheek. *Will that come to pass?*

None can escape fate. Your only choice is how you'll face it. Choose wisely.

Anskar remained at my side, looking on me with brow

furrowed. I craned my neck. Princess Arína still sat watching me at her bench. She turned a shade of red when her eyes met mine and my heart filled my chest.

Humans. Full of life and breath as I was. Strangers, aye, but strangers like me.

The king cleared his throat. "Boia? Will you pledge your loyalty?"

I nodded.

He passed the arm ring to Anskar. "Then kneel."

The earthen floor pressed against my knees.

The king stood over me and I kept my eyes on his boots. "Boia, son of none. Do you swear loyalty to me?"

I choked, then found my voice. "I swear."

"That you shall give in times of need."

"I swear."

"That you shall keep no secret from me."

"I swear."

"That you shall make my enemies your enemies, no matter who they be."

I faltered.

The king cleared his throat. "Look up. Let me see your eyes." His gaze pierced me. "Will you stand with the folk of this land? Will you be the light against the dark?"

Nobody deserved to die as I saw in my vision. Not Anskar. Not Arína. Not even Ulf. "I will."

Anskar grabbed me by my left wrist and pulled me to my feet. He spun me around to face the crowd, held my hand high and slipped the ring over my arm. "Then rise, Boia Elfin-sun, defender of the realm."

As soon as he said the name, the amulet blazed with heat. Light shone through the wool of my tunic as though from within me. Men fell silent as it filled their vision. The light was all but blinding, but they could not look away as the power of Freya washed over them.

Princess Arína stood. "The light of the goddess," she cried. "Hail the Seether! Hail Boia Elfin-sun!"

The men took up the chant with one guttural voice. "Elfin-sun! Elfin-sun! Hail, hail! Elfin-sun!"

Your name, dear one, said the amulet. *Trust it. Embrace it.*

I mouthed the name silently. To me it seemed strange. Perhaps it belonged to somebody I knew when I was small, an imaginary friend or a sprite from one of Módor's stories. But I wasn't sure it belonged to me. Not yet.

Three things were certain. I was a child of two worlds. And I would die to defend both. Though it was my fate to fill Grethor's jaws, I could still do good before the end.

Had I known what was to come, I might have chosen otherwise.

PART II

BETWEEN WORLDS

Row against the wind
And you'll find
The Norns' fate
Around the cape;
In the waves you shall drown
A fool's doom awaits.
– Fáfnismál

MIST

"Keep up, Boia," said Anskar over his shoulder. "It's easy to lose yourself in the mist."

I grunted a reply and panted along the forest track to match his strides. The mud sucked at my boots and I slipped.

He caught me by the ring I now wore on my upper arm. "Are you well?" His face was full of concern.

"Fine." I spat on the ground, determined not to let my fear betray me.

"Good. We cannot face the beast if you're ill."

The beast. Grethor, my brother. I had no wish to speak of him. "Must you call me Boia?" The sun had risen and set three times since Anskar had given me the name, yet it still felt like a word from a strange tongue.

His brow creased. "You know the reasons."

"But we're alone."

He opened his mouth to answer, then we both tensed as wet leaves rustled in the woods. I reached for the amulet which hung from my throat. Anskar pulled his new-forged axe from his belt. Its edge gleamed like a devil's eye. We both waited, peering into the predawn gloom, but neither outlaw nor troll leaped from the pines. After a moment, Anskar relaxed but he did not put away his axe. "We are not alone," he said and kept walking.

In my fist the amber pulsed hot. From within it came the voice of the goddess, light as springtime. *You must stop fighting your name, dear one.*

"Enough," I said. "Not now."

Anskar turned. "Eh?"

"Nothing. Where are we going? Not tracking Grethor."

He shook his head. "Your heart is unprepared."

I hissed. "I took your king's oath, didn't I?"

"Our king, you mean. And you are not ready to face Grethor yet. That much is plain."

I gnawed the inside of my cheek, caught between wrath and relief. Anskar did not know how truly he spoke. Just a few days ago, my entire world had been the cave where I'd dwelled with my little clan. Then I had seen the terror my brother wrought upon humankind, the doom he would bring upon me. I had sworn to stand against him, protect this realm and all who dwelled in it. Never would I shirk my task. Yet when I thought of it, I felt smaller than the meanest dwarf.

Anskar spoke on: "These aren't stones under my brows. I see you flinch every time I speak its name." His voice softened. "It is no shame—you were its thrall a long while and that will take time to unlearn."

"How?"

"I cannot teach you, for I know nothing of seething. But I know someone who can. That's where we're going."

"Who?"

He took up his long strides once more and I fell into step

at his side. "An old friend. Speaking of which, I saw you and Princess Arína yesterday."

My face grew hot and not just because the sun was rising. Yesterday Anskar and I had gone to see the long ships off as they left for the summer raids. Arína had come to sacrifice for the protection of the warriors. I had hung back from the crowd of humans, overwhelmed by the vastness of the sea. Though I had heard of the whale road, it seemed too huge to be real. So wide that I could not see the other shore, the waters shining brighter than silver. How uncanny, that frail creatures like humans would cross it on strips of wood.

Seeing me at the back of the crowd, Arína had beckoned me forward. "Come, Boia Elfin-sun. It is right that a Seether should bless the voyage." I joined her at the altar and stammered a few words. There was no joy in having so many eyes upon me. And though I expected her to mock, she only smiled, slipped her arm around my waist and said I had done well. The warmth of her touch still felt like lightning. Perhaps it shouldn't have meant so much, but it did. Only...

"She doesn't know I'm a girl," I said.

"As it should be."

"Why?"

"Because things may become prickly otherwise."

"Prickly?"

"It's a kind of plant..." Seeing my muddled look, Anskar released a slow breath. "Never mind. I know it's hard, but the other warriors would turn on us if they knew."

"Explain."

"It would humble them to know their safety lay in the hands of a girl, and they have no wish to be humbled. And if they knew the king had deceived them..."

"Blood." I remembered well the murder in the warriors'

eyes that night. The king had many enemies even in his own hall.

"Aye. Best to forget the princess. It is a deadly errand, to love a king or one of his house. I should know."

Anger wrenched in my belly. "I didn't ask for this. The name, seething, any of it. And now you tell me to shun the one human who does not jeer at me."

He fiddled with the iron brooch that kept his cloak in place. "Forgive me. This is not something I expected. But I will not jeer at you. This I swear… Dóta."

My well of words was dry, so I walked ahead of him. No doubt he could have kept up, but he remained just near enough to keep me in sight.

The warmth of the amulet spread across my chest like a balm. *The warrior is wise in many things,* said the goddess. *But not in the ways of the heart.*

"Oh?" I whispered. "You know this?"

The songs of love and hate belong to me. I can teach them all, if only you would let me. The magic could be yours.

"Why would you do that?"

To help you, of course. The creatures must be slain.

"What of my mother? She isn't as bad as Grethor."

They are of one kind.

"They are my kin."

No kin of yours. Or mine. The amulet went cold and I clenched my teeth as I walked. The amulet had the power both to rankle and soothe. It had this in common with my mother.

A pang of guilt struck me at the thought. Módor had taken me in when my own blood kin abandoned me. And how had I repaid her? By running away the first chance I had. Back to the very creatures who had left me to die. Not that Grethor had given me much choice.

Over the last few days I had thought to search for my birth parents but had barely left the king's hall, watching behind a pillar as the men bustled about to prepare for the raids. There were so many little rituals to learn—the brushing of the hair, the picking of the teeth. The way humans would press their foreheads together and say tender words when they thought they were alone. Perhaps I might have asked about my parents, yet I had no inkling of where to begin. Better to rest, I had decided. There would be little time for it in the days ahead.

The trees began to thin, the path winding between a pair of low hills which rose from the earth like the knucklebones of giants. The mists drifted around them.

Anskar gave the hills a grim look and performed a warding gesture. "Mounds, the homes of the dead. Men have lived in these parts a long time. The old kings haunt the land still."

The wind sighed through the mounds. A chill passed over me as it stroked my cheek. "Can we not go around?"

He shook his head. "This is the border of my friend's homestead. The ghosts are meant to protect her house."

"So they're our friends?"

"The dead have no friends, but they can be appeased." He bent, unwrapped a bloody hunk of meat from his pack and laid it on the road between the mounds. All the while he muttered words beyond my ken. "They won't bother us now."

We hurried forward. Then I glanced behind, glimpsing a dart of movement at the edge of my gaze. The meat was already gone, but no vole or rat showed itself. I quickened my pace.

The mists were all but spent now and I could see a house at the heart of the clearing. Shaggy turf grew upon the walls—where it began and the forest ended, I could not say. Smoke curled from under the door which stood ajar. Nowadays I would call it a strange sight, but all houses were strange to me then. It reminded me of the mounds, though this was surely a house for the living. A pair of boots stood by the threshold.

Anskar cleared his throat. "Ah, you'd best let me speak first." He rose his hand and thumped on the door. "Twyla? Are you there?"

The door creaked open to reveal a woman adjusting her grimy kirtle. She brushed her greying hair out of her face to reveal a scar on her chin. Her mossy green eyes narrowed at the warrior. "Anskar? You've some gall coming here."

She slammed the door, leaving us no company but the wind and ghosts.

TWYLA

I HAD SEEN Anskar face down a snarling troll, no weapon in his hand but a broken axe. Not long afterward, he had not blanched as he met the blood challenge of Ulf Redmane and his followers. So it took me a moment to recognize the fear on his face as he stood before Twyla's door.

"What's wrong?" I said. "Why did she do that?"

Anskar made a noise in his throat, then knocked on the door again, more gently this time. "Twyla? Please, open the door. We need to talk."

"Ah, get you gone," came her voice from inside the house. She did not talk like other humans, her tones lilting. "I thought we agreed never to speak again."

"You agreed," murmured Anskar. "It matters little now. The kingdom is threatened. I wouldn't have come to you otherwise."

The door opened and Twyla's head poked out. She peered at Anskar's chin. "You've grown a hedge on your face." Then she glanced at me. "Who's this, then?"

Anskar spoke before I could. "One with much to learn about seething."

"Not so," said Twyla, pointing at my arm ring. "I don't teach man-children. War-makers have no use for my craf—" She stopped and peered closer at me, then stepped out from her turf house to look into my eyes. I dared not blink as she studied me. The amulet flashed with heat as the strange woman muttered to herself in another tongue. She waved her yellowed fingertips before my face and laid a hand on her breastbone. "By all Asgard... This is no war-maker, is it? Not a peace-weaver, neither. You're something else."

"I'm Dóta." I glared at her.

"And why are you garbed as a boy, eh? Playing make believe?"

"What's make believe?"

The lines around Twyla's eyes deepened as she smiled. "Aye, you're a strange one. I like that. I'm Twyla, daughter of Almund. I see you've already met my husband. Well, ex-husband."

"And land lord, last I knew," said Anskar, crossing his arms.

She finally took her eyes off me. "I pay your thrall sure enough. If the silver's missing, talk to him."

Anskar shook his head. "I didn't come here to quibble over pennies."

Her lips thinned. "You weren't joking about the kingdom being in danger, were you? Ah, how foolish of me. Like you'd ever joke. Very well, come inside."

Anskar turned to me. "You'd best remain, Dóta. Twyla and I... Well, there are things we must speak of alone." Seeing me shrug, he nodded. "I'll try not to be long." They went into the house, each keeping an arm's length from the other.

Twyla had been Anskar's mate, I gathered. What had

happened between them? A quarrel over treasures? No matter, I decided. It was none of my affair.

I sat with my back against the turf wall, gathering my cloak to keep the wet grass from soaking me. After a few breaths, I stood again. It was impossible to put myself at ease. The darkness between the trees at the edge of the clearing rankled me. I swallowed, unable to shake the sense of eyes in the shadows. The hairs upon the back of my neck curled as they did when Grethor sniffed my flesh. I flicked my bone knife from its sheath.

A scream rent the air. It came from the other side of the house. I glanced at the door, but Anskar and Twyla did not emerge. Fate had called me alone. My feet pounded the sodden earth. I prayed for the goddess's aid as I skidded to the rear of the house. The blood sang through my veins, ready for a fight.

A quick glance left and right. No sign of Grethor, nor any human. Just a few strange animals clad in white bristles, penned inside a low fence. Four legs like spindles, the horns on their heads sharpened as though for war. One of them was penned apart from the others. A doe, as I would soon learn. She stared at me with gold eyes, wanted to say something. Or so I supposed.

"Hello?" I took a step toward the animal.

She blinked, but did not answer.

"Did you see—"

Her teeth parted and a bellow rose from her throat, the voice so like a human's I took a step back.

Then I laughed at myself. This was all I had heard. I slipped the knife back into its sheath, then approached the gate. "What are you?"

The creature trotted up to the fence and thrust her head beneath my palm. Her hair was rough and made my skin itch as she rubbed back and forth. Up close, she had a peculiar musk.

"What do you want?"

No answer came but a whicker, and that's when I knew.

"You can't talk, can you? No more than Anskar's donkey." The golden eyes blinked at me and I couldn't help but smile. "Is it so with all who walk on four legs?"

The creature gave a longing stare at her fellows penned together nearby, her long ears down.

"Why are you all alone? Did you do something bad?" That's when I saw her belly was swollen on the left side. "Is it sickness?" I pressed my hand against the swelling and she did not shy away. My eyes widened as I sensed a flutter of movement, the warmth of flesh within flesh. Something stirred in her belly. "How?" I whispered.

Then my new companion stiffened and bolted to the other side of the pen. She pawed the ground with cloven feet, eyes rolling with terror.

A chill breath stroked my ear. "It's called a goat, sweet sister," said the familiar, sneering voice.

I whirled to meet my brother's glowing eyes. Grethor gestured at the hairy creature with one of his claws. He bared his fangs in a grin. "They're soft and toothsome. Perhaps I should have chosen something more like this for your first kill."

RUNES

GRETHOR LEERED and reached for my golden arm ring with one of his clawed hands. "Shiny. You always did like pretties, didn't you, thief? Did you steal it like the amulet?"

I backed away until the wooden fence post pressed against my spine. He thrust his face into mine, the dank smell of his breath dragging bile up from my gullet. A cold horror swept over my flesh and I wanted to shrink so small that he could never find me. Yet that was not my fate; I had seen the moment Grethor slew me, and this wasn't it. With shaking fingers I drew forth the amulet and brandished it at him.

The amber flashed in the sun and Grethor recoiled. He retreated a few steps, his slitted eyes on the amulet. My weapon, greater than tooth or blade.

At last I found my voice. "I'm no thief, Grethor. The amulet is mine."

He wheezed with laughter. "You have the magics, aye. But do you know how to use them?" I willed myself not to flinch and some of his slyness returned. "Thought you'd hurt poor Grethor with your seething, did you? And oh, you did. Hearing is sweet agony for me now, every rasp a bellow. But I should thank you. Your little curse made me stronger. Nothing can hide from me now. I hear every sigh, every murmur. I can hear your heart beating. Faster and faster, blood roaring in your veins." He licked his chops.

I gripped the amulet, called upon the goddess to help me end this fiend that called itself my kin.

Fear danced across Grethor's face at the sight, quickly replaced by a smirk. "Do it, then."

My hand shook. The amulet remained inert as a stone in my fist. *Not yet, dear one. First there is a choice you must make.*

Grethor smiled slowly. "Not so mighty, eh? Then you'd best listen to Grethor. I came to speak to you, sweet sister. To save you."

"From what?"

He nodded toward the house. "Men. They will do naught but twist your tender little thoughts. Against me, against Módor. She wants you back, you know."

"What?" I lowered my hand.

"She's a forgiving sort. For you, at least." He shuddered. "Such a thrashing she gave when I came back without you. You'd have liked seeing that."

"No." I lowered my hand a little. "I wouldn't."

"You say so." He sniffed. "She cried. I never saw her weep before. You know that? Great fat tears rolling from her eyes like gobs of tallow. Every night I hear her mutter how she lost her special one. Keeps me awake."

"Módor shed tears? For me?" A cloud passed over my thoughts. I leaned against the fence and crossed my arms. The goats penned opposite me stared at Grethor, the air thick with the stench of their fear. "You think humans so vile?"

He shrugged. "I watch my prey. And I listen."

"So you can glut yourself?"

"To fill my belly, aye. But more than that, much more. Understanding is worthy for its own sake. That's what our mother taught us, wasn't it? You want to learn a thing's true nature, you stalk it. Make it skittish. Let it know you're after it."

"And then?"

"It flees. Runs fast as its little trotters will carry it. But not fast enough. Soon you have your fingers around its throat. You squeeze, grip. Make the thing squeak! Draw blood if you want." His eyes flicked to my bone knife. My claw. "The eyes open wide. That's when you see."

"What?"

"Its soul, its gizzard. All that it is. Everything comes out in death." He chuckled. "I know you think me a monster— you've thought it since you were little. Don't pretend, lies taste bitter and I know you better than that. But don't you see, Dóta?" He leaned closer to me, a noble look on his face. "I wanted to teach you what humankind looks like inside. I know what it is to be a beast, unloved. That's why I chose Anskar for your first kill."

"You wanted to help me."

He swallowed. "To show you what you are, no matter your flesh."

"Aye? And what is that?"

He smiled without showing his teeth. "A killer. One of us. Part of our clan. Their souls don't look like ours. Are you so quick to forget, sweet sister? Humans discarded you like shite." He leaned closer. "All can be as it was. If Módor can forgive, so can I. Will you not come with me?"

The world blurred behind tears. A yearning for the comfort of rock walls. Cold and lonesome, perhaps, but there my only worry was the ire of Módor or my brother. A simple life. Far from confusion and doubt, no question of who I am or what I mean. The desire tugged at me, I will not deny it. And then: "How do you know his name?"

"Eh?"

"The warrior. Anskar."

"Heard you talking, didn't I? Every word. But you've not answered me." When I remained silent, the nobility dropped from his face. "I could drag you," he hissed.

"You couldn't."

"Módor said not to touch a hair on your head, but she's not here…" He reached to grab one of my curls with his long, tapering claws.

I slapped his hand away. "Don't touch me." I filled my lungs. "I'm not like you, never will be!"

My brother growled like a wounded animal at my shout. "That's what I told Módor, sweet sister. But still she told me to bring you back and I'm in no mood for another thrashing. So I'll make it plain. Come home, I'll spare these humans you love so much. Stay and…" He laughed. "What happens next will be your doing."

But I did not relent, quaking with rage. My voice was quiet but remained steady. "I've made my choice. Now I'll give you one. Leave me now. Leave this realm. Or you will burn."

He guffawed. "I see the bloodlust in your eyes. You're tainted as I am."

"No, troll," said a lilting voice behind me. I turned to find Twyla staring at Grethor, no fear in her eyes. In her hands she held a gnarled staff, runes carved along its length. "Nothing is so foul. Now do as she says."

Grethor smirked and took a swipe at her.

She side-stepped his attack. "Raise your amulet, Dóta. And get behind me."

I obeyed. The amulet grew hot, power building within it.

Twyla raised her staff. The air became cold and heavy, like winter had fallen in an instant. The bleats of the goats grew higher, more frantic. The branches quivered and wind hissed through them. Dead pine needles whipped at my face. The winds swirled around the tip of the staff and the runes shone with a blue flame.

Grethor struggled against the gale. Even with his eyes screwed shut, I could see fear on his face. Magic was terror to him, no matter his bluster. The roar of the wind must have been torture to his ears, yet still he reached for the staff.

Anskar ran out from inside the house, yellow hair flying, axe at the ready.

"No, Anskar," I said. "Stay back."

He was not such a fool as to rush into the fight, knowing a task that called for seething. Still, he made no move to flee.

"You shan't have the better of me, beast," said Twyla through gritted teeth. "For I am a servant of the raven god. You've no place in this world or any other." Then she chanted, strange words slicing through the squall. The same words Anskar had uttered before, though I still did not grasp their meaning.

As if in answer a figure drifted from the direction of the mounds. It was taller than I, clad in armor of leather and scale. A hoary beard, no mistaking it for a mortal man. For a moment I saw a flash of Anskar on its face, but its skin was blue as veins. All but the lips, coated with blood. A bronze torque around its neck. It glanced at me, eyes blazing cobalt. The dead king turned back to Grethor with a grin like that of a mountain lion which had just cornered a mouse.

Grethor opened his mouth and howled at the dead with all the ferocity in his heart. Seeing the ghost did not turn aside, Grethor sprang back. "Soon, Dóta. You'll come home soon enough." Then he turned and fled into the darkness of the pines.

Twyla lowered her staff. The glow of the runes dimmed, their power spent.

My heart beat three times before Anskar spoke. "It ran from you. I never knew you had such power, Twyla."

Her laugh was tired. "The power isn't mine, Anskar. How many times must you hear it?" She bowed her head to the dead king, who regarded her with cool eyes. "You have my thanks, old one," she said. "And you shall have more besides. Go in peace."

The ghost gave me one last, lingering look before it departed, little more than a wisp of the air.

"I see the threat, now. And I sense..." Twyla fell silent, as though listening to a voice I could not hear. Then she nodded. "Oh, how strange the weaving of fate is. Pull one thread, the whole unravels." She laid a hand on my shoulder, her grip harder than I expected. "Know that I would teach you because it is my fate. Not because Anskar asks it of me."

Some of the tension left Anskar's shoulders. "You have my thanks."

"For all that's worth." Twyla turned back to me. "The only question, then, young one. Will you have me as your teacher? I'd not take an unwilling pupil."

I hesitated. "Yes."

"Yes what?"

"I want you to teach me the ways of the gods."

"Why?"

"Because I need to slay my... I need to slay him. I swore an oath." Anskar nodded, but Twyla raised her chin. Was my answer not enough? "And because..." I swallowed, my throat like the world of flame. "I need to know."

Twyla smiled, clamped her arm around my shoulders and steered me into her house. She left her staff propped by the door next to her mud-stained boots.

QUESTIONS

"Boia? It's time to awaken," said Anskar.

I groaned and huddled deeper into my bedroll.

"Dóta," he corrected himself. "I must go."

Rubbing the grit out of my eyes, I sat up. Little rest had come to me in the night. Grey light seeped through a hole in the thatch above my head, revealing the soot which filled Twyla's house. "So soon?"

He smiled, his eyes bloodshot. He and Twyla had stayed up drinking vile stuff by the fire, talking in soft voices until Anskar had taken his sleeping bag outside. I didn't understand why they had spent the night this way, but few human deeds made sense to me. "I cannot remain. Too many memories here. And there is much to do."

"Like what?"

"The beast left a trail when it fled yesterday. I mean to track it."

I sat up, my muscles sore from sleeping on the hard earth floor. "Take me with you."

He shook his head. "Fear not. I won't be hunting, not

without you at my side. But we'll have no joy until we find its lair."

Joy. A strange notion. For what joy could I find, knowing Anskar sought the dark in which I was raised? I recalled the bones I had found in Módor's treasure chamber, all that remained of a warrior armored like Anskar. My mother had ripped apart the man's chain mail and cracked his ribs.

"Promise me you won't go into the cave," I said.

He leaned forward. "A cave, you say." When I gave no reply other than to chew my lip, Anskar's face grew stern. "I've been patient, Dóta. But I'll not have you play with the lives of men. Mine included. Is there anything you wish to tell me?"

I felt as though I was choking. Snot ran from my nose. I wiped it away with the back of my hand. The worst of it was that I did want to tell him, I just didn't know how. Or why.

The door creaked open. Twyla swept into the house, bringing a whiff of goat with her. She set a brush down next to the hearth, warming her hands by the embers. "Won't be long 'til we have a wee kid springing about." She turned to me. "Are you ready? Boots on, thank you kindly."

I pushed aside the bedroll and reached for my boots.

Anskar glared at me a moment and then his eyes softened. "You'll tell me when it's time. I'd not squeeze a stone for blood." He accepted a husk of barley bread from Twyla. Their fingers brushed together and they exchanged a long glance before Anskar pulled away and looked at me. Pride shone even through his weariness. "Learn well—fill your head with the mead of wisdom. Soon enough we'll drink the real thing. A toast to our victory. Meanwhile, be good to each other, eh?"

"Anskar," murmured Twyla.

He turned. "What?"

"I'm happy you came back, is all."

Gladness crossed his face, though it was drowned in pain. He gave a silent nod and strode from the house. The clomp of his feet made me think of Módor's tales of frost giants.

As soon as he was out of earshot, I asked Twyla why Anskar would not farewell her.

"That," she said with a raised brow, "is not a wise question. Now, lesson time. We've roots and herbs and mushrooms to gather."

"Mushrooms?" I said as I helped myself to some bread from the hearth. "They grow above ground?"

She gave me an odd look. "Aye indeed. Come along! The sun won't wait, she only burns so long." Twyla grabbed a leather sack. "Leave the amulet today. There are things you need to learn on your own first. No need to fear the troll, not around these parts. My ghostly companions will see to that."

"Sorry," I muttered to the amulet as I stuffed it under the bedroll. Its silence was sullen, or so I dreamed. A strange relief, that the goddess would not be whispering in my ear today. Making sure my knife was tucked in its sheath, I followed Twyla out the door. As we approached the edge of the clearing, I said: "Twyla, why does your house smell so bad? The burning dung kept me awake."

"My gods, you do cut to the quick! My house is older than most, so no chimney. The worst of the smoke escapes through the thatch, so I never saw the need. Anyway, the smell seldom bothers me."

"How come?"

"It takes dreadful cold to keep me inside."

"Why?"

"I, ah, once spent a lot of time cramped and seasick. If you know my meaning."

"No."

Her face darkened, blood filling her cheeks. "Oh, I—well, I was a thrall, wasn't I? That's how I got this." She pointed at the mark on her chin. "Mouthy now, mouthy then." She gave me a weak smile. "I prefer the woods."

Thrall. I had heard this word many times now, though I was no closer to its meaning. "What is a thrall?"

"You do come from far off. Well, we've one thing in common, then. Now come along."

I frowned, for she had not answered my question. Yet it was best to ask nothing more. What if she struck me like Módor did? Within moments I was pushing dewy branches out of my face as we tramped through the underbrush. Twyla told me the names of every herb and root she gathered. I recall few of them now, for my mind was on other things. Only a little time had passed since I had decided to ask no more questions, yet I found another on my lips. "What have mushrooms to do with the gods?"

"Ha! If only you knew," said Twyla. She pulled me into a crouch behind a tree. "Look."

A pair of bright eyes gleamed from beneath a bush. My heart lurched, thinking of Grethor. But no, these eyes were too close together, too full of mischief. They darted from me and Twyla to a clump of red-capped mushrooms nearby. Judging us no threat, the animal darted out as quick as my eye could follow. I caught a flash of gold fur, a puffy tail waving in the air. Nowadays I would call it a fox. Whiskers twitched as it sniffed at the mushrooms. The fox opened its jaws on one and bit off a piece. Then it spat out the morsel and slunk away, its pink tongue lolling.

When the fox was out of sight, Twyla approached the clump, motioning me to follow. She bent, plucked one up and sniffed it just as my mother would have. Then Twyla ran her tongue over the top of the mushroom. "Now you try. Lick it, go on."

I picked one, rolled it between my fingers. Sniffing it suggested nothing amiss. Yet the top of the mushroom gleamed a dangerous crimson flecked with white. Like a pustule. I raised it to my mouth. Twyla gave me an encouraging nod, and I ran my tongue over it. The taste was nothing like the mushrooms I had grown up with, so awful that my stomach clenched around my morning bread. It was slimy yet sucked moisture from my mouth. My lips tingled as though spiders danced upon them. I cast the mushroom to the ground. "It's poison!"

Twyla cackled. "To most, aye. The Red Cap has taken more than one life. Yet it will let the hardiest see the faces of the gods, fill them with the mad courage of Odin's berserk. You were right not to swallow, you're not ready for that yet."

The sinews around my mouth tightened as I glared at her. "You might have killed me."

"But I didn't. And you learned something."

"What, not to do a thing you tell me?"

"No," said Twyla, taken aback. Then she thought on it. "But I can see why you'd take that lesson. Think on this. The fox rejected the poison. Did you do elsewise?" My brow furrowed and I shook my head. "Nor should you. Human, animal, there is no difference."

"What about trolls?"

"Troll, dwarf, elf-kind. Even the Valkyries and Norns. Everyone lives for the sake of living. And until you grasp this, you cannot know the gods. Some are good and some cruel, but all of us are beasts like any other."

My mother's lip would have curled at such advice. Every time I had asked her about humans, she had chided me: *"They aren't like our kind, Dóta. They are beasts."* Yet she had made me part of her clan, had told me we were the same. I rubbed my temples. The mead of wisdom made my head hurt and there was so much more to drink in.

Twyla snapped her fingers in front of my face. "I can't teach if you're woolgathering."

I blinked out of my thoughts. "Eh?"

"Show me the wisdom you've gained today."

I mumbled the names of the herbs and roots and mushrooms she had taught me, the properties of the Red Cap.

Her brows crept up her forehead. "Your wisdom, I said."

Flexing my jaw, I did my best to recount what I had learned of humans and beasts.

Yet she rolled her eyes. "Show your wisdom by your questions, not your knowledge."

I gnawed the inside of my cheek. "My mother had little time for questions."

She ground her teeth, which were greyish and crooked. "Loki's balls! You had questions aplenty this morning."

I swallowed, tried to think. Grethor's taunts from yesterday came back to me. "What does the soul look like?"

"What?" Something told me she wasn't prepared for this.

"You said humans and trolls are all just beasts—do our souls look the same?"

"Perhaps you are not such a dullard after all," said Twyla. "These are wise questions. But they belong to another day. Let's be getting back. These mushrooms will take time to stew. If we're lucky, the goats will give us good dung for the fire." She tucked a few of the Red Caps into her satchel and ambled toward the house.

I held back a moment, watching her duck under the boughs. There was something else I wanted to know, more than anything else.

Who are my birth parents? And why did they leave me behind?

The question had not long awakened within me and would not rest. Still, I reckoned Twyla would not deem it wise.

DUTY

A FEW NIGHTS HAD PASSED. I was picking a bur out of the
pregnant goat's hair, trying to ignore her bleating. Twyla
assured me tending the goats and fetching water were part
of my training, like stargazing and talking of Norns and the
fates, but I suspected she just needed the help. She should
have asked, no need for tricks. I liked the doe, wanted to
ease her discomfort. Then came the sound of a horse
approaching from around the front of the house. My
muscles tensed, but I did not cease brushing until I heard
Arína's voice.

My mouth went dry, my heart thrumming like a lyre.
The princess always did this to me. I could not explain it,
not then, but I craved her favor as once I craved the sun. The
brush lay forgotten on the grass as I ran.

The princess's black horse stood tethered to a post
nearby, steam rising from its nostrils. She herself stood
muttering in the horse's ear. I stopped short at the sight of
her. Arína wore no kirtle, but a gleaming mail shirt like that
of Anskar. A shield was strapped to her back, a short sword
hanging from her belt. Her golden hair was plaited close to

her scalp. A war-maker and a peace-weaver in one body. Was such a thing possible? She turned and caught me staring, her face greyer than last time I saw her. No smile crossed her face. "Well met, Boia Elfin-sun."

I swallowed, wanted to tell her my name was Dóta. But no, she might not care for me if she knew I was a girl. Did she care for me? I had half expected her to greet me with arms outstretched. "Arína," I said. "Well met, princess."

She gave a single nod. "If only it were not under an ill omen. Grethor nears Valdskali."

"What?"

"It was near midnight and all was dark. Yet one of the villagers saw when she stepped out to squat—a pair of glowing eyes, watching from the shadows. The girl crept back inside and slid the bolt. That's when she heard the fiend's dreadful laugh, its glee like Loki's. Yet it came no nearer. Not that night."

"Nobody died?" I might have sagged from relief.

"Not yet. But some say they have seen the thing's face looking in on them. One old man swears its skin is like tree-bark, another reckons it has scales like an adder. All agree its fangs are longer than those of a dire wolf."

"Where would they have seen a dire wolf?"

"Gods know. But a feud broke out yesterday when a farmer threw a stone, thinking it was the monster, and hit his neighbor instead. Folks are frightened, Boia." She halted her speech. "Even my father."

"And you?" I said.

Her face hardened. "I am brave."

"I didn't mean—"

"I know. Of course you didn't." She sighed, no longer the bright-haired princess I had met that night in the hall.

"Are you weary?" I said. "Come inside, Twyla can give you a—"

She shook her head. "I didn't ride for one of her brews. I came for you."

"Me?"

"Are you ready to face the beast? Have you learned the magic you need?" Arína's eyes pierced me.

I looked away. "I've only been here a week since Thor's Day. The moon has hardly changed his face since I arrived."

"What have you been learning, then?" Arína reached out and pulled a strand of goat hair off my shirt. "Thrall's work?"

"Twyla's ways are strange. I don't know why she teaches me this."

Arína reddened. "So you've learned no seething? None? How do you expect to slay the monster?"

"I don't know yet." My words were hoarse.

"I see." The princess drew her sword and with one swipe sliced through the horse's tether.

"Where are you going?"

"To prepare. An attack is coming, I'm sure of it."

"What will you do?"

"My father trained me and a handful of other maidens. He kept it secret from his companions, even Anskar. When all else fails, we must shield the king." She slid her foot into one of the iron stirrups.

"You could stay here."

Arína stilled. "Eh?"

"This place is safe, Princess. Grethor cannot strike you here." I swallowed. "I wouldn't have you in his reach."

She planted both feet on the soil and stared. "No, Boia. My place is with my father. The men are away pillaging. Only we shield maidens protect the realm. Until you are ready."

"But... I don't want you in danger."

"Then learn fast. Because we're all in danger." The princess's eyes glistened, and she said in a lower voice: "There's something else, Boia. I couldn't stay with you anyway. I am betrothed now. All arranged long ago, but I was told just after you left my father's hall."

"Betrothed? What does that mean?"

"It means we can't be alone together." A tear streaked down her face and she batted it away. "We never could be, anyway. My father wouldn't allow it. He doesn't even know I'm here. And as for the boy I'm to marry..." She shrugged. "You met him at the Althing. Jörgen, son of Ulf."

"That boy who was with Redmane?" My first night in Valdskali, I had seen the sad-faced boy try and stop his father from spilling blood, yet still Redmane had sneered at King Hrut, called him swine. And many had cheered.

"Ten days from now the warriors will return from the first of the summer raids. Then I am to marry. It's the only way the king can avoid war with their clan. A kingdom might endure war or monsters, but not both."

"But... We can't talk to one another?"

"You have your duty, Boia Elfin-sun. And I have mine. This is the fate which the Norns have spun for me."

"I'm sorry," I said.

"As am I." And I think she meant it. She mounted up and tugged on the reins. The horse whinnied and trotted toward the forest track.

"Wait," I said. "There's something I need to tell you."

But she was already away, her horse kicking up dust.

I truly didn't know what "betrothed" meant. When Twyla explained it, I wept.

BIRTH

NO MATTER MY HURT, the sun still rose the next morning.

I had barely swallowed my morning meal when Twyla ordered me to grab a bucket. "There's a hot spring just a half day's walk from here. The water has healing powers." Seeing my hand moving toward the amulet, she shook her head. "You won't be needing it."

I muttered something, my thoughts dark.

Twyla blinked. "I know your wrath isn't for me. Speak."

No, she was the one I was angry with. "Why are we wasting our time? Aren't you going to teach me seething?"

"What in Hel do you think I've been doing? Seething is more than just words and power. It can take years to master—"

"We don't have years!" I snapped. "Grethor is out there right now and I'm stuck here with you."

"Calm yourself. There's work to be done."

"Thrall's work?" I said, remembering Arína's words.

Her face went white as bone, utterly drained of blood. I had never seen human flesh do that before. "Yes, Dóta.

That's exactly what it is. You truly don't know what a thrall is, do you?"

My innards went cold, fathoming the hurt in her voice. "No," I admitted.

"It's…" She fiddled with one of the thorns she used to fasten her clothes. "A human who must do the will of another. Serve. Your life becomes obedience. Some become thralls for their crimes." She swallowed. "Others are simply fated for it. So it was when the raiders fettered me and brought me here. They took me away from my mother, my father, my brothers. I had nothing but my belief in the All-Father, even if I knew him by another name then. Yet I am grateful—I could not serve the gods until I learned to serve humankind."

"But seething…"

"Is just another form of service. By Asgard, didn't you hear what I told Anskar? The power does not belong to me, but Odin. I am naught but the god's hand." She took a step closer to me. "First you learn to serve, humbling yourself. Know we are all of us nature's creatures. Then you can still your mind, taste of the mushrooms and breathe the burning herbs. Through them you can heed the voices of the gods and know their commands."

"But I can hear them now," I said, trying to keep my voice from shaking. "Freya herself speaks to me through the amulet."

Twyla looked away, her brows knitted. "Before the rites? I never heard of such a thing."

My pulse quickened, wondering how much to tell her. "My mother said something to me. She said the gods had reason to protect me."

"All mothers say such things. Ah, give me time to think on it. Go check the goats."

I wanted to slam the door behind me, only it might have fallen from its hinges. So I growled at the sky instead and stomped toward the goat pens, for there was nothing better to do. Twyla was naught but a foolish old woman, I told myself. She had deceived me, wanted to make me feel small, to make me a thrall like her. Whatever my destiny held, it wasn't that.

My anger fell away when I beheld the pregnant goat. Her tail pointed to the sky, her back arched as she rocked back and forth. She was digging with her hoofs. Her golden eyes begged me for help.

"Twyla!" I shouted. "Come, there's something wrong!"

The door banged open and Twyla came running. "What?" Then she saw the goat and relaxed. "A little earlier than I thought, but no matter. Be at peace, Dóta."

"Peace?" The doe made soft keening noises. Not screaming as she had when Grethor was near, but enough to tell me this wasn't normal.

"Go fetch a clean cloth. Seems we're to have a different lesson from what I had in mind."

I sped off to do as she asked, then returned at once. A long, silvery line of fluid now trailed behind the goat, glistening in the sun. "What do we do?"

"Now," said Twyla, settling herself down on a clean patch of hay inside the pen. "We wait until the babe is ready. There isn't much we can do but catch him when he slips out."

I closed the gate behind me and crouched beside her. "How can you tell it's a him?"

Twyla closed her eyes for a moment and breathed deep. "He has the soul of a war-maker. I can see it."

"Always?"

"I'm seldom wrong," she said, then opened her eyes.

"For now, just stroke her back. Gently, that's it. We need to keep her calm."

The sun had only climbed a little when the goat began panting, her voice growing shrill. Twyla's face became grave. "Stand back." She gently felt inside the goat and shook her head. "The hoofs aren't right."

"What does that mean?"

"This is going to be harder than I thought. I'll have to pull. Keep talking to her, sing a song. Show her there's nothing to fear."

Was there nothing to fear? I pressed my tongue between my teeth, willing my heart to stop fluttering. I crooned a song my mother had sung to help me sleep.

> *Fair maids shape the worlds' fates*
> *Three dwell beneath the ash*
> *Mothers all, daughters all*
> *Many are their children*
> *Spread far throughout Midgard*
> *Some gods, some elves, some dwarfs*
> *All wise, all proud, all feared.*

Perhaps recognizing the song, Twyla gave me a look so sharp it might have pierced bone. And yet I sang on. My voice was rough—I was no skald—but the Song of the Norns soothed the doe even as she strained. Before I knew it, Twyla cradled a bundle wrapped in cloth and the goat convulsed with weariness. "Here, Dóta," said Twyla and she shoved the bundle into my arms. "My work isn't done yet. Still the placenta to go."

I examined the kid as the doe pushed. The creature was tiny, fragile, its hair slick with sticky fluid. He had little stubs where the horns would grow, softer than my nails. His eyes were closed and he made not a sound. Limp as a wet rag. "Twyla," I said, "he's not breathing."

"A shame," said Twyla without looking up. "His sire must have been one of my neighbor's sheep. Half breeds are usually born dead and this one came out feet first…"

Tears blurred my sight, she spoke with such cold indifference. Couldn't this little weirdling have its chance at life? With a furious passion I wiped at it with the cloth and cleaned the gunk out of its nose. Desperately, furiously, I prayed for this waif to live.

Twyla wiped her hands and looked at me. "Dóta," she said gently. "He's gone. I know it's hard, but this is the way of—"

"No," I said and shoved the kid into his mother's face. The doe shied away from her young, more intent upon the long, purple husk of flesh she had just birthed. "Don't you know he's yours?" I said, my voice cracking under the weight of despair.

Twyla put a hand on my shoulder. "Not all are meant for this world. Don't feel bad, this is fate."

I shrugged her off. "Do something."

"What would you have me do? Even gods cannot restore the dead."

"But they can breathe upon an ember."

"Where did you hear—"

"The goddess told me," I snapped. "Please. We have to try."

Twyla sighed and laid a hand on the kid's head. She muttered a few words, no more than that.

Nothing happened. The doe continued to feast on her own flesh. The kid didn't stir and all was still.

Twyla turned to me. "I'm sorry, Dóta. I tried."

"I know," I said. "I know you did. Thank-you."

"Do you want to talk?"

"No." I rose from my crouch and trudged back toward the house.

Then a high, thin noise rose from the pen. The kid opened his mouth and gave another bleat. I spun around to find the mother goat nuzzling her young, licking off the last of the stickiness. He leaned into her, suckling. After a few moments, the infant wobbled to his feet, sliding on what was left of the placenta before he recovered. Growing in strength with every breath. He had just a sliver of life, but was alive nonetheless.

A tear spilled down Twyla's face. My brow furrowed in confusion. What was there to grieve over? She held out her arms and enfolded me. Her musk was of loam and pine and unwashed wool. She was a huddle of warmth and safety. Yet my own arms remained rigid at my sides. I stepped back, my senses aflame. This might have been a trap.

Perhaps sensing I would not return her hug, Twyla pulled back. She opened her mouth, then closed it. Her eyes fixed upon me, wide as the sea. A secret hid in those depths like the Midgard Serpent. Then she pointed over my shoulder, her face drawn in horror. "Look."

Smoke rose above the pines. My guts shifted, for I knew what lay in that direction.

Valdskali was in flames.

PREY

Dark smoke still rose from the king's hall when we reached
the top of the hill. The acrid stench made me gag, but the
hall continued to stand. The relief so overwhelmed me that
I might have died of it. For in a vision I had seen the Hall of
the Wolf consumed by flame and all humans within burned
to ash.

Not today, dear one, came the honeyed voice from the
amulet which gleamed upon my chest. *The hour is nearer
than ever before, but not yet.*

Yet I could not feel safe. Twyla and I stood at the base of
the steps before the threshold. Men and women in ragged
tunics—thralls—ran in all directions, their buckets sloshing
on the flagstones. They cast water upon glowing embers
which died in a hiss. The great oaken door to Valdskali
stood broken, gaping where it had been kicked in. Jagged
claw marks on the wood showed Grethor must have
smashed his way through. The door might have been woven
from dry thatch for all the protection it had given.

I exchanged a look with Twyla. She tightened her grip
upon her staff before we shouldered our way into the hall.

A few girls mopped red puddles from the floor. A cloud of flies hummed over the blood like bees upon nectar. My eyes smarted and my nose ran, the pall was so thick. Ash coated everything. The long benches at which the warriors had sat were now heaped in the corner, little more than a pile of splinters thanks to my brother.

I stepped aside for a pair of thralls dragging something heavy in a sack. A boneless arm flopped from the sack, pale fingers trailing on the dirt floor. A thrall with a shaved head cursed and tucked the arm back inside, but he stopped short when he saw me running up.

"Open it," I said.

The thrall hesitated but obeyed. Within the folds, the blank eyes of the king's companion Rokia stared upward at the beams of the roof.

I clapped my hand over my mouth at the sight.

"Did you know him?" said Twyla.

I shook my head. "Though he was kind to me, that first night I arrived here."

The thrall with the shiny scalp nodded. "Odin will have a place set out for Rokia in his hall sure enough, Elfin-sun. Blind or no, the old man did not turn when the creature came for the king. Stood right by the princess as she fell."

"What?"

"Even she was no match for it."

"Where is she?" I snarled, hearing the savagery even in my own voice.

He pointed. The princess slumped upon the throne. Blood dripped from her face onto the links of her chain-mail. Around her were perhaps a dozen other women, all clad in war garments as she was. Some stood, others leaned against spears. I do not recall making the choice to run to Arína's side, but I was there in less than a heartbeat. Three furious red lines raked her face from her brow to her chin. Her eyes roved as she looked up at me. It only came to us later that she was lucky to still have both. "Boia. You've come."

"Too late. I'm sorry, I'm so sorry."

She shook her head. "Not too late, not yet. We did our task, the king is safe. And the hall's still standing." She started to smile, but it made the gouges on her face bleed anew.

I snatched the amulet from within my tunic. "We can help." I glared at Twyla. "Can't we?"

"I'm no healer and neither are you. But we'll do what we can," said Twyla.

Arína shook her head as I leaned toward her, though her face was tight with anguish. She motioned toward a bronze-haired girl who lay prone before the stone shrine in the corner of the hall. The girl's woolens were stained a shiny red, her face whiter than milk. Still breathing, but I feared not for long. "Thora cast herself in the creature's path when it reached for me. Save her."

Twyla was already at the girl's side. She examined the claw marks across the girl's chest. Breaths gurgled deep inside, flecks of pink foam on the chin. "I can't do this alone," said Twyla. "Has the goddess taught you any words of healing?"

"None," I said.

"I know but a few. Listen to me and repeat this chant." When she was certain I could recite the words of power, Twyla stood over the girl and raised her staff. A cold fire lanced from the runes along its length and into the flesh. Yet the eyes of Grethor's victim remained shut, her breathing ragged.

I lifted the amulet and said the words, expecting to feel

the magic seethe through me. Nothing happened. "Come on," I whispered.

The voice had lost its warmth now. *As I told you before, I am not your thrall.*

"No," I muttered through gritted teeth. "But you must help."

What do I care if this human lives or dies? There is nothing special about her, no touch of destiny. This is her doom and she cannot flee it.

"You help her," I hissed at the amulet, "or I'll take you off and leave you off."

In my hand, the amulet flamed with scorching heat. I bit my tongue to stop myself from crying out—never before had I been burned. The goddess's voice thundered in my ears. *You think to threaten me? The amulet is but my instrument. Like you.*

My hand was throbbing, but I couldn't let go. "For every giving there is a taking," I said. One of my mother's favorite sayings. "Show these folks your strength. Give the girl her life and all will honor you."

The amulet paused as though thinking on it. The wounded girl's breaths became a rattle. Her eyes snapped open, spinning with agony while the goddess pondered.

"Or perhaps you'd rather be forgotten," I said through gnashed teeth. "The goddess who did nothing when the monster came."

You wicked, ungrateful thrall. Know that I do this for honor, not to appease your whims. Now speak my name and run through the words again.

The chant poured from my lips with new haste. The amber in my fist glowed bright enough for me to see the bones and sinews of my hand. Heat rippled and it fed the flames from Twyla's staff. I might have gasped as the pain seared through my palm. But I did not dare cease chanting.

"Enough," said Twyla at last and she sat down by the altar. Her face was lined with weariness. The bronze-haired girl was silent now, curled up on the floor in peace. Her wounds had already closed. Thora's chest rose up and down, her breaths deep and clear.

I fell silent, my throat raw and my head light. I felt like a wrung cloth, yet my veins were filled with rushing flames. How could I be so spent and yet so elated? I flexed my palm. The angry red mark still throbbed.

For every giving a taking, said the amulet, a sneer in the goddess's voice. *Surely you do not begrudge the girl your strength?*

This shield maiden lived because of me and Twyla. Though the goddess should have told me how it would work, I found comfort in that.

"Thank-you, Boia," said the princess. She was on her feet and watching. She had removed her mail and wore a torn woolen shirt. It seemed an effort for her even to stand.

"Let me heal you," I said, not caring about the cost.

"No," said Arína. "Do not weaken yourself further. I shall bear these scars as tokens of battle. Let our enemies see Hrut's kin stand firm."

"Well said, my daughter," said a calm, deep voice. King Hrut strode into the hall. He readjusted the wolf's pelt he wore like a cloak. The king laid heavy hands upon my shoulders. "Your magic has grown strong indeed, Boia Elfin-sun."

"We must hold council, my king," said Anskar. I had not noticed when he had slipped into the hall. He seemed unharmed. "There are choices to be made."

"Right as usual, Anskar." Hrut, Anskar and Arína walked

toward the back of the hall. Then the king stopped and asked over his shoulder if I was coming.

"What about Twyla?" I said.

Anskar's face grew flinty at the notion, but he did not protest.

Twyla didn't look at him. "I'll stay and do what I can out here."

The king nodded and we followed him through the oaken door into the next chamber. He sat down at the end of a long wooden table and we arranged ourselves on straight backed chairs. I sat as far from the king as I could, feeling small in his presence. All I wanted was to bathe my hand in cool water, anything to quench the fire that still dwelled in my flesh.

The king snapped his fingers and a thrall came to fill his cup. Hrut rubbed his temples as he took a deep draught. "A grim day indeed. But this Grethor is not long for this world, thanks to Arína."

"What?" I twisted in my seat, the pain forgotten.

"My king," said Anskar, sitting at Hrut's right hand. "I would know what happened. Boia too."

The king drained his cup and snapped his fingers for more. "It came early in the morning when all of us were snoring. Blasted craven didn't even have the decency to face me." Wine dripped from the tip of the king's moustache. "The demon has no mercy. The few warriors we had were dead before they could reach for their blades. The thing tossed them through the air like they were rags, dashed their skulls against the walls. I heard the crack."

I closed my eyes, thinking of Rokia.

The king spoke on. "Gods above and below. It didn't just kill. It opened its jaws and..."

His hands trembled as he reached for his cup once

more, but Arína pushed it out of his reach. "The creature feasted," she said. "Let us say no more than that." She tore a strip from her ruined woolens, dipped it into the wine and pressed it into her wounds. "I think someone must have knocked over a lamp, for the flames were already leaping. The girls and I formed a shield wall around the throne. Through the flames it came. Spear, axe, sword... Every blow failed. It threw its head back and giggled, bloody teeth gleaming. That's when I saw a way."

"My girl shouted for a bow," said Hrut. "I grabbed one from the wall, strung it fast as I could while she and the shield maidens grappled with it. Fierce as the Valkyries, you were."

Anskar opened his mouth, then closed it. I reckon he wanted to rebuke the king for hiding the training of the shield maidens. Yet he was not one to speak against his brother and lord in front of others.

"Not fierce enough," said Arína. "You cried out my name, Father, telling me to catch. And then the beast froze. At first I thought we must have wounded it, but it clamped those blazing eyes upon me. As though it had recognized my name. I nocked an arrow. One sweep of its claw and the maidens flew. It was coming for me like a night-spirit. Eyes rolling, wide as targets... And so I loosed."

"You hit him?" My chair clattered backward, I stood so fast.

King Hrut looked on his daughter, pride rising from him like sparks from a hearth. "The light in its eye snuffed out. The bastard reeled, dark blood all over its face. Hah! It bawled like a stuck pig. I don't think it will trouble us again."

Anskar gripped the edge of the table. "It's dead, then? Where is the body?"

The king scoffed. "An arrow in the eye? It'll perish of blood fever soon, no doubt. No man could survive that."

"Grethor is no man," I said.

Arína shook her head slowly and held the wine-soaked rag up to her face. It must have caused her pain, but she pressed all the harder. "The shaft didn't go in far enough, Father. Losing an eye only made Odin stronger, why would the demon be elsewise?" She shuddered. "It grabbed me by the hair and it…"

"Sniffed," I finished. "Grethor sniffed your hair." As he did to all his prey. As he did to me.

"And then it did this. One quick swipe." She motioned toward the cuts on her face. "*She likes the pretties.* That's what it whispered in my ear. And then it stalked out of the hall, leaving behind a trail of blood." She fell back into her chair, shaking. "I don't understand. Grethor could have slain the king. Could have slain all of us. But it was after me? And who's she?"

A long silence.

My guts might have been alive with worms, I felt so sick. For I could fathom the cause. Had Grethor not warned me? If I came home, he'd spare these humans I love so much. I shrank into my chair. This was my doing. "He is still alive, King. I know it in my heart. And he will only do more evil."

Hope died on the king's face. "And there I thought this was done. We must call off the wedding now. I cannot risk—"

Arína looked up. "There is risk in all things, Father. But we cannot afford to anger Redmane. We cannot afford weakness."

"But—" I started.

"The princess is right, Hrut," Anskar cut me off. "Boia, the creature has slunk off to lick its wounds. It's hurt and vulnerable. For the first time it knows fear. But I have tracked it. Its lair is on the edge of the Shivering Woods, somewhere near the lake. Now is the time. Are you ready?"

I turned from face to face. The king watching me, expectation in his gaze. Anskar, his brows heavy. And Arína's blood-stained face, so proud and fierce. Grethor had heard me and Anskar talking about her in the woods, I was sure of it. My brother only knew the princess's name because of me.

I rose, squared my shoulders, tried to look as fierce as Arína. "I am."

My hand ached anew.

And the amulet gave what might have been a laugh.

BOIA

THE AIR HAD GROWN heavy as we began the hunt. Dark masses gathered in the sky. They boiled with rage, stirred the trees with malice. Then tears of cold anger had streaked down upon our heads. I stuck out my tongue to catch a droplet, was surprised to find it wasn't salty. A flash from above blinded me for an instant. The boom of Thor's hammer shook the woods and a deer bolted across the forest path ahead, its ears pricked in terror. I knew how it felt—my brother had told me of rain, but seeing it was something else.

"A thunderstorm this time of year," said Twyla, walking at my left. "And getting dark early. It's not right."

Anskar hastened to my right side. "The land itself groans under Grethor's curse."

Twyla rolled her eyes. "Or perhaps it's just a storm."

"Either way, this is no fit beginning to our search. Any tracks will be washed away and we'll break a leg groping about in the dark. We should find somewhere to make camp for the night, make ready for the new sun's rising."

She nodded. "There's a sheltered spot under the cliff near here. We'll be out of the wind, at least."

Anskar hesitated. "We're not far from your house. Dóta and I can make camp, you don't have to—"

"I'm coming with you tomorrow."

"Why don't we all go to Twyla's house?" I said before Anskar could argue.

The warrior ran a hand through his beard. "It'll be quicker to make camp, I suppose. Let's not quarrel in the rain. Lead on, Twyla."

By the time we reached the site, the icy rain had soaked through our cloaks. I decided I did not care for the sensation of sopping wool against my hide. The rocky overhang gave some shelter from the weather, but not much. I sank down and perched upon a fallen log, wanting to help Anskar and Twyla put the tent up but unsure where to start.

I raised my hood and shook my head, trying to blink away weariness. I kept my burned hand stiff, careful to touch nothing with it. The wound had pained me when it happened, but had gone numb afterward. Then the anguish had returned, growing worse throughout the day. In my left I clutched the amulet, hoping it might share some of its warmth with me. Or healing, even. Heat fluttered from the amber and I caught a snatch of the goddess's harsh whisper in my ear. Angry words, resentful.

Something else too. The smell of char. The howl of a wolf. Golden sparks. Anticipation. Every sense ready. The same eagerness I had seen on my brother's face before a kill...

I rubbed my eyes and sat up, unsure whether I had been asleep.

The rain had died off, leaving the earth sodden and Anskar doing his best to start a fire in the dying light.

"It's no good," said Twyla, watching him. They gave no sign they knew I was awake.

"You couldn't..." Anskar wriggled his fingers over the wood. "Could you?"

"I'm a Seether, not a wonder worker," she snapped.

"Of course not. How foolish of me."

"Why don't you want me with you on the morrow?" she said. "Surely two Seethers are better than one."

He grunted. "Bet I can get this going with the right kindling."

Twyla crossed her arms. "You've still not forgiven me, have you, Anskar?"

The warrior gave up on the fire and reached into his bag for some hard tack. He bit down on it and chewed as he stared into the gloaming.

It was all the answer Twyla needed. "Fair enough. I've not forgiven myself either."

Anskar crumbled the remainder of his meal in his fist and looked up. "I wanted to. But you made your choice."

Twyla stared at him for a moment, then swept inside the tent, staff in hand and her satchel swinging from her shoulder. The light was spent now, but I still knew her face was a blank mask.

Anskar said a bad word. Not the gods' tongue, but it still held power.

"Who do you curse?" I said. "Her or yourself?"

He looked up. "Thought you were slumbering. How's your hand? You were brave for the king, but—"

"It's fine," I lied. "Why don't you want Twyla with us? Her magic is stronger than mine."

He shook his head. "I've seen what you can do. We don't need her."

I got up and sat down beside him. "You didn't answer me."

He got up and paced around his failed attempt at a fire. "You expect truth? Very well. Why didn't you tell me where Grethor's lair is? The lake's a bowshot from where we met, you had to know." When I said nothing, he muttered another ugly word under his breath. "No more secrets or lies. We need every scrap of knowledge if we're to face the monster."

"I..." The pulse roared in my ears. I was trembling.

"What?"

I didn't owe the clan anything, I told myself. Not loyalty, not love. Not after what Grethor had done. And yet I could do little more than choke out the words, glad Anskar and I could not see one another properly. Truth lay in darkness. "They took me in. Made me one of them." I clawed away my tears. "I was never Grethor's thrall. He is my brother. Don't you understand? All the time he was hurting people, I might have suspected, might have done something. But I didn't. I'm the monster, I'm the evil one."

"No," said Anskar. The anger had washed away from his voice and he was firm as stone. "You're many things, girl. Different. Confusing, maybe. A hell of a messy eater. But you are not a monster."

"I don't know if I can do this," I whispered. "It doesn't matter what magic I have. I can't slay my own kin."

Anskar said nothing. He stepped over the pile of damp wood and sat at my side. For an instant I feared he would try to put his arms around me, but he kept away. "Listen to me, Dóta. Do you know why I brought you with me that day? It wasn't because of your magic. It wasn't because I thought you could save the kingdom."

I sniffed. "Why, then?"

"Remember what you did to me, first time I came near?"

"I gave you a kick."

"That's when I saw you. So proud, so fierce. No feckless waif. You asked me why I was carrying a boy's clothes."

"For your son?"

"Aye. Sixteen years gone, my little war-maker." He laughed and I could hear how tight his throat was. "I never met him, never got the chance. He was gone by the time I got back from the summer raid. The clothes were an offering to his ghost. I leave a sacrifice in the Shivering Woods every year since my boy was lost. The dead can be appeased. But when I looked at you... I saw him. The hero he would have been, had he lived. I know it's daft. I mean, I know you're a girl. But it's truth. My Boia." His voice became husky. "Perhaps it's wrong of me to place that upon you. But I didn't see evil in your heart, Dóta. Not one bit."

Neither of us said anything. I wanted to dab at my eyes with the corner of my cloak, but it was too laden with water. "How did he die?"

Anskar laughed without mirth. "Ask Twyla." He breathed in and out, then stood once more. "Go to her, if you will. Then sleep, for we've killing to do in the morning. I'll keep watch over you both." He drew his axe and strode to the edge of our camp, staring into the night.

OFFERINGS

THE BLUE GLOW of Odin's flames rose from within the tent, bright as the hearth in Twyla's home. I swept aside the tent flap, baring my teeth at the flare of pain from the burn. Within the goatskin folds sat Twyla. A globe of light circled around her head. I wanted to ask how she did that, but more urgent questions clamored. Tears made tracks down her grubby cheeks. Still, I could not pity her. Would not, after what she had done.

"You heard that?" I said.

She rubbed away her tears. "I could hardly do elsewise, could I?"

"Is it true?"

She reached for me. "I didn't see your hand earlier. Sit down, let me take a look."

I glared, then relented.

She stretched out my fingers and tutted. "I've seen worse, but bad enough. It's a high price the gods ask of us sometimes. I've something that'll help." She reached into her satchel and produced a flask, the light still bobbing over her head.

"One of your poisons?"

"Goat's milk." She poured some upon my palm, spilling a few drops onto the tent floor. The pain ebbed to a dull throb. "You'll want to bathe that every day if you don't want a blood fever. A shame we have no waters from that spring I mentioned this morning."

Was that only this morning? It seemed as though it had happened in another age. She had helped me bring the half-goat into the world, had shed tears at its birth. Was she sad that he had a place in the world? She hadn't seemed to care that it was born without breath, after all. "Twyla," I said, "you have to tell me."

She did not let go of my hand but circled my palm with her thumb. Her touch was light and she took care not to go near the red mark. "Ah, young one. You deserve an answer, don't you? Very well." She took a breath. "Know that I was alone, barely older than you are now. Life was naught but my master's whip. You've met him, I believe. Ulf Redmane."

My eyes widened. "I know the man. Cowardly, cruel, craven."

She nodded. "Aye, you've the measure of him. My homeland was far away and I was dead to all I had known. I didn't care what happened to me. Nothing remained but my faith in the gods. No, that's not true." Twyla shook her head. "I had love. Anskar wintered at Redmane's homestead. The king sent him to talk cattle." She chuckled. "Anskar was young too, as foolish as I was. But his beard was like gold, his shoulders so broad. More than that, though. His eyes. Kindly, they were. The kindliest eyes I've ever seen. We kept each other warm that first winter, no matter the risk."

"What risk?"

She shrugged. "There are penalties for laying with another man's thrall without permission. And perhaps I'd do elsewise now, but we were too enmeshed to care. Love between men and women is dangerous that way, Dóta. There's nothing safe about it."

"I know," I said, trying to keep my voice from betraying me. Thoughts of Arína passed through my mind, but I pushed them aside.

Twyla fell silent, her eyes full of memory. "I was more than his conquest. I'd be his wife, for pride was still in me and rashness in him. For a year I saved to pay for my freedom. Anskar would sneak in what silver he could. My bride price, we called our little hoard. And soon enough I left Redmane behind. Anskar gave me my little cottage. And we were happy. Yet still his king disapproved. You must know Anskar was the finest warrior in all the land, stoutest in the shield wall. Why would he give himself to a freedwoman? I must have seethed some spell over him, folks said."

"And did you?"

The god's light cast a long shadow on Twyla's face. "Every night I'd make offerings to the Norns, ask them to spin me a greater fate. And one of them answered my prayers, aye. She came to me in the night. Beautiful, she was. Slender, her hair rippling like a waterfall. Sharp of face, perhaps, but beautiful. Just appeared on my doorstep." Twyla leaned forward. "Then I raised my torch. By the fire's light I took a closer look. It wasn't right, she wasn't a fair maid at all. Her left side covered in scales, fingernails long and gnarled. She looked on me, her eyes like coals."

"Her eyes glowed..." The fathoming was near, just out of my grasp. "Her teeth," I said. "What were they like?"

"Eh? I don't remember, just ordinary teeth."

Yet my hackles refused to settle, for something was still amiss. "Go on."

"She said I could have the marriage I yearned for, all I

wanted. But she wanted something in return. For every giving…"

"A taking," I said, my voice little more than a croak. "Her price?"

"My firstborn. She was a Norn, she said. No matter what she looked like. She could alter my fate if I left my babe in the Shivering Woods, hers to take. There'd be other children, she said. But none so loved as this one. All I had to do was let her in." Twyla lowered her head. "And I did. Oh gods, I did. Anskar and I married in the spring. First time he ever did a thing without Hrut's say-so, I reckon. Right before he left for that's year's raid. And it wasn't long before I felt life within me."

My heart pounded against my ribs like a prisoner against a cage. "Right, then," I said, my voice aquiver. "You wanted me to ask a wise question, Twyla. So answer me this. Did you give me birth?"

Her eyes sparkled. Then, no more than a whisper, the words came out. "Yes, Dóta. It's me. I'm your mother."

"How long have you known?" I hissed. "Did you know this when—"

She shook her head. "I thought it, but couldn't trust myself. Not until today. When I heard you singing the Song of the Norns…"

"But…" I shook my head. "A boy, Anskar said. You bore him a son, not a daughter."

"You know I can see the child within, sense its soul. I'm seldom wrong. Seldom! My child had a war-maker's heart, I was certain of it. And Anskar was so happy, he'd have his Boia. It meant so much to him."

"But I was a girl." A shard of ice formed in my heart.

"I couldn't explain it… Your soul didn't match your body. I was so sure of what I'd seen but—"

I snatched my hand back, wanted to flee, to strike Twyla, to curl up in a sniveling ball and cry. "Damn my flesh, I wasn't the son you wanted. A weirdling, a freak."

"You're not a—"

"You're not my mother, you never were!"

"Dóta, wait—"

But I wasn't listening. I was already out of the tent flap, leaving the light behind. How could I have expected anything else from Twyla? She was a beast like all the rest.

"Dóta?" Anskar's voice came from the dark. "Where are you going?"

I ignored him and ran past, crashed blind into the woods. I didn't know where I was going, didn't care. All that mattered was getting away from these monsters who wanted to twist me, enthrall me, cast me away. I tripped over something, toppled to the ground, threw out a hand to save myself. Agony ripped from my burned palm as I scraped it against a rock.

"Dóta? Where are you?" Twyla called from nearby.

I threw myself behind a bush as they approached, clutching my hand against my chest. The amulet pulsed as if waiting.

"Come back, girl," called Anskar. "Where did you go?"

I willed myself to become still as a stump until they passed. Then I uttered the worst curse word Anskar had taught me. He didn't know. I was sure of that. Anskar wouldn't keep this from me. Would he?

An owl gave its dire call. Shrews riffled through the underbrush. Somewhere Anskar and Twyla still hunted me. I was surrounded, creatures everywhere, animals like me, but they weren't my kind, they were beasts. Big, too big, an endless world. I wanted the closeness, the comfort of the

gloom, to pull my sheepskin over my head and shut it
all out.

Módor had told me the truth, was the only one who had.
By Asgard, she'd tried to warn me, had told me of good and
evil and the fates... I needed to be certain, needed to know,
needed the touch of one who loved me more than any other.
I was hers, she had told me, her child, her little Dóta and
that was my true name and I didn't care what Anskar or the
goddess or anyone else said.

I took one step, then another. How long I walked, I can't
say. The dank smell of the lake wafted on the breeze, beckoning me onward, driving out all thought, all pain.

Soon, Dóta, I told myself. *You'll be home soon enough.*

DESCENT

The mist was so thick that I could hardly see the waters of
the mere. The smell of rot filled my nostrils. This reek
would only grow worse when the sun had risen. I stood
naked upon the shore, chilly mud between my toes. The
predawn wind upon my bare hide made me shudder and I
hugged myself. Only ten days ago I had loathed the feel of
clothing against my flesh, but now it felt strange to stand
exposed under the sky. I baulked at the idea of plunging into
the frigid eddies. Yet home lay at the bottom of the lake. The
only home I had ever known or ever would, I told myself.

And yet...

What if Módor didn't want me? After I had refused to
come back when she called? After what Arína had done to
Grethor?

Arína. I squeezed my eyes shut and her poor damaged
face loomed before me. Had Grethor not promised he
would leave the humans alone if I came home? This was
right, this was my place. I belonged to the shadows beneath
the earth. And the princess would be better off without me.
Of that, there could be no doubt.

You must descend. There is no other way, dear one, said the amulet, which lay against my bare skin. Deadly calm had returned to the goddess's voice.

"Are you talking to me again?"

I will help you see truth. You shall have my strength and power to fulfil your task. This I promise.

I released a slow breath of relief, for I was not as strong a swimmer as my brother and would be going against the current. I plucked up my knife from the pile of clothing which lay by the water. Between that and my amulet, I had all I needed. No need to take my arm ring. The first shock of cold made me squeak as I waded out. By the time the waters had reached my shoulders, my blood was screeching through my veins. Holding the handle of the knife brought pain to my burned hand, so I clenched the blade between my teeth. Filling my lungs, I dived into the darkness.

My muscles went rigid as the waters overtook me. Blindness robbed my eyes, for no light pierced the murk. I grappled with the panic tearing through me and pulled myself further into the depths. All I knew was that I had to get further down, down, down. The entrance to the cave was near, I just had to reach... My fingers brushed against the slime of the rocks just as my lungs began to scream for air.

The amulet blazed to life, a torch under water. The bottom of the lake lay bare under its light and I saw the gash that would lead me to Módor. A new power coursed through my limbs, a vital heat. I swam with a frenzy like nothing I had experienced before. Every stroke hauled me through the water with the strength of a shark as I entered the tunnel. By the light of the amulet I caught a flash of the red adders staring, cowering. They knew to fear me now. I barely had time to savor their terror before rising from the passage into the underground cavern.

The light of the amulet winked out as my head broke the surface of the water. I hauled myself onto the rocks, choking for air, my hair streaming. Brackish water burned my throat and nostrils as it gushed from my belly. Then I collapsed and lay face down on the stone floor of the cave, thrilled but drained and sore all over. The glow of the mushrooms was a familiar comfort, telling me I had returned.

Do not lower your defenses, Elfin-sun, whispered the amulet. *She is near.*

Then I yelped as something heavy fell on me from above, enveloping me like a blanket. It took me a moment to recognize the roughness of my old sheepskin. I turned over to find Módor's eyes glowing red-orange. She stared down at the amulet against my thin chest.

"So you did take it," she rasped. "I hoped Grethor was lying to me. That thing is an abomination, child. It belonged to the man who came seeking my death. The goddess's last thrall." A hiss rose from her throat. "Have you come to slay me?"

I shook my head, not trusting myself to speak.

"Then take it off now. Cast it into the water."

The amulet cried out a warning. The goddess's fury rumbled through my head like distant thunder, but she was too late. Slowness was unwise when it came to my mother's commands. I slipped the leather cord over my head and cast the amulet into the pool. There it drifted on the ripples. Yet I could feel the eye of the goddess lingering upon me, full of reproach. Without the amulet I felt like an armorless warrior.

"Good girl," said my mother. "No need to sully this moment with the games of the goddess. And you've kept your claw, I see."

I held up my knife. "I've come home, Módor."

She sneered. "Have you?"

"You were right," I whispered. "About the world, about humans. About everything."

She regarded me, her face like stone. I bit the inside of my cheek until the taste of blood filled my mouth. Then she smiled, showing her pointed teeth. "I warned you about those creatures, didn't I? But you had to see for yourself, I suppose. Make your own mistakes. Foolish child. But fate led you back to me. Are you hungry? I've dried fish."

I shook my head and wrapped my sheepskin around me. Once I might not have cared, but now I did not want my mother to see me uncovered. "Where is Grethor?"

"Above somewhere. I've not seen your brother in days."

Relief washed over me. She didn't know Grethor was wounded. Yet.

"You must be famished." Before I could protest, she slipped out of the chamber. I had never noticed before, but Módor stooped, her arms longer than her legs. At last she returned, shoved a fish under my nostrils.

I took the hunk of flesh between my fingers, but could not bring myself to bite. I let it drop. "I don't eat meat any more. I can't."

Módor's eyes widened. "They have twisted you."

"I have changed. And I have learned."

"And what great wisdom have you gained from those creatures?"

And so I told Módor what I had found in the world above. My words echoed through the cavern. All the beauty I had experienced, all the terror. A doll left torn apart in the field. Warriors who grappled for sport. Mushrooms and the birth of new life. My voice broke when I told her of Arína, but I made myself keep going. Módor's face remained still and she said nothing of the princess.

Then I spoke of Anskar's cunning, of fetching wood for Twyla.

My mother bared her fangs. "They always were selfish beings, those two. Even before you were born, they'd lay together planning all you'd be. A life of service, that's what they'd have given you. Seething, peace-weaving, making war? Such was never your fate, I knew it. These things mean nothing to a child of fate."

"Módor," I said, putting as much care as I could into the words. "Anskar and Twyla. They are my parents, aren't they?"

She was silent a long moment. "They might have been your mother and father, yes. But did they sing you to sleep, lick your wounds clean?" She reached out and grabbed my hand, running her scales over the raw burn. I flinched, but she gripped tighter. "And look what Twyla's path has brought you. Nothing but pain."

"Please, Módor, you're hurting me."

She released me, jumped back. Almost shocked. "But I could never hurt you. You are my Dóta. Though I hear you go by another name these days."

I cradled my throbbing hand and held it in the water, letting the coolness do its work. "It doesn't matter what they call me. I came back, didn't I?"

She cocked her head. "You did, you did. And a good thing too. Will you not let me feed you?" She picked up the fish again.

"Módor," I said, willing my courage to rise, "I have to know the truth, all of it."

She nibbled the fish. "It's good, see? Still juicy."

"Módor..."

Her eyes flashed. "Must I tell it again? I happened on you in the Shivering Woods, took you in, raised you—"

"But you didn't just happen on me, did you? Twyla said you came to her and…"

"Human lies."

"Then tell me what really happened. You just said—"

"Enough!" She tore the fish in half, leaving its sinews ragged. "Let's just have supper, leave aside this whole thing."

"You told me once the gods spared me for a reason. What reason? Why did you want Twyla to leave me in the woods?"

"That stupid girl. Always meddling, could never leave things alone. She thought to cheat me, but I showed her." Módor laughed, though it sounded more like a growl. "You want the truth? Very well. I have never lied to you, Dóta, not once. I saw you even before you were conceived. It was I who brought you into this world, even if another carried you in her womb. Just a tug at the strings of fate, no more. A special child, one born between worlds. One meant for a special purpose."

"I don't understand."

"You were meant to help me, Dóta."

Once I would have offered myself without question. Instead I sat down slowly on a rock. "Tell me what you want, Módor."

"You know I came from somewhere else. And I was banished, sent to live out my days here in this cold lonesome world. I don't belong here. And what was my crime? Love, Dóta. As simple as that."

"Love."

"Have you never wondered who Grethor's father was? Your brother was not a foundling as you were—from my own loins I gave him life. What greater outrage could there be for the immortals, that a fair Norn should join herself to a troll?" She bared her teeth. "The gods summoned me to the World Tree to receive my punishment. Freya herself looked down on me from the branches, so proud and haughty. I had broken the laws of nature, she said. I had known a beast and was carrying its bastard. For the father, death. For the mother…" She sneered. "Freya could punish me a thousand times, it would never be enough. They sent me here to live out my days."

"Módor, I don't understand. You're a Norn? But…"

"Why am I ugly?" She chuckled. "Maybe it was the goddess's way of making things right. If I were a beast too, there'd be no wrongdoing. My nails were first to change. Longer and longer they grew, and I couldn't cut them. Then my eyes grew larger, my hair became green. My hide was next. Every tooth I had rotted in my head and fell out. These fangs grew in their place. Each time I looked in the water I saw less of myself. More than that, the hunger…" She closed her eyes. "They made me a predator. Blood was all I craved, while I carried Grethor. And blood is all I have." She snaffled the rest of the fish, bones crunching in her mouth.

I squirmed, remembering the horror I had beheld aboveground. Yet I was loathe to stop her tale.

"And so I was trapped here in Midgard with a squalling babe at the hip. Yet I had a touch of the old power still. Life and death were still my tools. All the humans had to do was let me in and I could pull the threads of fate. And so it was that I brought you about, Dóta. Can you not see? You are my claw. You were never meant to serve the gods, but be their master. You can bring me back, restore me to my proper place."

"That's what I was meant for."

"I had to have you, I knew it before you lay in the crib. The greatest treasure I've ever had." Módor's eyes shone.

"You're such a good girl, so brave, so kind, so special. You want to help me, don't you?"

I toyed with the bone knife Módor had given me. In another lifetime, it now seems. At last I looked up and met her fiery eyes. "There is one thing more I need to know, Módor."

"Name it."

"You said all you wanted was blood. Human blood?"

Módor stared. "I am not choosy when it comes to my meat. Not like your brother."

"All the years he'd go back and forth to the surface, you knew he hunted the humans."

"Yes..." Her brow furrowed.

"My kinsmen."

"Hardly. My power flows in your veins. You belong to me."

"And Grethor, he'll go on hunting them."

She shrugged. "What of it? I couldn't stop him if I wanted."

I nodded and stood. "Thank-you, Módor." I pressed the handle of the bone knife into her claw. "You can have it back. I won't be needing it." Before she could reply, I shrugged off the sheepskin and stepped toward the river. I treaded with a doggedness that said I was on the right path.

"You're alone, child." Módor's words were venomous darts in my back. I didn't need to look at her to know she was swollen with ire. "Your little princess has already cast you aside. And fate is coming for her as well."

"You are right about one thing, Módor," I said over my shoulder. "You don't belong in this world. You or my brother."

I seized the amulet as I dived, kicking for the underwater passage that would bring me back to the light.

The mists were gone by the time I breached the surface of the lake. No fear of Módor following, for she despised to enter water. I stood bathing in the sun's golden warmth until the drips vanished from my hide. Then I reached for my woolen shirt and breeches and dressed myself, slipping on the golden arm ring.

"Dóta?" Anskar's voice came from the trees. "Is it truly my Dóta?" I looked up. His eyes were red, his expression fearful.

I looked around for Twyla, but Anskar had come alone. "It's me."

"I tracked you through the night." He cleared his throat. "I thought we'd lost you again."

So she had told him. I shook my head slowly. "I'm not lost, Anskar. I know what I have to do now, but I can't do it on my own. Will you walk with me?"

His face hardened with fresh resolve and he offered his hand.

No way was I ready to take it, not yet. But our footsteps were in time as we trudged back toward the king's hall.

DESPAIR

THE HALL WAS DECKED out for the wedding, but the mood was that of a funeral. Garlands hung from the carved wooden pillars and incense burned, ready to cleanse the place for the new couple's arrival. Yet there was no laughter, no jesting. Deathly silence, the thralls' faces tight with worry. On the grass outside Valdskali, the warriors caroused and jeered at one another, filled with the false warmth of drink. The men had returned yesterday and were ready for the three-day bridal feast. I flinched at the rough echo of their voices as I made my way to the back of the hall. If I could hear them, so could my brother.

My innards coiled with dread at what was to come. The skalds would sing of this day. For good or ill, none could tell. I flexed my hand in anticipation, my newly-healed flesh tingling.

It took some time to find Arína's chamber. I pushed the door open to find a dozen pairs of startled eyes staring in my direction. The princess sat with her back to me, surrounded by her shield maidens. The girls' armor shone like mirrors.

The maiden with bronze hair drew her knife and glared. Some thanks for saving her hide, I thought.

Arína did not turn. "Who is it, Thora?"

"The Seether boy."

"Boia. You shouldn't be here." Arína sighed. "Would you girls wait in the hall?"

"Princess..." Thora didn't lower the knife.

"Go." The girls shuffled past, Thora casting me a vile look. When we were alone, the princess beckoned me forth and I moved to her side. My chest ached at the sight of Arína's face. Her skin had been scrubbed and she wore blue war paint over the scabbed claw marks. Flowers were twined through her hair, though she still wore the same white kirtle as the night we met. She was wild, fierce, like a goddess herself.

"Arína," I said. Everything wanted to come out, but there were no words.

She stood and grasped my forearms. "How is your hand?"

"Better. Your wounds?"

The princess shrugged. "My bridal wash stung worse than an asp's bite, but it will heal." She paused. "I'm glad you came, Elfin-Sun. I wasn't sure you would."

"Just call, I'll come. That won't change."

Without warning, she pulled me closer, pressed her forehead against mine. Our noses were touching. The clean smell of her skin, the warmth of her breath on my face. She closed her eyes. So did I. My heart swelled. Never had I been so overwhelmed, not even by the glittering sea.

At last she ran her thumb over the golden arm ring. She pulled back, gave me a watery smile. "For a moment, I might have believed that, Boia. But all things change." She glanced toward her bed. The pelts had been cleaned, cushions set out for tonight. "There's something I need you to do for me." She stood and retrieved a band of leather knotwork from a table by her bed. "My crown of maidenhood. I've had it since I was a child. Will you…"

"Eh?"

"Will you put it on me? This is the last day I'll wear it." She placed it in my hand, sat down and looked up at me.

"Oh," I mumbled, not quite sure what to do. I tried to recall everything my brother had said about crowns, then pushed the memory to one side. Thinking of Grethor would not make today any easier. "Are you sure you want to do this?"

"Yes." No hesitation, no doubt.

Not daring to speak another word, I placed the crown atop her head, careful not to upset her braids.

A knock came from the door. "Princess?" said Thora. "Redmane and his clan have arrived with the gifts. It's time."

I moved toward the door. "Be safe, Arína."

"You too."

I swept out of the chamber, trying to keep my face from crumpling. My fingers brushed the amulet hanging around my neck, found it freshly polished and smooth. It tingled under my skin. *Is your heart ready?*

"Is yours?" I said aloud. A passing thrall gave me a strange look as my footsteps clattered through the hall, but I cared not. "I need you with me. No vanishing today."

You shall not be alone—I am always with you. You need not fear, long as you mind my commands.

Somehow this gave me little comfort. I stepped from the hall and saw the crowd gathered on the hillside. Great earthen bowls sat upon a table, already full of blood from the animal sacrifices. Their contents were thickening in the sun. The sickly smell reminded me why I didn't eat meat anymore.

Nearby, two groups of warriors were playing what I would come to know as a tug of war, the air rank with their sweat. I side-stepped as a man lost his grip on the rope and tumbled to the ground. His companions guffawed to see him lying dazed in his armor. Mead sloshed from their drinking horns. The fallen man roared and tried to get up, his face red and foam at the corner of his mouth. His eyes were shot with veins of red and they reflected an ill light.

Anskar stepped from the crowd and helped the warrior to his feet. "Here, brother. Got your axe all right?" Seeing the man nod, Anskar clapped him on the back. "Let's get you another drink, eh?" He steered the man over to a cauldron from which the thralls ladled mead.

The sun had not yet finished its climb through the sky. Any other day, it would have been too early to fill men's bellies with mead, but this was not like any other day.

Anskar caught my eye. "Everything's ready out here. Princess coming?"

I nodded and Anskar rejoined the men. He bustled about, telling them to drink up. The warriors resumed their game, champing like a stampede of cattle. Loud, too loud.

My eyes flicked downhill toward the village, but there was no sign. Not yet.

A knot of red-haired men stood watching the tug of war. They took no part, but rested their hands on swords and daggers. These warriors were the only ones steady on their feet, drinking from their own water barrel.

Ulf Redmane mocked me with his skull-like grin. A surge of hatred ran through me, for I had not seen him since the Althing. My first night in Valdskali, Ulf had shamed me and tried to start a feud. "It's our Seether. Caught your creature yet?" The men around him hooted with mirth, but I gave them no heed. There were other things to worry about, no point grappling with the father of the groom.

I spied Twyla hovering near the cauldron. She snapped the clasp on her satchel shut as she saw me coming. She leaned upon her staff and we exchanged a silent nod. I began a slow circuit of the crowd, wary as a rabbit among wolves.

A shrill horn sounded, heralding the arrival of the bride and the king's family. Through the crowd I glimpsed him leading his daughter by the hand up to the sacrificial bowls. The shield maidens formed up, flanking Arína and the king.

The red-haired groom stepped out from among Redmane's kinsmen, flourishing his cape like the milk drinker he was. Young Jörgen Redmane had none of his father's guile, yet he could never be good enough for Arína. He grinned at her, showing gaps between his teeth. And his skin was blotchy. And his ears stuck out. I turned my face away from the ceremony, not wanting to look at him. Or her.

Ravens circled above the bride and groom, eager to dip their beaks in blood.

My pulse began to race. Arína was too exposed in the open.

The people of the village gathered around the bride and groom. I stood back from the crowd, kept the amulet at hand. Only once or twice did I glance in their direction. Despite myself, I could not look away. I caught a few snatches of songs praising the gods. Neither King Hrut nor Redmane smiled as they traded the swords of their fore-bears, nor did Arína meet her new husband's eyes as he placed a ring on her finger.

Then the king took a bundle of twigs, dipped it in the

blood and spattered the red onto Arína's white kirtle. She held her shoulders firm, her face betraying nothing.

King Hrut commanded the groom to kneel before him. He spoke a word in the boy's ear, and then Jörgen rose and plucked the crown from Arína's head. A pang ripped through my chest as he dropped the leather crown of maidenhood to the earth and ground it beneath his boot.

Folks cheered, all reaching to touch the couple, give their blessing. I might have wailed, but my voice was crushed beneath the wolf-howls of the warriors.

She was lost to me.

I squeezed my eyes shut, allowed myself despair.

Perhaps if I hadn't given in for the moment, things might have turned out different. Yet that was not how this day was fated.

My eyes snapped open as screams erupted from the crowd. Ravens cawing, black wings flurrying. A confused tangle of bodies, people fighting to get away, nostrils wide with fright. Some of the warriors fought to get closer, fumbling for blades. Over it all, a familiar gurgling laugh.

I battled the crowds to the spot where Arína had stood, fears rushing like flames. She was nowhere. I prayed the shield maidens had gotten her to safety.

Grethor stood at the heart of it all, gripping King Hrut by the throat. My brother raised the king over his head. Just moments ago, Hrut's eyes had been full of love and pride in his daughter. Now they bulged, his face turning purple.

Grethor's face twisted in a delighted smirk, his empty eye socket dripping black. Then he cocked his head and tested the air with his forked tongue. "I know you're here, sweet sister. Your little friend half-blinded me, but I can taste you already. I hear your poor broken heart."

"I'm here," I said, and stepped out from the mass. "Let him go."

"Very well." With a cackle, Grethor slammed the king to the ground. A wet crunch and Hrut's head lolled, his body limp. A cry of sorrow and rage burst from the crowd. Grethor flinched from the noise, covered it with a one-eyed sneer.

"What have you done?" I whispered.

"Me? Nothing." He pointed where his eye had been. "This was your doing, you and that bitch of yours. But don't worry. You won't have to live with it long." Then he ran at me, a blur of motion, his claws outstretched.

No rowing against the wind. This was my doom.

ASH

For a heartbeat I froze.

They say the Valkyries descend and your forebears greet you in Valhalla when death comes. But I was surrounded by the living as Grethor charged.

Time ceased to circle through the ages and I heard not even the croak of a raven.

A thousand thoughts danced through my head.

This was it. The moment of my death. In my vision I had seen this, knew that in an instant I would feel Grethor's claws around my throat—squeezing, crushing, stealing my life's breath. I had hoped to do some good before he ended me, but it had come to nothing. Failure.

And yet something rankled me, for this was not the vision I had seen. Where was the empty battlefield, the haunted wind? The goddess had shown snowflakes falling from the sky, yet this was summer. More than that, in the vision I had been without my amulet. And I had been alone.

I glanced left. Anskar's lips were parted, rallying the men with a war cry. To my right, Twyla's hand was raised toward the sky. Blue flames gathered along the edge of her staff, a deadly power filling the air. And then I saw Arína striding from the rear of the crowd. Still clad in her kirtle, a flaming arrow nocked in her bow, shield maidens at her back. Her face was vengeance.

I was wrong. My Valkyrie had come. And I knew I was not alone.

As one body, the warriors and maidens formed a shield wall between me and Grethor. They did not break before his charge, but roared and chopped at him, axes flashing, faster than my eyes could see. Not a hint of fear in them, no sign of fleeing. They were blood-drunk, filled with the mad frenzy of the berserk. Twyla's elixir had done its work.

Confusion filled Grethor's face, then a cruel laugh escaped his lips. He raised a branch-like arm to sweep aside the fighters.

"Now!" I cried. Hollering a din of battle shrieks, the warriors and maidens hammered axes against shields, stamping their feet. The earth shook with the clamor.

Grethor pressed hands over his ears. He advanced no further, curled on the ground, his groans filling the air.

Twyla's eyes flashed toward me. "Dóta!"

Grethor looked up, his lopsided face a rictus of pain. "Make them stop, they're hurting me."

I squeezed my eyes shut. I couldn't let him poison my resolve.

"Please," I whispered to the goddess. "It must be now."

Relish filled every one of the goddess's words. *Let us end this beast.*

The wrath of the goddess crackled through me, the flames filling my very flesh. My skin glowed golden, heat rushed through my eyes. As though fire were pouring from my heart.

I stood over Grethor and he cowered beneath me.

His one yellow-green eye was round as a coin, its light flickering. "I didn't mean anything by it, I was just playing." Drops of his dark blood seeped from the empty eye socket like tears. "You believe me, don't you?"

"I do." I spoke only a whisper, knowing he would hear every word. "It's a game to you. But I warned you and you didn't listen."

"What will you do? Slay me?" He laughed until it became a hacking cough. "I was trying to help you, sweet sister. And you know that, yes? I needed you see what you are."

"I know what I am." A single tear splashed to the ground. "And you were right. We are alike, more than you know." I raised my hand. Molten rage filled me.

"No, Dóta, no! Please, you're better than this, better than me, I—"

Golden flames erupted from my fingertips and slammed into his chest. He held up a clawed hand to shield his face, but there was no hiding from my wrath. His hide sizzled, the fire rushing around him, through him, pouring down his throat and into his core. My brother's screams were twisted, dreadful, inhuman.

A storm of fire seethed through me and I bared my teeth in the joy of it, unrelenting. My lips formed words of love and hate. Not my spell, but that of the goddess. Where my fury ended and hers began, I can't say. Her wildness became my own and I poured myself into her curse.

The anger boiled up, so long had I held it back. And I enjoyed punishing him, I admit it. Not just for what he had done to Arína and the other humans. Not just for his part in Módor's lies.

For every time he sniffed my hair. Every time he made me feel small. Every time he touched me.

Twyla stood on the other side of Grethor, her staff raised. Her flames were such a bright blue they almost blinded me, but I could not look away. They joined mine, the colors swirling brighter than Bifröst.

Enough, said the goddess at last.

I fell to my knees, trembling with exhaustion. I felt as though I carried a yoke on my shoulders.

A blackened, twisted figure teetered where my brother had stood. A statue carved from charred meat, a madman's dream. And yet a light still gleamed in its face. It reached for me, begging, desperate. "Sister…" it rasped. Then the light of its eye went out. Toppled forward, collapsed into a mound of ash and cinders and bone. The skull rolled to rest at my feet.

I closed my eyes against the sight, but his fanged leer would haunt me all my days. "Goodbye, brother."

All around me, voices were roaring, crying, screaming their victory. Hands pounded my back, telling me I had earned my arm ring. I could just hear folks chanting "Elfin-sun! Elfin-sun! Hail the troll slayer!" But I was numb to all feeling. I was surrounded by humans, but never had I felt less like one of them. For I had become the worst of all beasts. A kin slayer.

Twyla's lips were blueish and she was trembling almost as much as I was. Was she talking to me?

"What?" I said, blinking.

"I asked if you're all right."

"Am I alive?"

"Aye."

"But it was going to be the world's ending… The goddess showed me Ragnarök."

Twyla's laugh was hollow. "You sound dismayed."

I showed you what you needed to see, dear one.

All things became fuzzy and dark. I swayed. If the goddess's reply disturbed me, I was too worn to care. Just had to lie down a moment, even in the middle of the field.

When I opened my eyes, I was wrapped in Twyla's cloak. It was warmer than my sheepskin, I thought, and allowed myself to drift again.

I recall little and less of the rest of the day. How long I lay there, I can't be sure. Only jagged images remain of what I saw.

Men stumbling, downing more and more mead. They kept toasting each other as though they had defeated the monster themselves.

Anskar cradled the broken body of the king, pressed his lips against his brother's forehead. The first and only time I saw my father weep.

Ulf Redmane and his clan were sauntering toward the king's hall. That shouldn't be. I raised a hand and pointed feebly, but nobody saw and I didn't have the strength to stop them.

Arína sitting on the ground beside me, her knees against her chest. Her eyes wide and staring into nothingness. Where had her courage gone? A Valkyrie no more, but a child in mourning. She was far away, did not hear her shield maiden's comforting words. I reached for her hand and squeezed it. The princess blinked as though realizing I was there for the first time. And though her face remained pale and bleak, she returned the squeeze.

Neither of us said a word. Neither of us had to.

SHIMMER

I WOKE IN THE GLOOM. For a panicked moment I feared I had returned to Módor's cave. But the lingering stink of Twyla's hearth told me where I was.

She and Anskar lay together by the embers of the fire. Both fully clothed and an arm's length from one another, but still together. He was snoring, but her eyes were open and fixed on me. "Careful," she whispered, gesturing. "Don't wake her."

The princess lay on the floor beside me, her eyes moving beneath her lids. She grunted in her sleep as I eased back the bedroll and tiptoed around her.

"Gave her some stew and put her to bed," whispered Twyla. "I didn't know what else to do. There's to be an Althing in a few days to choose our next king. Until that's decided, it won't be safe for her. Come, let them sleep." Twyla beckoned me to join her outside.

The two of us slipped into the night. We stood a few paces apart and I craned my neck to look upon the river of stars. They have never lost their wonder for me, though in those days they were naught more than a scattering of bright lights in the sky. In the years to come I would learn to spot the shapes of Aurvandil's Toe, the Wolf's Jaws, the Shimmer Road. The darkness seemed to grow deeper the longer I stood there, though the stars burned brighter for it. Beneath the endless sky, I still could not quite believe I lived.

Inside the house, Anskar drew a gasping breath. How could a human make so much noise sleeping?

"I forgot he snored," said Twyla. "I might have to get used to that."

"You might." Neither of us said anything for a moment, then each of us started to speak. "You first," I said.

"Dóta... We didn't abandon you. You understand this, yes? I almost died of grief when I found your crib empty. I loved you so much."

"So much that you agreed to give her what she wanted. You did abandon me, before I was even born."

Twyla breathed in sharply. "I was a fool and made a fool's bargain. I didn't think what I was losing, only what I had to gain."

"He was right to leave you."

My words cut her and I was glad of it. "I left him. The shame..." She shook her head and swore. "I'm sorry, Dóta. And I know that's not enough, but it's all I have right now. Can you ever forgive me?"

"I'm going to check on the goats."

"All right." Twyla went back inside, but she left the door open for me.

I was too tired to feel anything as I stepped toward the goat pens. Just wanted to look upon my little weirdling as it slept. Let it remind me that we can change our fates.

Anskar gave another snore from inside the house. Just another human thing to bear. I could hear it even out here. Then I stopped short. The night shouldn't have been so silent. Owls should have been hooting, shrews snuffling. The goats...

I raced through the dark.

The doe lay with her head upon the ground. The kid I had helped bring into this world nestled against her side. I might have thought they were sleeping.

The bone knife lodged in the half-breed's throat told me I was wrong.

Suspicion feathered the back of my neck, the sense of being watched. I turned toward the woods, saw a pair of eyes glowing like coals in the night. They blinked once, then vanished. Leaves crackled as she fled.

Somehow she had found a way out of the cave. Neither the living nor the dead could stop her. My mother would not rest until she had her revenge.

The ordeal was far from over.

PART III

WELL OF FATE

The ash tree stands tall
Yggdrasil is its name
Sprinkled with bright water
Dew flows from it into dales
Always it stands green over
The Well of Fate.
– Völuspá

TRIUMPH

THE HEARTH HAD NOT BEEN LIT that morning. Three pairs of human eyes stared at me, each heavy with fatigue. Throughout the night, the sound of a squirrel picking at a hole in the thatch of Twyla's roof had sounded like the grinding of giants' teeth. None of us had slept well, haunted by the day before.

The wounds to Princess Arína's face had begun to close, but some hurts run deeper than bloodshed. Her father's body was not yet ready for the pyre, it was so fresh. Yesterday we had seen the king struck down by a monster's fury. It was meant to be Arína's bridal feast, but death had corrupted the day, filled her with such grief that I had feared she would not wake. Yet here she was. Pale and wan, her brow low, but alive. Even a Valkyrie needed time to heal.

Anskar's eyes were bloodshot and he moved slower than normal. Looking back, I'm not surprised—yesterday the warrior had drunk mead mixed with a potion that destroyed all fear. No doubt his head felt like it had taken a blow from a war hammer. More than that, Anskar had held Arína's father in his arms, watched his friend die. His howls of grief had rent the air. The love between companions goes beyond that between men and women.

Twyla stood at his side, her hand on his shoulder. She was watching me, the lines of her face taut. The two of us had talked late into the night. Of fate, forgiveness, truths. It was not long since I learned she had carried me in her womb. Whether that made her my mother, neither of us could be sure. After we talked, I had remained outside and gone to check on the goats. That's when I had witnessed it.

"You're sure, Dóta?" said Twyla.

"I know what I saw. Módor's eyes watching me in the dark. It was her who slaughtered the animals." I held up the bone knife I had pulled from the baby goat's throat. Once I had called it my claw, but now the dried blood on the edge sickened me. Twyla flinched from the sight, perhaps recognizing it. After all, she had met Módor before.

"I don't understand, Elfin-sun," said Arína. "Who's Módor?" She turned to Anskar and Twyla. "And why do you keep calling him Dóta? That's a girl's name."

Even in the mires of grief, Arína was no-one's fool. We'd only met a short while ago, but in some ways I already felt the princess knew me best. Even so, I was not ready to reveal myself to her. "Módor is Grethor's mother," I said at last. Not a lie, even if not the whole truth. "As for the name…"

"A joke. A Seether thing," said Twyla quickly. "Forgive me, Boia."

Arína opened her mouth as though she was going to ask something else, but thought better of it.

Anskar's face grew stormy. "Grethor had a mother?"

"Most creatures do, Anskar," said Twyla.

He crossed his arms. "You might have told me."

"I didn't think it would come to this," I said. "She always seemed…"

He huffed. "What? Gentler? That troll hag raised a beast."

My heart stilled at his words, but I could not bring myself to answer.

"Anskar." Twyla's tone might have cut ice. "You know she is more than that. A fallen Norn has many powers."

Anskar grunted and sipped water.

Arína shook her head. "The beast-mother has no claim to vengeance. Her bastard stole my father's life, so Elfin-sun took his. The blood price is paid, nothing owed."

I picked up a clump of ash from the fire, crushed it between my fingers. "She will not see it so. For every giving, a taking."

Then I sat down upon my bedroll, held my head in my hands. More than likely ash now marred my hair, but that didn't matter. Something was wrong within me. Needles pricking my insides, a headache pounding. A familiar discomfort.

I was eleven when the blood had first come. Módor didn't tell me what it was, would not even look at me. She just sent Grethor to hunt and brought me fresh moss. Whenever it happened, she would banish me to the furthest corner of the cave until it stopped.

"What's wrong?" said Arína.

I shook my head. "Nothing." If I said it, then it might come true.

A knock on the door spared me from having to explain further. I leapt to my feet and dived under the bedroll for my amulet. As soon as it touched my flesh, a quiver of the goddess's excitement swept over me.

Anskar already gripped his axe. "Is it her?"

I shook my head. "Módor wouldn't knock."

"She might," said Twyla.

"Anskar!" The rough man's voice came from outside.

Arína froze, recognizing it belonged to Ulf Redmane. Her new father-in-law.

"Open the door, Anskar," said Redmane. "We know you're in there. It's no secret this is your woman's house. No need to fear, we'd have words with you, that's all. There is much to discuss now Hrut is gone."

The princess glared at the door. "I should speak. Hrut was my father, after all."

Anskar shook his head. "That's why you mustn't. We don't know what he's after, but it's safest for you to slip away." He cleared his throat. "A moment, Redmane. I'm not dressed."

"Well, hurry up," said Redmane.

Anskar turned back to Arína. "Listen, I know Ulf Redmane. He won't care that you were to be wedded to his son. The bedding never happened, the ceremony wasn't done. Not yet."

My heart leapt. Did that mean Arína could still spend time with me? Looking back, I see that was a selfish notion, but an honest one.

"And what will you do, Wind-Rime?" said the princess.

He shrugged, slyness filling his grin. "Most likely he does just want to talk. Doubt he'd be bold enough to try anything foolish. We could still make an ally of him. But I wouldn't have you near while I negotiate. Your inheritance may depend on it."

Arína bit her lip, then nodded. "There's only one way out."

"Not so," said Twyla, looking up at the hole in the thatch.

"Come on, Anskar," said Redmane, his voice growing louder. "The day's wasting."

I reached for a stool and placed it under the hole in the roof. Arína took my hand and hoisted herself up, the roof creaking under her weight.

Anskar locked his gaze on Twyla. "Remember that spot we made camp, the first night we set out to hunt Grethor? I was going to meet some friends there today. If I don't come by sundown, I want you to take the princess and flee. Cross the whale road, find the hill folk, be anywhere but here."

Twyla stared into his eyes. "Anskar…"

His face twitched in a smile. "Don't worry about me." They held each other in a tight embrace, pressed their foreheads together. Then their lips touched. A kiss. I paused, staring. Never had I seen humans do that before. They broke apart and he glanced at me.

"Anskar!" shouted Redmane. "I've waited long enough."

"Patience, Ulf. I'm coming." Anskar pushed Twyla away gently. "Go on. Just in case."

Twyla grabbed her staff and held it up to the gap in the thatch. Arína's hand came down and seized it, then Twyla clambered up to join her on the roof, clutching her satchel.

Anskar turned to me. Feelings flickered across his face like a torch in a gale. "We'll talk soon, Dóta. I promise." Then his face hardened. "Got your arm ring? Take your knife, your amulet. Guard the princess, you hear me? She deserves to rule."

Goodbyes were for softer creatures. I nodded, wrapped my fingers around the knife handle and pulled myself through the hole in the thatch.

The three of us pressed ourselves against the roof, the dry thatch making my face itch. From the other side of the house came the muffled voices of men. Redmane and Anskar were talking, though I could not make out the words. After a few moments, I heard the door bang open.

Footsteps, somebody tearing the house apart. Searching for us.

I peeked out over the top of the house. Two men stood on either side of Anskar. He relaxed as he talked with Redmane, carefree in the sunshine. As though the two of them were discussing the price of cattle.

A lanky boy came out of the house, pushing his red hair out of his eyes. "Nobody in there, Father. Just as he said." My eyes narrowed as I recognized him as Jörgen, son of Redmane. The boy Arína was supposed to marry. I shot a glance at her, but her face remained a tight mask.

Redmane grunted and stroked his beard. The scars around his hollow eye socket were livid in the morning sun. "Good, Anskar. I wouldn't have you cheat me, by Odin's spear. I've a proposition you'll find most interesting."

Arína stiffened. Even that was enough to make the roof groan.

"Come on," whispered Twyla. "The thatch won't hold."

I nodded and slid over to the far side of the house, where Redmane's men couldn't see. Then I jumped to the ground, just missing the fence of the goat pen. I tried not to look at the fresh carcasses strewn about.

Arína pointed toward the woods. "Quietly now."

We crept as low as we could and made as little noise as possible. The pines were so close I could spit at them when one of Redmane's men gave a shout. "There they are! Knew he was lying!"

Something streaking through the air. I hurled myself to the ground. An arrow slammed into a tree trunk where my head had just been.

Jörgen charged through the clearing toward us, his crimson hair flying. His eyes were fixed on Arína and he grinned so wide I could see every tooth in his head. He was looking at her the way my brother would look upon his prey. The youth wielded an axe in his hand, sharp enough to cleave her skull.

I stood between him and Arína.

Time grew still.

A rush of the goddess's might rose from the amulet. *My power. Use it!*

"No," I whispered. "He's human."

You can protect the girl. All you have to do is let me in.

He bore down on me, raised the axe. A feral grin on his round face.

I held the amulet before me, thinking to frighten him. He was uncowed, his nostrils stretched in bloody rage...

Let me in! Now!

I didn't hesitate, didn't think, craved the power of Asgard in my flesh. Instantly the fever of the goddess swept through me. Hot pinpricks of anger within my womb, a seething rage which rose through my belly to escape through my fingertips. The goddess's wrath enveloped me and I let it.

This whelp would not take Arína. I raised my hand.

Jörgen's tunic erupted into flames as though coated in pitch. The axe dropped from his hands and fell to the grass with a thump. He stopped short, his eyes wide with shock. Then his jaws parted in a scream which made the ravens take wing. He toppled to the ground. Rolling, desperate to put out the flames even as they roasted his flesh. A sizzle like fat dripping onto a hearth, the smell of charred meat. I willed the goddess's fire to burn brighter, to make him ash.

His cries did not last long. A swift agony, then nothing. Smoke curling over bones.

A savage pleasure ripped through me, triumph roaring through my chest. The same elation I had felt when I drove my knife into the serpent's eye. The same which I had felt as I slew my brother.

I was no-one's prey.

Across the clearing, before Twyla's house, Ulf Redmane stared. Shock and disbelief crossed his face. Anskar stood beside him, his mouth open and eyes wide.

And it might have been a dream, but my brother's gurgling laugh echoed through my head.

My elation shriveled. I clapped my hand over my mouth, breakfast rising through my gullet. What had I done? The boy had been just as human as me, but I slew him, made him suffer before he died. More than that. I enjoyed it. I'd thought myself human, but Grethor had spoken true. I was a monster.

Then Redmane's one-eyed face twisted, his wrath terrible as the hanged god. "Murderer! Outlaw!" he screamed. "Seether, you killed my son. You hear me? My son!" He motioned to two of his men, who kicked Anskar's legs from under him. Anskar sprawled to the ground and Redmane grabbed his axe. They seized him under the arms and started to drag him away.

My claw. I still had the knife, could save Anskar, fix everything...

Twyla took a step toward the men, her staff raised.

The princess threw out an arm to stop her. "He knew the risk. And there'll be no more seething today." She turned to me. Was that fear I saw in her eyes? "Do you heed me, Boia? We must flee."

I bit my lip, hard enough to draw blood. Then I remembered Anskar's last command and nodded.

The princess led us through the pines, never once glancing behind her.

OATH

My shadow had grown by the time we reached the campsite. It was here that Twyla had revealed how she had birthed me. I had only ever seen it in the dark before. A grassy place, partly sheltered by cliffs. A brook burbled from the woodland nearby, flowing into a great river. White flowers swayed in the breeze, tended by tiny winged creatures with yellow stripes. If the times were not so dire, I might have thought it beautiful.

After checking we weren't followed, Arína threw herself on the ground and turned to Twyla. "I don't suppose either of you brought any food?"

Twyla blinked. "If I'd had more time, princess..."

"No matter. How easy is it to get to the top of this cliff? It'd make a good lookout."

"There's a path, but we'd have to double back."

"Then this place isn't safe," said Arína. "Too easy to get hemmed in. We must go to my father's hall at once."

I shook my head. "But Anskar said—"

Arína kept her eyes on the top of the cliff. "It doesn't matter what Anskar said."

"He told us to wait here, that there were people coming. A safe place."

At last she rounded on me, her gaze hard enough to make me flinch. "Don't you understand, Boia? He's not coming back. No place is safe, not after what you did. Redmane has no path now but revenge."

I looked down at my feet, knowing she spoke truth.

A tear of anger spilled into one of the cuts on her cheek. "You foolish, foolish boy. Why did you have to kill him?"

"I did it because—"

"I know why you did it," she snarled. "You boys and your honor. Had to prove yourself, had to save your darling princess, wanted to be a hero. But warmakers don't build kingdoms, Boia. It's peace-weavers. Jörgen and I could have been bedded and the marriage would be sealed and this whole thing would be done."

"It wouldn't." I raised my chin. "Did you not see the way Redmane's son was looking at you? He was going to kill you, Arína."

She glared at me, then stalked off to the edge of the campsite.

"Princess," Twyla called after her, "it's true. I know the Redmane and his clan. Don't forget, I was his thrall once. There is no cruelty beyond his doing."

The princess's shoulders hunched, but she would not look at either of us. In the space of a day, her entire world had gone askew. I wanted to hold her, offer comfort, for I knew how it felt to be lost. Yet some instinct warned me against reaching for her.

Leaving Arína alone, I sat down upon a fallen log, plucked at strands of grass. My headache was growing worse and I felt like a hollow gourd. I pulled out the amulet and dangled it by the narrow strip of leather. Sunlight filled the amber, made it shine with inner flame. Once the goddess had refused to help a human girl who needed healing. But she had not hesitated to strike down a mortal who stood in her path.

Twyla stood over me, blocking out the sun. "Did you mean to do it, Dóta?" she said softly.

"I didn't mean to, didn't think..." But that wasn't true, not completely. I don't recall making the choice to end Jörgen's life, but I had done nothing to hold back the tide of power. It had overwhelmed me, swept me away. And I had enjoyed the rush, the knowledge that I could take life if I wished. The gate was open and Grethor's death had been the key.

Twyla studied my face. "Killing that boy was not murder, no matter what Redmane says. It was justice."

My cheeks burned. I could not look at her.

"Even so... It's no easy thing to take a life, but you'll have to keep on living." Seeing the look on my face, her eyes filled with pity. "I've never killed anybody, Dóta. That is not my place. But you? You have the soul of a warmaker. I saw it the moment you were born. You may have to kill again before this is done. Men do it all the time."

Some of the guilt sloughed from my shoulders, yet the feeling of uncleanness lingered. I felt the urge to wash, to scrub the killer's stink from my hide.

Twyla spoke on: "But when you slay another, be sure it's your will, not that of the goddess."

My brows raised. "What happened to us being thralls of the gods?"

She shrugged. "Even a thrall has freedom in her own mind. The only question is what you'll do with it."

I toyed with the amulet. "I swore an oath. Not just to the king, not just to Anskar, but to humankind. To be the light against the dark." I squinted up at her. "I can't do that as a strengthless waif. But I will not take life if I can help it." I slipped the amulet over my neck.

It lay against my flesh and the smugness of the goddess pulsed from it. *You need me child. Admit it.* To that, I had no reply.

Twyla nodded at my words, her eyes solemn. "Good." She gestured toward Arína. "And give her time. She lost her father only yesterday."

None of us spoke for a while. I was just getting up to drink from the stream when the clink of iron and the creak of boiled leather pricked my ears. A band of armed men approaching. Arína and I exchanged a wide-eyed glance. She drew a knife from inside her clothes. My own was already in my hand. The runes on Twyla's staff glowed, ready to unleash a wave of magic if they were Redmane's followers. We pressed ourselves against the tree trunks, prepared to leap upon the attackers.

The sound of footsteps halted at the edge of the clearing. "Who's there?" said a familiar voice. "Anskar, is that you?"

"You need no weapons, Boli Butterworth," said Arína as she stepped out from the pine with a grim smile. "Or is it Boli Blood-axe?"

"Princess," said Boli. He stepped from the shadow of the wood into the light and gave us a gap-toothed grin, beckoning a dozen or so men to follow. "My gods, I'm glad you're alive. We'd heard... Yesterday Wind-rime said to meet him here." He looked around. "Where is he?"

"Redmane has him," said Twyla. She quickly told Boli what had happened. When she reached Jörgen's death, Boli's friends edged away from me. One of them cursed and made a warding gesture my way. Yesterday they had cheered as I slew their monster. Now they were afraid of me.

Boli himself nodded and ran a hand over his bare scalp.

"Good, I've been dying for a scrap with Redmane and his brood. But we can't leave Anskar to his fate. By Tyr's hand, we'll butcher every milk drinker who gets between us and him." He drew his axe and the men roared in agreement.

Arína nodded slowly, turned her knife over in her hand. "Anskar's a friend to my clan. My father's milk brother. They stood together in the shield wall. Every one of us owes him our lives. We shall not abandon him. And yet one may succeed where a dozen fail, especially when he wields the power of a goddess." Arína raised her eyes to me. She did not need to speak the command for me to heed it.

"I can move quicker without armor," I said. "Let me save him." Even as I said the words, I had no idea how I'd do it.

Arína's face did not soften. "Good. We shall follow behind, fast as we can. After that—"

Butterworth's face reddened. "We make Redmane regret crossing Anskar. Or you, princess," he added as an afterthought.

"Will you come with me, Twyla?" I asked. "He may need healing."

She ran her fingers through her tangled hair, her eyes darting left and right. At last she shook her head. "I'd only slow you. Go now, I'll follow. Go!"

Without another word, I tore back the way we had come, following my own footprints. The underbrush did little to slow me as I crashed through the woods, the bone knife in my hand. Besides seething, it was my only weapon.

And what are you going to do with that knife? The goddess's voice came unbidden into my mind.

"What I must," I huffed through gritted teeth. "Now are you going to help me or not?"

We'll see.

No time for frustration. Just ahead I spied the arrow still

lodged in the tree from this morning. Twyla's house stood lonely at the heart of the clearing, the hole in the roof just visible from here. A quick glance showed nobody about. I crept through the long grass toward the house, but found no sign.

I leaned against the turf wall of the house, kneading my temples. They could have taken Anskar anywhere. I didn't know these woods, didn't know anything. The night was gathering. This wasn't my world, I didn't belong here. Some guardian I had turned out to be.

Then I looked up, for I was not the only guardian here. I looked down the muddy path. At its end stood the houses of the dead. I muttered the words Anskar and Twyla had used, chanted in a sing-song voice over and over.

The birds continued warbling and the wind to sigh. Maybe I had gotten the words wrong, or maybe the goddess's magic had no sway over the dead. No help was coming. I sank to the ground, despair weighing on me. My hand brushed against something sticky on the grass.

A drop of blood, half-dried. And there was another clinging to a bent stalk. Redmane's followers had tried to conceal their trail, but that was difficult if they dragged a bleeding man. The droplets led into another part of the woods: deeper, darker, clotted with webs. A hand clenched upon my gizzard and tightened with every step. A raven cawed up ahead and I followed its voice.

In the heart of the woods stood a great ash tree, gilded in the last light of day. I paused before it, filled with awe. Its limbs were like finger-bones. It towered over the fir trees surrounding it, Yggdrasil on Earth. A raven croaked within its branches, calling me forward.

A human shape swung on a rope from the lower branches, spinning like a beetle caught in a web.

"Anskar!" I ran to him.

Redmane's men had bound Anskar's arms to his sides, hung him from the tree by his feet. His face was a mess of bruises, his long hair trailing to the ground. A dark wound in his side dripped into his eyes.

They had not slain Anskar, hadn't given him the honor of a painless death. This was a twisted sacrifice. And a point-less one at that, for Anskar was no willing victim. Did they really think giving him to Odin would bring victory?

"No, no, no." I found the sturdiest looking branch I could reach, pulled myself up to the bough from which Anskar hung. Tears leaked from my eyes as I hewed at the rope with my knife. This man had sired me. Only weeks ago he had been a stranger, but now he meant more than I dreamed. My father would not die because of me.

Leaves crunched on the ground beneath the ash.

The warrior wore rings in his ears and a skullcap on his head. A leather vest covered his chest. His pale hide beneath was covered in tattoos, his piggy face full of cruel laughter. He levelled his bow at me, an arrow already nocked.

Let me in...

I hissed, ignoring the whisper in my head. Had Módor not once said those exact words?

I grasped my knife-blade between two fingers and flung it at the man. He side-stepped with a laugh. The bow creaked as he pulled the string taut. He closed an eye, aiming carefully. He was in no hurry, for where did I have to run?

Let me in, said the goddess. Her voice louder, more insis-tent. *You must.*

My flesh was already tingling, warmth rippling from the amulet.

This man wanted my blood. Naught but a beast. At the

sight of the glowing amulet, the sneer fell from his face. His mouth hung slack.

No choice, I told myself. No choice. But I couldn't, shouldn't, didn't want—

A shriek pierced the woods. Movement flickered behind the bowman and I caught a flash of a hooded figure moving faster than any human. He turned to face it, but slow, too slow. A pair of clawed hands had already snared him around the chest, fangs tearing out his throat. A gout of blood. The man gave a whimper as he fell, his eyes rolling.

The figure crouched over him, pinning him to the ground, her crimson robes covering him like a shroud. She faced away from me as she drank from his veins, yet I could not mistake her.

Smite her. Smite her now!

I wanted to sprout wings and fly, anything to get away. And yet I could not leave Anskar to her.

At last she stood and turned. Never before had I seen Módor's face by daylight, her mottled skin the pale green of blight. Her eyes were dark pools rimmed in fire, alive with mirth. She grinned wide with pointed teeth, wiped the blood from her lips, and stepped over the body of her victim.

Once again, the goddess's power seethed through my sinews, the molten anger building behind my eyes. Her voice thundered in my ears, driving out all other thought. *LET ME IN!*

FIRE

THE GODDESS's power roared through me and my hands quivered. I commanded them to cease, but it did no good.

Módor plucked up the knife, turned it over in her clawed hands and slinked toward me. She smiled just as she had when I had done something wicked as a child. "Oh, Dóta. My poor addled girl. It's not time to play. Will you come down from there?"

Do as I command, whispered the goddess in my ear. *You can defend yourself better with both feet planted.*

I dropped to the ground, clutching the amulet to keep it from flying. It took me a few heartbeats to regain my feet, swooning as though I had drunk a skin of mead. Red flashes filled my sight.

Destroy this creature. She must be punished for what she has done.

I ignored the goddess, strained to keep my mother's face in my gaze. "So you want to talk. What have you to say? Have you come to slay me like you slew the animals?"

Módor blinked and tucked the knife into her crimson robes. "How could I slay my own daughter?"

"Don't pretend—you know what I've done. And I'm not your daughter, I'm his." I motioned upward at Anskar's body.

Her mouth twisted in an ugly sneer. "Is this the man you call father? Such a slender thread of life, so easy to twist. I was both mother and father to you, was that not enough? He could never offer what you needed."

"Oh yes?" I said. "And what was that? He has shown me more of humankind than you ever could." And then a thought came to me. "Did you have something to do with this sacrifice?"

My mother laughed, though it was empty of joy. "Humans killing humans. I did not need to intervene and nor did the All-Father. Fate has come for the warrior as I knew it would." She threw her hood back, revealing her pointed ears. "Do you like my robes? If only you could have seen me when I was young and beautiful. I wore garb like this every day. But that was before the goddess came. Before she filled your head with lies." Módor glared at the amulet.

"The only lies are yours." Malice dripped from the amber into my heart, dark and burning as serpent's venom. I gave way to the anger, the outrage, let it reign within me. My hands were weary from shaking, yet I could not stop them, did not want to...

... For this creature was abomination, less than the meanest goblin. It had given itself to a troll, the lowest and vilest beast in all nine worlds. It deserved to be stripped and flogged before all the gods, chained up and cast into the gloom of the mist world. If not for the soft-heartedness of the gods of the spring, it would have been...

I blinked. How could I know such things? Something is wrong, said a voice in my head. My own, I realized, then brushed it aside.

My hands had stopped shaking at last. Calm filled me, the magic and I becoming one.

"The gods are here, daughter of Norns. And they lend strength to their thrall." My lips formed the words and the sound came from my throat, but they did not belong to me.

Módor's mouth fell open. Then her face flushed dark. "Dóta," she said. "Dóta, this isn't you."

My teeth gnashed together. "Who are you to tell her what she is?"

The knife flashed in one of Módor's hands. From the other she extended her claws. "Let her go, Freya."

"What will you do? Plunge your dagger into her? Such caring."

My mother faltered. For the first time, I saw fear in her eyes. The same fear I had seen on Arína's face. "Release her. She doesn't belong to you."

"Does she not?" A dark laugh rose from the depths of my belly. It was loud, twisted, and sounded nothing like my laugh. "Long have I watched you torment this one, Norn. You gave her life, do you think that means she's yours? For every giving a taking..." My hand was yanked up as though on a silken chain.

"Dóta," said Módor, "you mustn't listen. She will betray you to your death. Do you not recall the bones of the last man to bear the amulet? What do you think happens when you displease her?"

My lips curled in a smirk. "Dóta is gone. She cannot hear you. She is part of me now."

Lies. I heard every word. I wanted to curse, to scream. But my voice was smothered as though someone had shoved a cloth down my throat.

Módor's voice shook. "Dóta, I know you're in there." Her eyes shone like she was weeping.

The glow of power swept through my veins, visible even through my hide.

She did not try to flee, but dropped the knife. "Very well. If you can hear me, know that I forgive you. For everything."

Tiny flames danced at my fingertips and my mouth watered at the knowledge that this creature would die at my hand. Why not? I was already a kin-slayer, wasn't I?

And yet...

Something inside me railed against the killing. Perhaps I was a monster, but I couldn't slay my own mother, whatever she had done.

"You're still my daughter," whispered Módor. "We are kin, you and I."

My hands shook once more. I strained against the invisible fetters even as they bit into my wrists.

I won't do it, I thought. The goddess could not silence me even if she held my body in her grip.

"You are mine," the goddess said in my voice. "My thrall."

And yet I was more than that. From the corner of my eye I spied Anskar hanging limp above me. His blood ran through my veins. I was human. Human! I threw myself upon the notion and gripped it tight in my mind. Every sinew in my body ached from the strain, my heart dashing itself against my ribs. Sweat dripped down into my eyes as though I was pumping the bellows of a forge.

My hands were blazing with the fires of the goddess, reflected in the terror of Módor's eyes. Those eyes had watched over me since before I was born.

"Stand, Dóta!" Módor cried. "Fight!"

A cry ripped from my throat, resounded through the woods and the darkness beyond. My scream, my voice.

The weight fell from my shoulders. The flitter of raven's

wings filled my ears. And I knew she was gone. The goddess had fled from me.

And so I raised my hands and cast a stream of fire into the heavens. The flames skimmed the treetops and the wood caught light.

The only sound was the crackling of burning trees. Módor watched me, her pale face filled with awe. Fires bloomed all around us, the heat scorching.

I stumbled, my vision growing dark. Cold inside now.

Chilly arms caught me, lowered me gently to the ground.

"She's gone, Dóta," Módor said. "You did it. You are free." She stroked my hair with her long fingers. "There now, nothing to fear. Sleep, my girl. I shall watch over you."

I opened and closed my eyes, struggling against the weariness which threatened to overwhelm me.

Anskar still swung from the rope above my head. And above him, the ash tree stretched beyond the roof of the world, its branches swaying. Floating sparks and embers mingled with the stars.

The light broke into shards of rainbow before my eyes slid shut.

WAR

A BLAST of wind wrenched me back to wakefulness, icy as the breath of frost giants. It was still night.

"Good, Boia. You're awake." Arína's face filled my vision, lit by the crackling flames.

"Arína?"

"I'm here," she said.

The bitter smell of smoldering bark told me I still lay beneath the ash tree. "Módor—" I sat up again.

"The beast-mother was gone before we arrived. I saw her footprints. Your magic must have driven her off. Now calm yourself."

I eased back. What was Módor's game?

Arína's eyes were full of concern. She reached and brushed a fir needle from my hair. Her eyes met mine and my heart swelled like the ocean beneath the moon. I reached out and stroked her cheek, careful not to touch the claw-marks. She did not pull back, but cupped my hand beneath hers. She closed her eyes for an instant, then stood, throwing a fearful glance over her shoulder. For we were not alone.

No sign of Módor, nor the man she slew. Best not to dwell on what she had done to his corpse.

Twyla stood nearby, her staff raised. She muttered a chant under her breath, aiming at the fires. Another frosty breath of wind came from the staff-tip, quelling the flames. Finishing her spell, she glanced at me and the princess and raised an eyebrow. "Are you all right?"

I nodded.

"Good. Same can't be said for him." She nodded behind me.

I eased myself up and peered over my shoulder. Anskar's friends had cut him down from the tree and lowered him to the ground. Now he lay wrapped in blankets. His eyes were hidden behind swollen lids, not moving.

Boli Butterworth kneeled at Anskar's side, his head lowered as he prayed. Some of his friends stood around, torches in their hands.

The princess stepped back as I ran to Anskar's side and grabbed him by the shoulder. "Anskar?" I shook him. "Come on, Anskar, wake up."

Boli shook his head. "He won't wake."

"He's not—"

"Not yet," said Twyla. "His spirit lingers, though his body's broken."

"I can help," I said. "We can fix this, Twyla."

She closed her eyes for a moment, listening. To the voice of the All-father, perhaps?

"Please," I said. To whom, I didn't quite know.

Twyla's face grew solemn. Then she nodded. "We can try. Remember the words?"

The amulet was already in my grasp. I pressed my lips together, ready to summon the power of the goddess. If she tried to take control of me again, I would throw her off. I'd done it once already.

"Stand back, all of you," said Arína.

Twyla raised her staff and held it above Anskar's chest. The sweet notes of her healing song fell from her lips, calling forth the cold fire.

I clutched the amulet and chanted the words, steeling my heart against the goddess. But the amulet remained cold and dead as marble in my fist.

Twyla fell silent as beams of blue light shone from her staff. They crept across Anskar's body, probing the soft flesh of his side. He began to shake, flopping on the ground like a salmon. In a few heartbeats the swelling in his face went down and the wound ceased its weeping.

Twyla's hand wavered, her staff dropping toward the ground. "I can't do this on my own."

I started the chant again, determined not to fumble the words. No rush of power, no feeling of exhilaration. Just nausea sucking at my insides. "Come on! Why won't you help me?" I shouted at the amulet. Yet no answer came. The only voice in my head belonged to me.

"Enough," Twyla whispered. She sank down and hugged herself. "I've given all I can, Boia. No more." She looked up. "What happened?"

I stared at the amulet in my hand, no more than an ill-made trinket now. "I don't know. The goddess has always come when I called before." Yet that was a lie. Freya had let me taste the power when it pleased her. Still, that wasn't all of it. If not for the goddess, I would have died so many times over the past days. Why had she saved me?

To win my trust. So I would let her into my heart. And now that I had shunned her, she had abandoned me.

"Will he wake?" said the princess.

Anskar now lay still. The wound in his side had closed, yet his face remained contorted in pain.

Slowly Twyla shook her head. "The bleeding is inside him. This is beyond my skill."

As if in answer a shrill voice sounded through the woods. It came from far away and carried neither words nor song. Just one dread call.

At the sound one of Boli's friends muttered. "A hunting horn. It's over. We may as well hand ourselves to Redmane now. Perhaps he'll spare us."

"Boar piss he will," muttered Twyla.

Boli wasn't listening. He was staring at Anskar, his face grave. "There's still time for one thing." He drew his axe.

"What are you doing?" I said.

His thick brows lowered. "Anskar is my friend. My captain, the best of us. When the cold winds blew, he lent me his blanket. You think I'll let him die a sniveler's death?" He raised his weapon.

Twyla made no move to stop him. "It's what he would want," she said. "Better to feast in Valhalla than endure Hel's blight."

"You can't," I said.

"Stick to seething, weeper," Boli growled, "this is man's work."

I hissed and reached for my knife, only to find it gone.

"Stop." Authority rang from Arína's voice.

Boli's hand froze.

She raised her chin at him. "Stay your hand, Boli. He may wake yet, for Valkyries only come when it's time. Is this any way to start a war?"

"War?" Boli muttered. All vigor had bled from him now.

"Redmane has already won, daughter of Hrut. What hope have we without Anskar?"

"Hope remains." She held out her hand for the axe. "So long as we stand."

After chewing his lip, Boli pressed the handle into her palm.

Aína held it up so the moonlight gleamed on the polished edge. "We will not shirk the call to battle. Now is the time to rally. We must gather every warrior and shield maiden." At her words, my heart gave a great surge; this was the Aína I liked best.

"Aye," said Twyla. "You'll throw rocks, will you? We are no army. You cannot fight a war without food stores, Princess." Twyla's voice cracked. "Nor will sword-smiths work for free. And no place in the kingdom is safe now. Where are we to hide?"

All voices fell silent. Aína lowered the axe, her eyes on the ground.

I mulled over it, toying with the amulet. No point asking it for help, not when Freya had left me as she did its last bearer. For an idle moment I wondered who he had been, where he had come from. How had he gotten into our cave?

The notion struck me like one of Aegir's waves.

I released the amulet and pushed up my arm ring. "I know somewhere."

The horn of Redmane's hunters blew again, nearer this time.

Boli tensed as though ready to flee.

"Hold," said Aína in a harsh whisper. "We don't bolt like hares." The princess fixed her eyes on me. "Speak, Elfin-sun."

"The place. It's a cave. Not too far from here."

"This is madness," Boli hissed. "There's no such—"

"You wouldn't know it. The only way in is underwater."

Arína's brow creased. "That doesn't help, though. Our armor would drag us to our doom."

"No." I shook my head, my thoughts jostling. "The warrior who bore the amulet before me, he wore battle clothes."

"Eh?" said Boli.

"All I found was his bones, but he was still in his mail." Mutters broke out and I talked over them. "But he couldn't have swum. There must be a tunnel or something."

Shrewdness pierced Arína's gaze. "How did you find it?"

I faltered, suddenly wishing I had said nothing. Never before had I told Arína of my rearing, nor anyone else. Even Twyla didn't know everything. The idea of revealing myself before all these strangers tasted of shite. But what choice did I have?

"You asked me once where I came from, Arína. This is it." I swallowed. "The lair of Grethor and his mother."

Twyla's face grew harder than flint, but her eyes filled with sorrow.

"You were the monster's thrall?" Boli did not bother hiding his scorn.

I shrugged. It was close enough to truth. "There's fresh water and fish and mushrooms to eat. And there's gold. Lots of it."

Greed flashed in Boli's eyes, then he turned to Arína. "Do we trust him?"

The princess released a slow breath.

The hunting horn blasted again, close enough to fill our ears.

"Find the beast-mother's trail," said Arína.

"Right then," said Boli. "Come on, lads." He passed

Arína a torch, then he and the other warriors left, bent close
to the ground.

"As for you, Elfin-sun…" Arína frowned. "I'd have words.
But not yet." She turned away to follow Boli, then froze. She
turned back to me. "Boia, you are wounded."

"Eh?"

She pointed. I looked down to find a smear of blood on
my thigh. My face flushed with heat and my shoulders
clenched. All the other things that day had driven it from
my mind. I tried to brush away the stain, but that only made
it worse. "It's nothing," I stammered. "Just—"

But Arína was still staring as though she had never seen
me before. Her hand crept over her mouth, her eyes widen-
ing. "I—I didn't—you?"

"Please, I—"

She glanced at Twyla, then back to me. "Dóta. That's
your true name, isn't it?"

Twyla laid a hand on my shoulder. "It is. She is Dóta,
daughter of Anskar. And me."

I shrugged her hand off. "I don't know what my true
name is, Arína. Or where I fit. But I do know…" Tears stung
my eyes. "I feel…" The flow of my words failed. I bowed my
head.

"You deceived me. Both of you."

"I didn't mean—"

"Why didn't you tell me?"

Boli's shout rose from the trees. "We found it, Princess!"

"Good," said Arína, still looking at me with fear and
doubt written on her face. She shook herself. "Very good.
Gather Anskar up and lead on, we've a battle to win."

Boli slung Anskar over his shoulder, the yellow-haired
warrior still limp. Then the princess held her torch by her

head. Its light flickered, pale and feeble. As she turned to follow the men it went out.

"Arína," I called after her. "I wanted to tell you." I sank to my knees, the dew soaking my breeches. "Please," I whispered. But there was no point.

She was already gone.

BREATHE

As a child, I thought I knew the darkness. Yet now I kneeled in the abyss. Nothing lay before my eyes but midnight blacker than woad. The weight of the ash tree pressed down on me, even if I could not see it. The light, that's what I was meant to be. But I could not do that when darkness wrapped itself around me like a cloak of undeath.

No sign of the princess. She had turned away from me as Twyla did before I was even an inkling of the gods. And now Anskar too. I choked back a sob. If being human meant this kind of pain, I didn't want it.

Twyla snapped her fingers. "You still with us?"

I swallowed my pain. "Yes."

"Here." She pressed her hand into the shadows until it found mine. "Come, on your feet." She pulled me up, then gripped my hand in hers. Not sure what else to do, I squeezed back. Her skin against my palm was rough and covered in calluses, but warm. "Just hold on. Dawn will be here soon."

The low, mournful voice of the hunting horn rolled over us. It sounded further away now.

"Think they'll make it?" I said.

"If they're meant to. Are you well?"

"Well enough."

She clucked her tongue and let go of my hand. Bottles clinked as she searched her satchel. Then she pressed a bundle of cloth into my hand. "Rags. You know what they're for?"

"I can guess." I unbuckled my belt and fumbled with a rag until it was in place, then tightened the belt strap again. "Won't you need them?"

"Not yet. No need for shame, it happens to everyone."

"Everyone?"

"Every woman. Even if you have a war-maker's soul."

"Another human thing to learn."

She grunted. "You should have said something, I might have given you something for the pangs."

"I should have said a lot of things." Bitterness crept into my voice.

"Perhaps. Have you told her how you feel?"

I shook my head, then realized Twyla couldn't see me. "I couldn't know what she'd say."

"You never do. Gods know I didn't with Anskar." She sighed. "This Boia thing was his idea, wasn't it? I might have known."

"It doesn't matter now. I've already lost her."

"Was she yours to lose?"

I let go of Twyla's hand and crossed my arms, glaring at nothing.

"Peace, Dóta. I'm saying not to give up yet. Give her time to do what she must. And freedom to choose how to act on her heart."

I wiped my nose on my sleeve. "Do you think she'll choose me?"

"Dunno. But she cares for you an awful lot."

"Then why did she get so angry?"

Twyla laughed softly. "I don't think she would have if she didn't. But I've seen the brightness of her eyes as she looks at you. That can't be hidden. And yet… it's just not time yet for either of you. You'll know the right moment." Her voice grew heavy. "And when it comes, be truthful. Because years are too precious to waste."

Silence fell between us. Not an empty silence, for it did not ask to be filled. Twyla's head drooped on my shoulder. I thought of shrugging her off, but allowed her to snore. My eyes slid shut and I might have snored myself.

A tapping echoed between the trunks. I opened my eyes, looked up into the branches of the ash tree. A pair of curious black eyes peered down. The red-furred creature held an acorn in his paws, the bristles of his tail wagging. A squirrel: Grethor had spoken of these. He rapped his prize against the side of the tree, then leapt to the ground, scampering in search of better fare.

Twyla now lay nestled between the roots of the ash tree, her satchel under her head.

I stood and stretched, my limbs stiff and the rags still clenched in my hand. The boughs of the trees had emerged from the darkness, clad in silver-grey light. Not a hint of the Redmane or his ilk.

My gut gave a grumble, but I felt no urge to squat. For I had barely touched a morsel or drunk a drop yesterday. I sniffed and tracked the scent of river water on the breeze. The coldness of the stream was delicious against the rawness of my throat. I rinsed out the rag I used last night then replaced it with a clean one.

As I leaned over the stream, the amulet spilled from

under my collar. I looked into its amber depths. "Are you there?"

The goddess did not answer, not that I thought she would. Making sure the amulet was secure on its leather band, I slipped it back into my shirt.

I glanced back. The ash tree rose taller than a dream, Twyla resting at its feet. Once more I heard a raven cawing from the top of the tree. And though it sounds daft, I heard the warning in its voice, telling me it wasn't time to leave this holy place. Not yet.

Trying to recall Twyla's lessons on herblore, I picked berries and shoved them into my mouth. Then I spied a flash of crimson beneath the bushes. For an instant I thought it might have been that furred creature from before. But no, I was the only beast around here. The red came from the caps of mushrooms growing from the earth. I picked one of them, turned it over in my hands and pressed my tongue between my teeth. The mushrooms' white spots glistened in the morning sun.

Glancing over my shoulder to make sure no-one was watching, I ran the tip of my tongue over the mushroom again. Once more the urge to gag overwhelmed me, but I did not cast the Red Cap to the ground as I had before. Instead I put it with the rest, then made my way back toward Twyla.

She was already sitting up and leaning against the trunk of the ash, watching me approach. When she saw the mushroom in my hand, she turned her head to one side. "And what do you think you're doing with that?"

"You told me once the Red Cap would allow the worthy to see the faces of the gods."

"Only if it's brewed just right, otherwise it'll be a most

painful death. Lucky I still have some of the potion—give the mushroom here, it's folly to eat it raw."

I passed it to her. "Can I see the potion?"

She pulled a clay bottle from her bag, its wax stopper sealed tight. "Shouldn't we be heading off? I reckon we can still catch up to Arína."

"I need my seething back. I'm no use without the goddess."

"Well that's not—" She stopped and squinted. "You're not asking…"

"I am."

She stared at me for a long moment, then nodded and reached into her bag once more. "We'll need mugwort to do this right."

"We?"

"This is the final test for a seether."

"You think I'm ready?"

She didn't look up from her rummaging. "In truth, I can't teach you much. You already hear the voices of Asgard louder than I can." She pulled out a few dried sprigs. "You were born for magic."

I let out a slow breath, weary of hearing what I was born for. "I can do this by myself."

"All right, perish if you want. Even the wisest of us would not try something so foolish. Let me be your guide." Her voice broke. "Dóta, I know I wasn't much of a teacher and less of a mother. But I can do this for you if you trust me." She held out the bottle.

I hesitated, then closed my hand over it. "This doesn't mean you're forgiven."

"I know. Now sit."

I seated myself beneath the ash tree. This might have

been a sacred space, but the roots still formed a hard seat. "Now what?"

"You've a full belly?"

I nodded.

She piled up the sprigs of mugwort before me, grumbling they weren't as fresh as she'd like. "Now. Are you sure you want to do this? The gods might show you things you don't want to see."

"It's the only way to save Anskar. The only way I can save the kingdom."

"Are those good reasons?"

I gnawed my lip, thinking back to my first encounter with Twyla. "I have to know. To understand. To touch the face of the goddess. And if she won't help, I want her to look me in the eye and tell me the reason."

"Then drink."

I sipped. The potion tasted of honeyed mead, though the tartness of berry juice lurked beneath. And something else, sharp and deadly. She grabbed the bottle and tipped it so the potion glugged down my throat. The potion sizzled in my belly, hotter than wine.

"You pass the first test. Your body didn't reject it. And good thing too, else you might have ruined your shirt. Now we begin." She waved her staff over the sprigs. Instantly they sparked and ghostly smoke rose. "Breathe deep, Dóta."

A pleasing scent that didn't make me cough, filled my lungs with heat and coolness at the same time. The tension in my muscles eased after a few breaths and I half-closed my eyes.

"That's it. Just breathe." Twyla circled the fire, the smoke curling around her staff. She chanted in a rough voice that didn't belong to her. Deeper. Harsh words, frightening. And yet I did not want to cover my ears. Like a saga where you want to know the ending though you dread it at the same time. Her voice rose to a bellow...

She seemed tall as a giantess, her tangled curls loose, but no doubting she was human with her soft hide and round, round teeth.

Human.

For some reason the thought seemed funny. Something bubbled up from deep within. A belch? No, a giggle, a giggle! Joy and peace and all would be fine. The sensation grew like a beanstalk, soaring up into my head until my laugh became sobbing and laughing and crying all became twined like knotwork. I rode on the air as though on an eight-legged stallion.

And the squirrel sat watching me from above, whiskers twitching as he sniffed.

The sunlight streaming through the leaves fractured as they had when I had slipped from the waking world. Lights flashed and I would have seen them even behind closed lids.

Then a sudden fear gripped me, limbs tingling. Night falling. I crashed from the back of the stallion, spun through empty air. Legs pumping, no ground under my feet. Tumbling. The world had gone dark, the shadows returned. Had to run, escape, bury myself underground and not come out, had to—

"Twyla!" I cried. "Something..." I struggled to find words. "Something wrong." I squeezed my eyes shut.

"Ohh humm, nothing is wrong." The voice was high and filled with malice, and I did not know who spoke.

"Twyla..." Solid ground beneath my feet, a blessing.

"Gone, gone. You're all alone."

I opened my eyes to find myself standing in a world of purple twilight. A thousand colors danced like dragons across the sky, shimmering and shifting. There were no stars here. A hill climbed toward the heavens and atop it stood the ash tree. The same as before, but bigger, its branches stretching into the void. So huge it filled my sight, the only thing in this realm sharp and unblurred. In its upmost branches a light twinkled like a beacon.

I blinked, fathoming how far away the tree was. How could that be? I had been right underneath it before.

Yet these were not the woods of Midgard. At the feet of the tree lay nothing but rubble strewn upon the earth, the jagged outlines of broken halls. A ruined, empty place, a chill wind rasping.

"Where am I?" I said, my words slurred.

The same voice cackled. "Home is where she is, humm? Nothing wrong, he is safe."

"Who—" I looked around to find the voice and startled to find the squirrel sitting atop a boulder just a little taller than me, his eyes sparkling with cunning. Then he opened his mouth. "Where is here, mighty war-weaver. Not the place between worlds, ah no. Just your pretty little head, eh? Best place for a peace-maker."

I stepped back, my jaw falling.

"And who?" continued the squirrel. "Oooh, who is you and who is me and that be we. Ratatoskr is the name. And I will guide you to the hall of the gods."

GUIDE

ANIMALS DID NOT SPEAK, I was almost certain by now. Yet here was a creature who had more to say than I did. "That is... Yggdrasil?" I said, pointing at the tree. "The true Yggdrasil?"

The squirrel shook his head. "No, no. A fool's question. There is no true thing, not here. You, me, this place. All of this rattles in your skull, humm? Like those round teeth of yours."

"What do you know of my teeth?"

"Ratatoskr knows everything, he does. All the wisdom in the world, right here." He tapped his head.

I frowned. "But who are you?"

"Ratatoskr already tells. Some call me messenger of eagles and dragons, yet they tell fibs. Nobody, that's me."

"Nobody's nobody. Your true name, now."

"Ratatoskr has no true name. And if he does, there's no truth to it. No more than your naming, eh Boia? Or is it Dóta?"

I rubbed my forehead, trying to drive out the haze. "This is madness."

"The madness you crave. Perhaps Ratatoskr walks with you a bit and tells you a few things he knows?"

Of all guides, I wouldn't have chosen this prattler. Yet this was my test, and I would not fail. Hardening my face, I nodded.

He leapt from the boulder and clung to my shoulder. "Look. That is our way." He pointed toward a path which wound through the rubble. Had it been there before? "On we go, yes. Onward to the gods."

With a sigh, I took the first steps, trying not to wince at the touch of the squirrel's paws against my hide. Before long, we came to a fork in the road. The right-hand path went into the light, a smooth pass up a gentle slope. The other led downward, through a narrow pass full of mist. The way was strewn with bones. Sickly plants poked through broken cobblestones. A darker path, yet it held no terror for me.

"Which way?"

"The right path. Much quicker, much easier. The light, that's what you are wanting. Gods are up there. Going down is dangerous, yes. Monsters dwell beneath the tree. Vile creatures, you don't want anything to do with them."

"Fine." I trudged up the path. The steps led around the side of the hill.

"Good, good." He settled. "What do you seek from the goddess, eh?"

"Wisdom."

"Humm, wisdom. Such lies you spin, you should teach Ratatoskr."

"I've never lied. My brother could always tell."

"But lies are all you know, not honest like me. You seek forgiveness, of course."

I stopped walking. "I need no god's forgiveness."

"Then what do you want, humm?" I heard the grin in his voice as he leaned into my ear. "Is it love?

My teeth hurt from grinding. "It's power I seek."

"Oh, power. Aye, not wisdom, now you speak true. And what will you do with power? Kill? Of course, killing is easy. Fun too."

"No," I said. "I hate killing."

"More lies. You seek power to kill, but killing is power for your kind."

"My kind?" My loathing for this creature grew with every heartbeat.

"Calmness, calmness. You grow so tense your shoulder is uncomfortable. So much anger inside, such hate. Still, I don't judge you, of course I don't. You can't help it, little whelp. Just a beast, after all."

A tear spilled down my cheek and I flicked it away. Yet I had no reply.

He chattered on: "No, not even that. A troll in human flesh. No soul to speak of, foul as all your kinsmen, human and other."

"Be quiet."

His head bobbed up and down at the edge of my sight. "No secret is safe from Ratatoskr, he gnaws until he finds it." He sniffed. "The killer's stink still hangs on you."

With a snarl, I grabbed the creature by the tail, tired of carrying him around. Ratatoskr squeaked as I hurled him onto the dusty path. His bones crunched. He shuddered, gasping for air, legs twitching. Then the poor twisted body lay still.

I swear I never meant to do it, but I had. Taken a life. Not just a life. This creature was supposed to be my guide through this world. Gods, was I made to cause harm? The squirrel had spoken truly.

I sank down, reached to stroke the red fur. His body was hard and cold underneath. Then I shrank back and hugged myself. These hands were shaped like those of humans, but they may as well have been claws. Never again would they touch another living creature. This I swore. Arína deserved better. So did Anskar. My world should have more. Ah, but where was my world?

I turned, started back down the hill.

A shrill laugh rang out behind me. I spun around to find the squirrel hopping on the spot, rubbing his paws together with glee. "Oh, such pain! I am dying. Poor Ratatoskr." If he had been hurt, he showed no sign of it now. He turned a shrewd eye upon me. "But she hates killing and he loves healing, oh yes. Just like the mother."

The back of my neck grew hot. "You tricked me."

"Oh no. That is not Ratatoskr's nature."

I resumed my strides up the hill. "Follow if you must, but I'll not bear you."

My feet ached from hiking so far. Yet the tree was no nearer. Peering down the hillside showed I had not climbed at all. How could this be? I lifted my legs and put on a fresh spurt, building to a run. Every step was a goat's leap, but still the hilltop grew no closer.

"That's it," said the squirrel, running beside me. "You walk the right path, keep going this way. You'll get there and the goddess greets you with gifts."

I stopped, licked sweat from my upper lip. "Why should I believe you?"

"What truth can Ratatoskr tell? He has naught to spare."

His words made me frown. "No truth to your name. That's what you said."

The squirrel straightened, his hair on end. "No, I never."

"This path leads nowhere. And you speak nothing but lies." I turned my back on him once more.

"There's always truth in a lie, Dóta Elfin-sun," said Ratatoskr behind me. Hurt in his voice feigned, no doubt. "That's why we believe them."

Not concealing my disgust, I walked on. The little bastard sniggered to himself but didn't try to follow. For that, I was grateful—I couldn't trust myself not to kill him again. Better to be my own guide than trust one who would lead me astray.

Nothing he'd said was true, I told myself. And yet... He had said so many things I believed myself. But if this was some kind of fever dream and this was all happening inside my head, it would make sense.

But that was a lie too, wasn't it? All of this was real.

I halted when I reached the place where the ways parted. I peered down the trail of shadows, spiraling downward. The path remained choked with weeds. The end lay hidden behind the fog, but my guide had said monsters waited there.

Monsters like me.

Willing myself toward courage, I took my first steps down the path. It didn't take long to figure out it was cut into the side of a ravine, steps leading ever downward. To my left, a wall of granite. To my right, a sheer drop. I peered over the side and saw nothing but an endless void. Shivering, I quickened my pace. The bones crunched underfoot. Even through the soles of my boots they were like teeth nipping into my toes. The gloaming thickened as I descended. Looking up showed empty grey where the lights had danced.

Movement slithered in the shadows ahead.

A pale hand reached from a crack in the cobblestones.

Its fingers were long and thin like the limbs of a spider, the fingertips black with rot and yellow-white underneath. Ragged nails chewed short.

I froze, already reaching for the amulet. With a start, I realized it was gone. No defense against the specter.

The hand grasped at the air, seeking life. I stared, expecting the living corpse to burst from the ground. The fingers twitched, not quite awake.

The dead would not be denied, but I had no wish to tread on the grave. Who would bury a body beneath the road? Was it some kind of trap? No, not a trap. A test.

I glanced up at the rock wall. A ridge, a handhold. I leapt to grab it, scrabbled to find a grip. Hanging above, I inched along, the tip of my boot just inches from the hand. It reached like an eyeless creature, knowing prey was near, but not quite close enough to sniff out.

My hand closed upon a jagged stone atop the ridge. It sliced into the flesh of my left palm. A cry burst from my lips. I lost my grip and held on by my right hand, dangling from the ridge. A drop of blood splashed onto the ground and seeped through a crack.

The cobbles broke apart, bits of stonework flying. The air filled with moans, the sweet-sick scent of decay. The breath of the dead. A hundred hands exploded from beneath the ground like sharks in frenzy. A hand grabbed my ankle and pulled me down. I slammed to the ground, the copper taste of blood on my tongue. Already hands had snared my wrists, my feet. They clung tighter than irons, all driven by a single will. Hands all over me. Groping, squeezing, clammy death covering my eyes. I tried to scream, but wraith fingers were already pushing into my mouth, reaching down my throat, grabbing at my voice, determined to rip it out.

"Not today, you dead," said a woman's voice.

"You've had your time," said another.

"And you'll have your chance again," said a third. "But not yet."

Instantly the hands released me, retreated under the ground and left me half-buried beneath the soil. A hand appeared before me and I flinched away before seeing it was a live fleshy pink, the fingernails trimmed short. I grabbed it, felt myself lifted out of the ground.

I gagged, rubbing my throat and spitting out blood before I looked up.

Three kindly faces smiled down at me, their eyes aglow with warmth.

"You are lost, little weirdling," said a plump woman with rosy cheeks. She brushed dirt from her green kirtle.

A woman with hair the color of frost jabbed at me with her walking stick. "Lucky we heard you shout. Mind you, it would have saved everybody trouble if you just called for help in the first place."

"I didn't know there was help near," I said.

A third girl smiled, clapped her hands together. She was willowy, her hair like autumn flame. "Dóta will always be like that. Won't you see, sisters?"

"You know we never have," said the old one.

I blinked and stood. How could these women be sisters? All of them wore the crown of maidenhood, but that was all they had in common. That, and their pointed ears. "Who are you?"

The elder rolled her eyes, but no-one answered.

"The squirrel, he said I'd find monsters here," I said.

"To him, we probably are," said the maid of the green kirtle.

My hands balled into fists. "You haven't answered my question. Who are you?"

The youngest blinked. "But of course you'll recognize us, Elfin-sun. We're kin, after all."

"You should have known us right away. We have always tended the Well of Fate," said the eldest. "Gods know you've sung plenty of songs about us. You and your mother."

"I am Verdandi," said the young woman. "The becoming."

The old crone crossed her arms. "Humans always called me Urd. You may as well too."

"We don't know each other yet," said the girl with the red hair. "But will you guess my name?"

"Skuld," I whispered. "You are Norns."

"The Norns, as it were," sniffed Urd.

"More than that," said Verdandi with a gentle smile.

Skuld beamed and threw her arms around me. "You'll call us your grandmothers, Dóta."

ECHO

I PUSHED SKULD AWAY. An embrace was the last thing I wanted right now. "What did you say? Three grandmothers?"

"Gala is our daughter," said Verdandi. "You know her as Módor, of course."

"I don't suppose we'll ever see her again," said Skuld.

Urd clucked her tongue. "That was her own fault, the silly child. It's what she deserved for getting tangled up with that nasty troll boy."

"Hush, sister," said Verdandi. "Not now."

"But..." I said, feeling for the words. My mother had a name and parents of her own. Looking back, this ought not surprise me, but there it was. "How?"

"Think on this, dear weirdling," said Verdandi. "You have a mother and a father, parents of the body. Yet you would not exist were it not for our little one tugging at the strings of fate. Though she is not so little now."

"Three parents brought you into this world, pet," said Urd. "Thus it always has been for Norn kind. All our daughters are past, present and future joined in the flesh."

"But you're all girls."

"Are we?" said Verdandi, raising her brows. "We appear so, I suppose."

Urd raised a gnarled finger. "Hasn't always been that way, mind you."

"And may not yet be," murmured Skuld. "Someday things could change. After all, who knows?"

"Don't you?" I said, my brow creased.

A dreamy look filled Skuld's eye. "Oh, I might. But not yet. Our births will ever be sundered, even past Ragnarök and the new day's dawning."

Urd tapped her stick on the ground. "Come along, the hour's already grown late."

"Late for what?" I said.

"Your test, silly," said Skuld. "The moment nears. Follow me, I'll show you."

She pointed. As if responding to her command, the mists parted to reveal the path led to the mouth of a cave. The entrance stood at the bottom of the ravine. Golden light shone from within.

"Come, you'll like it. It'll feel homely." Skuld beckoned, then lifted her dress and skipped ahead. Only as she slipped inside the cave did I notice she went unshod, though it never occurred to me that she might suffer an injury.

With a sigh, Verdandi followed. "It is time."

"Past bloody time," growled Urd and bustled after, leaning on her walking stick. "Come along, pet."

I cast one last glance behind. The pale hand had already crept back to the surface, ready for its next victim. Not staying to gawk, I ran to catch up to Urd. "Why was Módor banished?"

"You've already heard, haven't you? The slattern offered

herself to a troll. Gave birth to a monster. You ask me, her fate was her doing."

"Why, though?"

"Oh, but she was a naughty one, always picking up strays. It was her who first pitied Ratatoskr, you know. Trained him as a pet."

"Eh?"

"Why do you think he took such an interest in you? I wager he said a few things not to your liking."

"Grethor's father," I said, trying to change the subject. "What was his name?"

She blinked. "He had a name..." Then Urd shook her head. "Too long ago."

"What was he like?"

Urd shrugged. "He was a troll. Hulking, scaly, yellow eyes. Big chompers." She opened wide and showed me her own, though I counted more gums than teeth.

"Was he bold or craven? Wise or foolish?"

"He was angry. Angry at the way his kind were shunned. Enough to make anyone angry, I suppose. But there was one thing he never understood. There was never a place for him in this world. Or any other. And we told him so."

I swallowed, finding the words familiar. "So you're saying he deserved death?"

"I'm saying he should have known his place. Even the frost giants would not allow trolls into their realm. More wretched than the meanest human. They're animals, hiding in the fringes of the woods and snatching prey where they can. He didn't woo our Gala so much as she felt sorry for him."

That was not what Módor had said. Nor the goddess. But it would not do to quarrel with a Norn, not when the object of my journey was so close.

She kept talking: "And I'll tell you something else." She leaned close enough for me to smell the cabbage on her breath. "He was hungry. A troll's belly is never full."

"Did he..." I swallowed. "Did he slay humans?"

"And ground their bones for meal." She smiled and patted me on the arm. "Don't worry, pet. What you did, you did without choice. You've never been like him."

"What am I, then?"

Urd laughed. "That is the real question, isn't it?" We now stood on the threshold of the cave. Up close, the dappling of the light showed it was reflected from water. She gestured. "Come inside."

I stepped around the spikes which grew from the rocky floor. When I saw what lay inside, there was no point hiding my gasp. The cave's top soared higher than the vaulted roof of Valdskali. The walls were lit not by glowing mushrooms, but by veins of gold that pulsed bright as though from the forge. Living gold, my mother had called it. The veins ran around tree roots which snaked down from the surface. Each root was thicker than a man's waist and fed from a great pool at the center of the chamber. The air was warmer than any cave I have ever beheld.

The three sisters stood at the edge of the water, staring at its surface.

Skuld waved me forward. "The Well of Fate. Will you not look into the water?"

My shuffling footsteps echoed as I approached. The waters shone like liquid gold. The surface showed the roof of the cave, rippling even without wind.

"A dragon dwells in those depths," said Verdandi. "Always chewing the roots of the world tree."

"Do I have to fight it?" I said.

Verdandi's eyes brightened. "Nothing so simple. The past, the present, the future. You must face them all."

"So all I have to do is look?"

Urd chuckled, not a pleasant sound. "The test has already claimed many, pet. But since you're keen... What would you like to see?"

I smoothed back a stray hair. "The beginning."

"Of the worlds? The knowledge may break you."

"No. The beginning of all this. Show me where it started." I looked her in the eye. "I want to see why the goddess punished Módor."

Urd glared at me. "I told you."

"Sister..." said Skuld. "Won't you—"

"I swore I'd never look upon her again. Or that awful boy."

"This isn't about your wishes, Urd," snapped Verdandi. "This is Dóta's choice."

"Fine." Urd slammed the butt of her stick into the water, breaking its surface with a splash. She turned away.

A nightingale's song filled the cave.

When the waters settled, they no longer reflected the roof. A grove of fruit trees appeared in the depths. Leaves of yellow and crimson flittered through the air. Autumn, I would call it now, but in that instant I thought I looked upon the world of the light elves.

A maiden danced beneath the boughs. She wore a robe of shimmering red, her skirts gathering around her as she twirled. Her black hair was twined through her crown of maidenhood, her skin like the petals of elder flowers. I started as I recognized the curve of her face, the points of her ears. Módor only wore that look of wild joy when she looked upon her hoard. But Gala swayed to the nightingale's tune.

She was young, so young. As young as me.

And then the brushes rustled and she froze. A figure emerged from behind the bushes, growing so tall she had to look up. The troll's chest was deep, his abdomen well-muscled, his shoulders broad. His face was not hard or cruel, but filled with warmth. He might almost have been comely, if he were not covered in scales. He made no move toward her, nor did he flee. He shuffled his feet and smiled. His mouth was full of pointed teeth, but his grin was still shy.

So this was Grethor's father.

Gala relaxed and returned his smile. A new spark kindled in her eyes. And slowly she began to twirl once more, then reached and pulled him into the dance. Soon they were both laughing, their eyes locked on one another, spinning faster and faster until they collapsed on the ground. They lay together for a moment, still panting.

Then he leaned over and picked up a fallen apple from the ground. Holding it between two delicate claws, the troll held it out to the Norn. His lop-sided grin was full of tenderness. She reached, then hesitated. Her eyes darted up to the sky, their light dimming with fear. And then she shook it off and accepted the fruit. A look of relish crossed her face as juice ran down her chin. She offered it to him. He ran his forked tongue over its white flesh, shuddered, then bit off a chunk anyway.

The woods grew dark and the surface of the water once more showed the cave's roof.

"A sad tale, pet," said Urd, turning back. "She threw it all away for a monster."

"He didn't seem like a monster," I said.

"They never do, Dóta," said Verdandi.

Urd's shoulders hunched. "He tried, oh yes. Managed to

stay away from meat just long enough to fool her." The old Norn's face twisted. "But in the end, nature always wins. He got hungry. By the time she found out the truth, it was too late. He'd already planted his seed in her belly."

Skuld gave a sigh. "Oh, but things might have been different."

Seldom had Módor laughed, except when Grethor stumbled and hurt himself. And yet her eyes had always grown distant when she talked of his father. "Did they love?"

Verdandi crossed her arms. "Does it matter?"

"She suffered for him. And out of that suffering I was born."

"Well, I couldn't have foreseen that, could I?" said Urd. "But yes, they loved each other, for all the good that did them. They couldn't hide from the goddess, though. Not after she found out."

"But surely she knew from the start?" I said.

"Oh no," said Urd with a toothless smile. "They are strong all right, these young gods. Always have been. But they don't know everything."

"Then how?"

Urd's lips tightened. "I told her, of course. Gala would foul our bloodline with troll spawn? So be it. Let her live with the punishment."

"There must be more to it."

"Why? I'm done here." Urd spat and shuffled out of the cave.

I made to follow, but Verdandi grabbed me by the shirt. "Urd's ways are hard. But you mustn't hold it against her. She has eyes but cannot see what is in front of her. She's blind as the rest of us."

"Eh?"

Skuld smiled sadly. "None of us will be able to see

beyond our own domain."

"That's how it is," said Verdandi. "We can see one side of fate with perfect clarity. As for the rest, it's a mystery. Only when we're together can we tease out the truth."

I clenched my jaw so tight my neck's sinews stuck out. The anger ran through me, but I would not give in to it. "Let's get on with this."

"Very well." She waved a hand over the waters and they stirred.

The first thing I saw was a clawed hand resting against a curved wall. The fingernails were long and coated with blood. Módor was garbed as in the days of her youth, but her face was green as I knew it. Sharp cheekbones and hair of emerald, the gnarled and scaly skin. It took me a moment to recognize she crouched by the walls of Valdskali.

Carnage spilled across the grassy hillside. The clash of iron against iron, two forces grappling to seize the hall. The screams of the dying rose. Warriors and shield maidens crying for Valhalla's welcome. Men clad in battle gear hacked at one another, slicing through chain mail and sinew and bone. Blood sprayed from severed limbs, filling the air with red mist.

Módor held her tongue out like a child tasting snowflakes, her eyes alight with hunger. The bone knife was in her hand once more. The gentle Gala was gone now. In her place hovered a demon waiting for her feast.

"What is this?" I whispered.

"War," said Verdandi. "Do you not know what it looks like?"

I shook my head. When Arína had spoken of it, war had seemed a magnificent thing. But where was she now?

Fear clutched my chest when I glimpsed the princess in the heart of the fighting, a dripping war axe in one hand and a wooden shield in the other. Her mail was torn, her cape mere shreds. Her left side was so dark with shining gore, she looked like Hel herself. Her own blood, or that of her enemies? She was panting, swaying on her feet.

Ulf Redmane's scarred face twisted in a snarl as he advanced toward Arína and raised his sword. Seeing him coming, Arína crouched and raised her shield. Yet her grip on it was already wavering as Redmane's sword crashed down and hewed into the wood. She tumbled back, tripping over a corpse. Panic splashed across her face like boiling oil and she raised her arm against his blow...

"No, get up! Get up!" I cried aloud. But she couldn't hear me.

The surface of the lake trembled once more and the image fell apart. When the water stilled, the inside of a wood-paneled room formed upon it. I recognized it as Arína's chamber with its luscious pelts and cushions.

Twyla sat upon a wooden chair by the bed, her staff across her lap. Her eyes were closed and her lips moved silently. Praying, I knew. On the bed lay two figures. One of them was covered in blankets, the face turned away so I couldn't see. The other...

Anskar's hair poured across the pillow, neatly combed and trimmed. His hands were folded across his chest as though he lay upon his bier. His eyes were closed, but sweat pooled upon his brow. Even in sleep, his mouth was tight with pain.

Twyla stood and mopped his brow with a cloth, still whispering. She leaned forward and kissed him.

"Anskar?" I said. "Anskar, you must wake up."

Twyla's eyes widened. Had she somehow heard me? She whirled to look upon the other figure on the bed. She ripped back the blankets to reveal—

A droplet fell from the cave roof into the water, shattering the scene. Like waking up from a night-spirit's fever.

"Wait!" I shouted, turning to Verdandi. "Bring them back. I have to know—"

Verdandi's eyes were closed. "I know what you saw in the well. Your heart guided you. But the magic does not work twice."

I wheeled upon Skuld. "Will Arína die? Will Anskar?"

Skuld would not look at me. "All things shall come to pass."

"What kind of answer is that?" I shouted, my voice mocking me with echoes. "What do you see? Tell me!"

"It'll never matter what I see." Her eyes were like the sun and moon, they shone so bright. "Won't you understand? If I tell you they live, you will only fight to make sure it happens. If I tell you they die, you'll fight to save them."

"Probably." My shoulders slumped. And then I girded my heart with steel. "On with it. The final test."

Verdandi's lip twitched. "You think you're ready?"

"Honest? I'm not sure. But I don't have time to linger here."

"It is true, your days go on," said Verdandi, musing. "Even now your body wastes away while we speak. Very well. The final test. But this is where our ways part, I fear."

"Everyone faces the last test alone, Dóta," said Skuld. "But we may meet again." She put her arms out to hug me once more. And though I could not return it, she still patted me on the back. "I'm glad to see you, granddaughter. All your tomorrows. You'll do great things, if you can trust yourself when the moment comes."

Verdandi raised a hand. "Farewell, weirdling."

I glanced at the water. "Wait, what do I—" But they were already gone. Just empty air, like they had been figments.

By myself again. Perhaps that was best. Even now I cannot decide whether I care for my grandmothers.

I sank down beside the waters and stared. They remained placid and showed nothing but the cave. No sign of the dragon. Not even a wave lapping the shore. After a few moments, I stood and rubbed my hands together. What was my task? Peering into the depths revealed nothing.

I leaned forward to consider my own reflection. Just me. Last time I had truly looked at myself had been Módor's cave. There was little difference between that face and the one I saw now. Hair the color of dun, matted and tangled. The same stupid nose and soft hide. So skinny even I thought I looked boyish. And those eyes. Those hateful little eyes.

The eyes of a killer.

I tore my gaze away, sickened.

Outside the cave, the light remained greyish. Time was growing short, that's what they'd told me. Yet did time pass here as it did in Midgard? Most likely not.

Something moved in the corner of my eye and I whirled to meet it.

A figure rose out of the waters and stood upon their shining surface. Gigantic, veiled in mist. She wore a pelt like a cape. Beneath the hood I saw only shadows, a pair of bright eyes gleaming. "Can you name me?"

"Módor?" I whispered.

The figure laughed, not unkindly. A woman's laugh, I thought, but could not be sure. "No, Dóta. I'm not your mother, though I can understand why you'd say so. Perhaps this will help." She reached to pull back her hood.

I readied myself to look upon the face of a monster. But nothing could have prepared me for what I saw.

EMBRACE

HER FACE HELD A HARD BEAUTY. No doubting this was a
woman, but none would dare call her a peace-weaver. She
was godlike in her furs, a golden brooch shining upon her
breastbone. On her right arm she bore an arm ring like
mine. The token of manhood. Beneath her eye she bore
rune marks. War paint, I thought at first, then realized the
runes had been etched onto her skin. What did they say?
The words were too small to make out, but I knew they
carried power. Strength rose from her like heat. She almost
reminded me of Anskar, with her hair like sunshine.

"Can you not name me?" she said.

"Are we of the same blood?"

"You don't know how right you are." She drifted closer,
right to the edge of the water. "Look into these eyes, Dóta.
Tell me what you see. Are they the eyes of a killer?"

The green of her eyes made me think of the elf stones in
Módor's hoard. They were sharp, filled with both sorrow
and joy. Like Twyla's eyes.

"No," I breathed. "It can't be."

Her lips curled in a smile, showing round teeth. "Eyes

for spying and teeth to devour. Isn't that what Módor told us?"

"You're... me?"

"You'll be me." She laughed again and shook her head. "This is so strange. I remember standing where you are, looking through your eyes. Hel, I remember hearing me say that. Your head's hurting, your monthly blood has just started and you don't know what's coming next."

I blinked, still reeling from the shock. "But..." I opened and closed my mouth like a landed fish. "My hair."

Her shoulders shook, her laugh rich and deep. She flicked her golden locks from side to side. "A gift of the Wind-rime. And the sun and salt." She paused. "There's so much to say, but I don't think I have long. Our name. You must say it."

"Dóta?" I said, my brow beetling in confusion.

She cocked her head. Did I do that when I was thinking? "That's what Módor called us."

"I never thought to call myself anything else. Not until Anskar came along. But now there's another name."

"Boia," she said. "The son Anskar wanted. The warmaker Twyla saw growing inside her."

"My true name, the goddess said."

She rolled her eyes and stroked the golden brooch on her breast. No sign of the amulet, but it might have been hidden under her shirt. "Ah, Freya. You'll meet her soon enough. But who is she to tell you your true name? You are a child of two worlds."

"And I will die defending both," I said, recalling my oath.

"Not for a while, I hope. For both our sakes. But that's not what I meant. You and me, we're different from most. Not quite a peace-weaver and not quite a warmaker but both."

I lowered my head. "I don't fit."

She reached out and touched my chin. Not the icy brush of a ghost, but solid. I looked up and met her gaze. In her face I saw caring, her brow furrowed in concern. "But there's something you haven't figured out yet. Nobody fits, not really. They just do what's expected of them. Even Anskar was made for peace, though few would know it."

"There's no place for me in the world," I said. "Not anywhere." My brother had used those words to hurt me. And I had used them to hurt my mother. An old curse. I didn't try to staunch the tears, just let them course down my cheeks.

She wiped away my tears with her thumb. Her voice was calm, free of doubt. For she knew exactly what I needed to hear. "Oh, young one. The adventures you'll have, the things you'll see. And you don't even know it yet. You will walk in new lands, see wonders you can't dream yet. You will face down tyrants and kings, wrestle with giants of the frost and walk across burning sands. You will carouse with elves and pump the bellows with dwarfs. And soon you'll climb the world tree." Her eyes darted to the roots of the tree snaking down from the roof. "And you will have love. I promise you that."

I gave a sobbing laugh. "Who would love a monster?"

She pointed at the runes on her face. "Can you not read?"

I sounded it out, my lips moving.

Kindred.

She leaned so close our foreheads were almost touching. "You say there's no place for you in the world, but the world is your place. The weirdlings, the misfits, the wanderers. The ones caught in between. Strangers like you, they shall be your kin. And as long as there are humans who care for you, you'll never be alone."

"My name," I whispered. "I've had it all along, haven't I? A truth wrapped in a lie."

She nodded but remained silent, giving me courage to speak.

"Arína gave me another name. Elfin-sun. A name to drive out the dark. I do come from two worlds." I swallowed. "And I live to honor both." I straightened and filled my lungs. "I am Dóta Elfin-sun. Seether. Slayer. Child of three parents and heir of fate."

The words filled the cave and power filled me. Not the burning intensity of the goddess's flame, but the vitality of new life. The veins of gold in the walls blazed in answer, making the shadows flee. By their light I saw a gap in the roof. One of the roots of the world tree extended from it, beckoning me to climb.

"Well done." Her eyes shone with pride as she held her arms out.

And so, for the first time, I embraced myself.

She was crying when we broke apart, her cheek wet as I wiped away her tears. "Forgive me," she said. "I weep because I'm not ready to say farewell."

"Must we say farewell?"

"You don't, not yet. As for me…" She took a deep breath. "Goodbyes really are for softer creatures, aren't they? Just one thing more. Be kind to Twyla. You'll need each other."

"I will."

"I know you will." She nodded and I knew she was steeling herself for her next words. "All my love to days past, Dóta. Until we catch up…" She sank back into the depths of fate, the waters folding over her.

Wrenching my gaze away from the pool, I looked up at

the gap in the roof. The way upward. Yet to reach the surface I'd have to pull myself up from under the earth. I shuddered, recalling the way the hands had tried to pull me underground. Yet the world of the gods lay atop the World Tree.

I lifted a foot and hooked it around one of the gnarled roots of the ash. Bit by bit, I inched my way upward until my head bumped against the roof. Fresh air flowed from the hole in the cave top. No way to go but up. I groped for a handhold. The fingers of my left hand smarted as loose pebbles ground against my gashes, but still I managed to squeeze myself into the crack. If only I had eyes like Grethor. He would have relished this, thought it was a game. But what point was there in wishing for what could not be? My teeth set as I hauled myself through the suffocating darkness.

At last I spied a light overhead. It lent new strength to my limbs, made me push harder until I reached the surface. Pulling myself out of the ground, I lay sprawled on the earth. Dirt covered every part of me and my head throbbed, but I had made it. I stood atop the hill at last. But the last stage of my journey still lay ahead.

I looked up, beheld Yggdrasil in all its majesty.

The ash tree of Midgard seemed stunted and feeble compared to this. All the cosmos whirled around the tree, a whirlpool of color in the sky. The limbs spread beyond my sight. Módor had told me tales of Yggdrasil, said the branches spread into every world. As a child, I couldn't picture it. And words cannot shape it now.

Infinity. A word unknown to me in those days and too short for its meaning. Yet it is the only way to describe the tree that stood between the worlds.

How to climb such a tree?

One branch at a time.

I reached for the lowest bough. The leaves rustled against the wool of my shirt as I began my ascent.

How long I climbed, I cannot be sure. Days, it seemed, though that is impossible. After a time I stopped noticing the weariness of my limbs or the burning of my sinews. My hands grew numb from cold and my breath rose before my eyes. My chest was screaming, my eyes growing dark. Yet nothing mattered except reaching the top. With every moment, the beacon atop the tree grew larger.

Only once did I make the mistake of looking down. A wind rose to shake the stars. The branch on which I clung swayed and I clutched at it in desperation. I couldn't die here, I told myself. The final test at the Well of Fate had shown me that. Yet my pulse would not slow as the icy blasts buffeted me and the leaves whipped at my face. I clamped my eyes shut, praying for life.

Yet what god would answer? Better to die with eyes wide.

Clouds drifted beneath me. The brains of a giant, crackling with thoughts. Far below the clouds lay the flat disc of Midgard. The world was full of lands, all covered with mountains and lakes and forests and ringed by sea. It glittered and churned like a bed of sapphires. There I saw the coils of the Midgard Serpent at play in the waves. And beyond that... I strained my eyes, could just make out the blurred outline of mountains at the edge of the earth. The unknown, waiting to be explored.

I closed my eyes once more, clung tighter to the branch. A fall from this height would leave me nothing more than a red smear on some mountainside.

At last the wind ceased. My insides feeling like water, I took up the climb once more. I did not stop until I ran out of sturdy branches. The maelstrom of color filled my sight.

The glowing threads of light changed from red to orange to yellow to green and blue. All the colors of the rainbow.

Bifröst. The light was not in the tree as I had thought, but danced just above it.

The spindly branches at the very top of the tree creaked as I put my weight on them, but that would not stop me. I reached, stretched my fingers as far as they would go. The tips of my fingers tingled as the energy caressed them, but I could not reach further.

"Come on!" I said through gnashed teeth.

The bough beneath me gave another groan. Something snapped.

Never would I be damned as a failure. So I did the only thing I could.

I leapt.

I should have plummeted into the void, should have heard the wind roaring in my ears and seen the ground rushing up to meet me.

Instead I floated like a feather on the breeze.

The rainbow caught me, carried me into the sky. I was rising on a current of wind. The colored lights streaked past, all becoming one, forming a tunnel. Nothing held me down, I was untethered. The weariness and the bruises dripped away.

A point of light at the end of the tunnel swelled and engulfed my sight, so fantastic it was blinding.

I raised my arms. Flying toward the light, soaring on raven's wings to the world of the gods.

ASGARD

Next I knew, hard-packed soil lay beneath my feet.

It took a moment for my sight to return. When it did, I rubbed my eyes, sure they were playing tricks.

The hall was lit only by the embers of the hearth-pit. The embers gave little warmth. Once this place might have been as grand as the Hall of the Wolf, but it had been a long time since it had known cheer. The mead benches were covered in webs and dust and the air was heavy with the stench of mildew. Yet someone still lived here; the glowing coals told me as much.

Asgard was not the glorious realm the sagas had promised.

"Hello?" I said. My voice echoed through the hall.

An empty chair stood before the hearth. It was grimy, coated in filth. As I approached, a creature with a long, bare tail darted from underneath. It regarded me with shiny red eyes, its pink nose twitching. Deciding I was unworthy of its notice, the rat scurried away. I picked at the grime with a fingernail to reveal a layer of gold underneath.

"So, thrall," said a voice behind me. "You've come. I knew you would."

I stood up straight, but did not turn. "Freya."

"You dare speak my name?" She laughed. "You are a bold one, to show such disrespect. Now turn and face me, Boia."

"My name is Dóta Elfin-sun."

"It matters little to me, in truth."

I flexed, ready to fend off an attack. None came. At last I turned to face the goddess.

Freya wore a cloak of glistening black feathers. A golden amulet hung from her throat. Almost like my own, but far more precious. These I had expected from the old tales. And yet her face was not beautiful, but thin and wasted. Her hair was like the webs which hung from the pillars of Asgard. The eyes glaring at me were pale and rheumy.

"So," said Freya. "Now you see." Her voice remained smooth, not an old maid's wheeze. "Does it make you feel good to see my face?"

"No," I said truthfully.

"Nor should it." She grimaced and held her bony hands over the hearth. Rings gleamed from her big-knuckled fingers. "It used to be something, this place. It will be again. One day it shall endure the siege of the dead. And then we gods will have our day once more. Until then, we wait."

My eyes narrowed in suspicion. "Is the All-Father here?"

She shook her head. "He wanders these days."

"Where are the other gods? Your thralls?"

"You're the only thrall here. As for the gods, they're asleep. Guard your voice, Thor would not like being woken. And throw some more wood into the hearth, would you?"

Thinking there was no point catching my death, I did so.

Freya rubbed her fingers together. The power fizzed and

sparked, but nothing more happened. She closed her eyes and concentrated until a tiny flame appeared at her fingertip. She shoved her finger under the log until its innards glowed. "You wonder why I look this way, why my powers are so feeble." She glanced at an empty dish on the bench nearby. "The apples of immortality are gone now. Soon it will be time for me to rest as well. It's why I brought you here."

"You didn't bring me here," I said. "I came on my own."

"Of course you did," said Freya with a laugh. "And I suppose you took back your body by your own strength. And did a raven not call you onward? I wanted to talk to you, for you to understand. Every one of your deeds is my bidding, thrall. You'd do well to remember." She stroked the golden amulet.

"Why?" I said. "All this to punish Módor?"

"That little fool? I knew you weren't meant to serve her. You could not be my instrument, so long as you were in her grasp. And your brother's. Though it was amusing to make the trolls suffer, was it not? Don't pretend, you enjoyed what I gave you. And that was just a taste. I will give you more."

"Why me?"

"Ha. Mortals have been asking that question since the dawn of the worlds." She stared into the coals. "I was not lying when I said Ragnarök is coming, for the wheel is ever spinning. Asgard's day is over, as I'm sure you can see. Humans are turning to new gods now. They whisper of the Warrior-Christ. His worshippers haven't reached your kingdom yet, but they will soon. You will know them by the strange amulets they bear." She turned and looked at me. "And as we gods sleep, all worlds shall be overturned in fire and war. But then Midgard shall be remade and all begins again. Just spokes on a wheel. All of this has happened before, countless times. And all shall happen again. But this time will be different. Because of you."

"I don't understand."

She reached out and snared me by the wrist. "In all the versions of the world, there has never been a creature like you. And there never will be again. A Seether born of magic and war, made to shape the fates." Her grip tightened. "With you as my instrument, humans will not turn their backs on us. My power alone isn't enough anymore. But together? They've already witnessed what a servant of Freya can do. In healing, in killing."

Horror crept over me. "That's why you wanted to help me kill Grethor. That's why you want to kill Módor."

Her eyes bulged. "Some fear you, others call you their hero. Either way, they will not forget us. We can break the wheel, prevent the world's ending. Together we will do great things, change the course of time itself. All you have to do is let me in once more."

"You say so." I shook my head. "I see your lies, goddess. You say I wasn't strong enough to throw you off before. If that's so, you could have taken me any time."

"A willing thrall is better than one who needs beating."

"Perhaps. But that thrall isn't me." I pulled my arm back and strode toward the entrance.

"She will die," said Freya, standing behind me. "The princess you cherish."

I stiffened.

"They all will," she continued. "All these humans you love so much."

I turned back to find her leaning against the throne. "The last one to threaten me like that is now a pile of ash. As you well know," I said.

"Not a threat, dear one. Just a fact. The sun and the

moon will be devoured in the last days. The seas shall rise and the dead shall walk the earth once more. Aría and Anskar and Twyla and every other soft-bellied human you care for will join the legions of the undead. And so will you. Unless you join me. Carry my light into the world."

I pressed my tongue between my teeth. She was twisting me, and I knew it. And yet I had sworn an oath. More than that, I would need her power to end the feuding. "We could do much good together."

"That's right."

"But I shall not be your thrall, goddess. I shall have freedom in my own mind. Never again will you make me act against my will."

Her lip curled in a smirk. "Who are you to decide the terms?"

"You didn't need to control me to punish Grethor."

Her face darkened. "That is more tiring. Why should I have to give up my strength for you?"

"Do you want my help or not?"

Her hands hardened into knobbled fists. Then she calmed herself. "Anything else?"

"Three things."

"Only three."

When I told her my desires, she shook her head. "Two of those are not my gifts to give. The third... It can be done. But why would you want this?"

"Your kind would not understand."

"You owe that creature nothing. She deserves a thousand deaths for her sins."

"And yet she can die but one," I said, and told her my plan.

The goddess listened. She did not like my notion, but she did not have to like it. It was enough that she agreed.

"And so, Dóta Elfin-sun," said Freya, "it seems your wish is my command. Let us hope it does not end in folly."

She walked up to me, her forefinger raised. The goddess pressed it between my eyes. The weight of sleep overcame me and I had the sense of falling, tumbling, spiraling down to Earth.

REST

THE SOUNDS of battle pierced my dreams.

I woke to find myself swaddled in blankets. The wool itched. My innards were roiling, the taste of puke on my tongue. I groaned and tried to open my eyes, only to find them glued tight. Helpless as a newborn. Fighting to still my panic, I went to sit up. A hand gripped my shoulder and held me to the bed.

"No, Dóta. Wait. Don't try to sit up yet. Twelve nights you have been under the potion's sway. It will take time to adjust." Twyla dabbed at my eyelids with a damp cloth until I could open them again. "Slowly. Nothing to fear. You're safe with me."

I opened my eyes to slits. The invasion of light into my eyes was agony, but Twyla held me until the pain ended. A warm huddle without chills. And I did not protest as she squeezed me tight.

At last I looked around to the familiar sight of pelts and cushions. Arína's armor was missing from its usual mount on the wall.

The war shrieks and clash of iron grew outside.

Twyla sat back in her wooden chair. All was as I had seen in the Well of Fate.

I glanced to my side. Anskar lay unmoving. "Any change?"

Twyla shook her head. "I heard you. Calling for him, though you didn't make a sound." She paused. "What did you see?"

"Many things," I said, already rolling out of bed. "I have to get to Arína." My legs buckled as soon as I tried to stand.

Twyla shook her head. "Give it time, I say. The battle's right outside. It's no place for you. I doubt they'd harm the king's hall. The doors are locked and banded with iron. You're safe here as anywhere else."

I sat down upon the bed, rubbing my legs to get the blood pumping. "It's not that. Arína. Where is she?"

"In the midst of the shield wall, last I knew. Her order was for me to watch over you and Anskar. My gods, that girl is magnificent. A week ago it seemed all but certain Redmane would make thralls of us. But that gold from your cave? She spent it well."

Twyla quickly told me the tale. Others might have hired mercenaries, or even just fled and kept the hoard for themselves. Not Arína, though. She granted gifts to every earl in the land and offered to pay all war debts. More than half swore themselves to her side by the end of the day. In the past days she had led the people from victory to victory. This hall belonged to her.

"That battle din you're hearing, that's Redmane's final push. If he breaks, he is finished. It won't be long now."

"I saw her battling the Redmane. He had her pinned to the ground. I have to go to her."

"You need to rest."

"Why?" I said, trying once more to sit up. "I've been

asleep for days, rest is the last thing I need. She will die without me."

"Are you certain?"

"No, but..." I sighed. "I asked the goddess to help. But she wouldn't. So it's up to me."

"Oh, Dóta." She squeezed my shoulder. "I'm afraid it's up to Arína and her companions. This is the worst part of battle. I know what you endure. He'd put me through it every summer." Twyla nodded at Anskar. "Arína has sent messengers to check on you every night, you know. Once she even came in herself, running between things. Never have I seen anybody look so worried."

"You mean..." I took a ragged breath. "She still cares? Even knowing..." I planted my feet on the ground and stood at last. I took a step toward the door, the dizziness already threatening to overwhelm me.

"If she's fated to return, she will," said Twyla.

"No way am I leaving this to f—"

"Dóta? Twyla? Is that you?" Both our heads snapped around at the sound of Anskar's voice. His eyes were halfway open, his eyelashes fluttering.

Twyla smoothed back his hair. "I'm here."

"Where's Dóta?" His voice was little more than a whisper.

The noise outside surged to a roar, so close it might have been just outside the door.

My soul was being pulled in two directions. Then I saw his hand twitch. He was reaching for me. And that's when I knew there was no choice. "It's me, Anskar. I'm not going anywhere." I took his brawny hand in mine.

His lip twitched. "Good."

Twyla looked up at me and patted her breastbone. Asking after the amulet, I knew.

I reached and felt the warmth of the amber through my shirt. The goddess was there, listening. But I could do nothing more than shake my head. Freya had made it plain she would do naught to save him. "I'm sorry," I choked. "If it weren't for me, Redmane never would have…"

But Anskar was shaking his head. "Nothing could have stopped Ulf. Doesn't matter now. I'm just glad…" He struggled to draw breath. "It's good we could be a family." His eyes had closed again. "Always thought I'd feast in Valhalla with my milk brother and my friends who perished on the raids. Instead I hear the calling of a darker realm. And yet…" He smiled. "I'm glad I came back. Better to endure Hel's tortures than miss this moment. Know you are my people. My wife. My daughter. I…" His words were thick with sleep now. He did not hear the clang and holler of war anymore. "I love."

"Rest, Anskar," said Twyla. "Your battle is done."

His hand trembled, then went slack.

No louder than a rasp, I said: "Goodbye, Father." I don't know whether he heard. All the tension in his face was gone, the pain lifted from him.

Twyla kept stroking his hair, her own face a mask of hardiness.

Outside, a new wave of noise rose. A hundred voices chanting one name. "Iron Heart! Iron Heart!"

I didn't know what it meant. Some human thing.

Anskar's hand was already growing cool. I let him go. "Twyla?"

"He's gone, Dóta. I can see it. His soul has already left." Her eyes were brimming.

"I know. Only… That thing he said. About us being his people." I took a breath. "I feel it too. You are… You are my…" I cursed myself. Why were the words so hard to say?

But I think she understood when I held out my arms, offered her the same comfort she had given me.

My mother broke down, her shoulders shaking with sobs. And I wept without shame, cried until my throat was raw and my face caked with dried tears. Our grief mingled into one, drowning out the chants of victory from outside.

GIVING

THE SOUNDS of battle had fallen silent outside. The hall doors banged open and a clamor of voices filled Valdskali.

Twyla did not protest as I got up and made my way to Arína's bedchamber door. She was still staring at Anskar's face, saying goodbye without words.

I poked my head out into the hall. Were these Arína's followers or those of the Redmane? I had no weapon except my magic, and I had no wish to use it on these humans whatever their side.

The rank smell of sweat attacked my nostrils. The hall was flooded with people, most of them in battle garments and all drinking the vile stuff humans seem to like.

I breathed a sigh of relief when I spotted Boli Butterworth on a mead bench, sharing a horn of ale with a pale-eyed imp. I recognized the youth as one I had seen on my first night in Valdskali. Foolish grins were fixed on their faces.

Catching my eye, Boli raised his horn and yellow liquid splashed to the floor. "Hey, here's our Seether. Our Seether's awake! Shame he's missed all the fun."

I thought about telling him Anskar was dead, but did not want this drunkard bursting in on Twyla. "Aría?"

"See for yourself." He motioned toward the carved wooden throne. There perched Arína, now clad in a clean grey kirtle. She seemed unhurt. A thrall stood to her side holding a bowl of water and a rag. She helped wash the blood from Arína's face.

"Arína Iron Heart! Our maiden king." Boli raised the horn in her honor and slopped half down his front as he drank.

So that was the name Arína had earned in battle. Fitting, I thought. She looked up, hearing Boli call her name. When she saw me, her eyes grew wide. The new king made to rise.

I pushed through the crowd as fast as I dared, making for the open air. The doors stood wide, letting the morning light fill the hall. Every part of me ached to share words with Arína. But there was something I had to do first.

I knew what to expect outside, but still wasn't prepared. Dead bodies lay strewn all over the hillside. The grass was a carpet of red. Flies buzzed over the carnage and ravens skirmished with stray cats for the spoils of flesh. They scattered as I approached. A tuft of red hair poked out from underneath one of the corpses. Ulf Redmane's one eye stared up at the sun, Arína's axe buried in his forehead. It worried me how the sight did not cause my belly to churn as it once might have.

This place had seen too much death in the past weeks. Part of me wanted to stay and guard his body, keep it from being marred by either man or bird. It was my fault he was dead, after all.

No, dear one. The task cannot wait.

"Do you know where she is?" I asked.

I can sense it. Can I show you?

"Yes."

An image I had seen before flitted into my mind. Elf-land, I thought. A place of autumn.

"I do not know the way."

Will you let me guide you to the place?

Too numb to argue, I nodded. Nowadays I chide myself for a fool, taking a stupid risk like that. After all, Freya could have led me over a cliff. But I was weary and heartsick.

Through the village, to the edge of the wood. From there I will show you the path.

The village streets were empty of humans. Smoke hung over all things. I do not remember the way to the orchard. All I know is the goddess carried me through a wheat field to a neighboring farm, not too far off.

The light streaming through the apple trees was brighter than that which I had seen in the Well of Fate. The trees were empty of fruit, but they were the same ones which grew in the days of Módor's youth.

I saw her there, leaning against a tree-trunk. Her red hood was up, but still I could see her face. She sniffed and wiped her mouth. She bore an expression I had only seen once before on her.

Shame.

"Let me speak," I whispered to the goddess. "Do nothing until I say so."

I sensed a wave of resentment from the amulet, but cared little and less.

"Gala," I said.

"Who knows that name?" She looked up, her fangs bared. "You. My child. Have you come to mock, or just kill? What manner of lies have you heard, Dóta?"

"More than I ever wanted," I said wearily. "What have

you been up to, Módor? Did you eat well this day? There's plenty of death to go around."

She looked away. "I didn't ask to be this way."

"I know," I said. "You are what the gods made you."

"The gods you serve now." She eyed the amulet.

I shook my head. "Freya will not toy with me like that again."

Módor's laugh was high and cold. "Did she promise you that? You cannot trust the words of Asgard, Dóta."

"Perhaps. But that is not what I've come to talk about. Come." I sank down onto the grass. "You were right, Módor. What you told me all those weeks ago. The world above is full of wickedness and lies. Humans are as awful as you always said. And yet it was here that I learned the truth of who I am."

"Oh yes," sneered Módor. "And what is that? A goatherd, a gatherer of mushrooms?"

Her words would have hurt once, made me feel small. No more. "I am your daughter," I said, and told her my true name.

When she heard it, Módor sat down beside me. "Dóta. I was still learning human speech, then. Same as you. I just wanted to call you "Daughter," but this new tongue of mine struggled with the word."

I nodded. "And you ceased to be Gala the day you took me in. You became my mother. My Módor. Me and my brother's." I took a deep breath. "Did you mean it when you said you forgive me for Grethor's death?"

Módor was silent for a long moment. She looked around the apple grove, her red eyes haunted. "Yes. I knew what he was, but didn't try to stop it." She looked down. "Didn't try to stop myself, either. I knew trolls could live on things other than flesh, but my every instinct... I didn't know what to do with the killing urge, the thirst. So I just went on."

"I don't know if this helps any," I said, "but I forgive you too. Because I know what it's like to lose control."

Her scaled face was empty of feeling as she pulled the bone knife from beneath her robes. The jagged tip flashed in the sunlight. She cut a furrow into the grass between us, then planted the knife in it. "You saved my life," she said. "You stopped the goddess that night. For every giving, a taking. Our feud is done." Then she poured earth over the hole she had made, burying the knife.

I pulled out the amulet. Módor flinched away from the sight, but I slipped it off. "Wait, Módor. For all you've done, it was you who brought me into this world. Will you not take my gift in return?"

She eyed the amulet with dislike. "You're offering me..."

"A chance. More than either of us deserve, but here it is." And I whispered in Módor's ear what I was offering.

She stared. "I didn't raise you for this, Dóta. You were meant to change my fate, not seal my doom. I was an immortal, a Norn!"

"Even so, it's the best you're going to get. Take my hand." I held out the amulet in my palm and closed my eyes.

She could have done anything in that moment. Fled, ripped out my throat. Instead I felt the rough chilliness of her palm against mine. We clasped the amulet together.

It came alive with warmth.

The goddess's fury awakened. This was her chance.

"No," I said, opening my eyes. "Not unless you want to be forgotten. Not unless you want to face the world's ending again."

As you wish. Let us begin.

The song fell from my lips. Flashes of brightness danced

from the amulet, forming a band between our wrists. They circled us, the heat growing in intensity as I sang.

Her hide was the first to change. The greenish scales flaked and dried, carried off by the wind. A new skin grew in their place, creamy as it had been when she was a Norn. Next, her hood flew back and her hair went from emerald to glossy black. It began at the roots and spread to the ends. She blinked and the red glow vanished from behind her eyes. She choked and spat out pointed teeth. Round white teeth like mine sprouted and filled her mouth. Her hand against mine grew shorter, the razor-like fingernails falling away. Her palm became soft and warm, vital heat flowing within it.

But I did not cease my song until her tapering ears became like round shells.

She looked down, admired her body. She ran a trembling hand over her cheek, her lips. "The hunger is gone. I'm me again."

"You always were," I said. "We truly are of like kind now. Both of us beasts. Flesh of my flesh. You'll grow old, but you'll have your beauty, so long as your heart remains true. That's how it is for humans."

"I will not forget this, Dóta. Not ever."

"Remember it next time you feel the urge to taste meat."

At last she let go of my hand.

Then she turned and walked into the trees, giving me one last longing glance. No words. She simply disappeared. And to this day, nobody has seen her again.

INHERITANCE

I STEPPED DRIPPING from the pool, wearing nothing but the amulet around my neck. Hugging myself to keep warm, I glanced around until I found my old sheepskin. After I had wrapped myself in it, I peered about. It was true, what Skuld had said. Módor's chambers were like those beneath the tree. Perhaps she had chosen this cave because it reminded her of home.

Just one last thing to do, then I would never go back to the cave. My kind was not made to skulk in the darkness, but live free.

As a child, I had never truly appreciated how small it was. These dark walls had been my entire world and even then I had not known all their secrets. Now the glowing mushrooms had been trampled underfoot, just a few giving off meagre light.

The treasure chamber was empty as I had expected. I could almost picture the men picking through for the finest loot. Like carrion birds. Yet there was no point resenting Arína or her followers for sacking the place. Not when I had invited them. And the gold had been used to make peace. It didn't matter anyway—I had my arm ring and that was enough. Now, as before, I only wanted to look upon the bones.

They still lay shoved in the corner atop the tarnished chainmail and sword. No doubt Boli and his ilk had deemed them worthless. Not to me.

I picked up the skull and held it up to the shaft of sunlight. The empty eye sockets stared. The warrior had most likely been dead as long as I had lived, but still he smiled with his round teeth. And I could not help smiling back. I bent and picked up his helm, stopping to admire the boar-shapes etched upon it.

The skull in one hand and the helmet in the other, I tiptoed through our cave to find the soft patch of earth where I had slept. Putting the skull to one side, I scooped up dirt in the hollow of the helmet.

Humans did not leave their dead to be picked apart by scavengers. I had learned this a few days ago.

Arína had declared there would be one mass funeral for all the dead, and she would pay from her own coffers. She did not want separate rites for her father, not when so many had suffered.

From my brother's attacks.

From my mother's hunting.

And from the war I started.

I didn't have the gall to stand with the princess as she spoke words over her father's body. Everyone in the kingdom had gathered along the riverbank in the early morning, laying garlands on the barges. Anskar and Hrut had been laid in the same long ship with swords and rings worthy of the royal house. The milk brothers would make their final journey together.

Twyla had sung the funeral dirge as the maiden king

helped push the boat out. Then all the others had done the same with their barges. I had whispered a word of power and flames leapt along the decks. The fleet of bones had drifted down the river and out of sight.

For the dead stranger, I could offer nothing so lavish. I placed his skull into the grave and pondered what words I should speak over him.

"I don't know who you were," I said. "I don't think I ever will. Maybe that doesn't matter now. All I know is that I wouldn't have figured any of this out if not for you. That's a debt I can't repay. And I don't have anything to put in your grave, except…"

I pulled the amulet out from under my sheepskin.

What do you think you're doing? The goddess's words were laced with menace.

This was reckless, I knew. A goddess didn't need an amulet to punish me. Yet Freya was not all-powerful, or all-knowing. This plan had only just come to me—if I had thought it through, the goddess would have known. Yet I sensed the rightness of it.

"I'm doing what I must," I said.

No. Do not do this. The strange men will come, bearing the sign of the cross.

"Let them. The amber belongs to the dead man anyway, remember? He served you, probably better than I did. And I won't be needing it anymore."

You still need me, you lying little—

"No. I don't think I will. Because Módor was right about one thing. You've given me no reason to trust you. You ask my permission now, but some day…"

The amulet burned hotter than a kiln. I dropped it into the shallow grave and poured earth over it before the goddess could scorch my hide.

Perhaps this was a mistake, but it was mine to make. For I knew one day I would hear the goddess's name and show nothing but scorn. What could she do to me?

I stood tall, looking down on the goddess. Her hatred still radiated from beneath the earth, but she could do no more harm today.

For an instant, I considered looking for the hidden tunnel. But when would I ever come back here? Instead I returned to the pool, dropped my sheepskin and dived. The red water snakes knew better than to attack me by now.

I broke the surface and swam to shore. Perhaps it was merely an inkling, but I thought my strokes were stronger than before. I cast about to find my clothing. There, hidden under the holly bush. It was mid-afternoon, the sky above still blue. Enough time remained for me to get back to Twyla's house before dark.

"Boia? Is that you?"

My muscles went rigid as Arína stepped from the woods. She wore a simple tunic today, an ancient broadsword strapped to her back. She wore no crown but that of maidenhood. The one I had placed upon her head. Yet the torque her father had worn gleamed on her neck. The maiden king looked upon my face, then the rest of me.

I saw no need to cover myself. Human shame was something I had only begun to learn. Besides, her eyes had seen all they would see. "No, Arína," I said shyly. "I'm Dóta Elfinsun. This is me."

"I can see that," she said. "You are beautiful." The king smiled, color filling her cheeks. "I knew. At least, I think I knew. Deep down. Or maybe I hoped."

"Can I get dressed? They don't call these the Shivering Woods for no reason."

"Of course. Forgive me." She shook herself, trained her

eyes upon the lake. Odd, that she seemed embarrassed about watching me dress. "I understand now why you didn't tell me. Twyla explained it."

"Oh?" I said, hitching my trousers up underneath my shirt.

"It would have been dangerous. I only wish you had told me sooner. Then I need not suffer so much doubt."

I laced my boots, then looked up. "What does that mean?"

She smiled. "Will you walk with me back to the village? I'm throwing a feast."

"Is that an order?"

"Will you come if I say yes?"

I snorted. "Only if you let me eat hard tack instead of meat."

"I'll let the cooks know." She reached for my hand.

I took it, our fingers twining. Her pace was brisker than my own.

With a start I realized I had walked this path before, with Anskar. When he first happened upon me. Was that the hand of fate?

I cleared my throat. "Where are your guardsmen? Should you be out here alone?"

"The king comes or stays by her own will."

"Forgive me. I just worry, that's all."

She blushed again. "I don't mind." We walked together in silence, the sun riding higher in the sky. By the time we sighted the distant lights of the village, the sky was dyed pink and gold. Not the blinding lights of Bifröst. The gift of another day's ending. We halted to enjoy it.

The breeze washed over us, carrying the tang of sea. I breathed deep. Once the sea had seemed endless, but now I knew better. There were lands out there, full of humans I didn't know yet.

The king breathed with me. "You're going to leave, aren't you?"

I could not lie. "One day, Arína. But not today."

"Good." She put her arms around my neck and held her body against me. She looked into my eyes. Into my soul. And in hers I saw both adoration and hurt. She pressed her lips against mine and I kissed her back as I had seen other humans do.

After a moment, she pulled away and turned toward the sea. Still, she had not let go of my hand. "When I found out, I was confused. Scared, maybe."

"You, scared?"

"You want the truth? Everything scared me that night. I had just seen my father killed. That is always a possibility for one of the royal house, but the killer..."

"Turned out to be my kinsman." Happiness shrank from my face.

"Grethor did this to me." She pointed at her scars. "Just to rattle you, and you said nothing. Can you imagine how that was for me?"

"And now?"

"Still confused. But also happy. It means I'm free to care for you in a way I couldn't for Boia, not when I was betrothed. But..."

"You're not ready."

"I want to be." Her eyes shone with tears. "Thank-you. For all you've done. You've rid my kingdom of a great evil and filled my house with gold. As for the rest..." She sighed.

I stood on my tiptoes. The blue haze of the whale road was just visible beyond the hills. "Twyla wants to visit her old country and I've agreed to come with her. She might not have much to teach of seething, but she still knows a lot elsewise. Maybe things will get easier." I swallowed, my chest tight. "I will come back, Arína. And perhaps then we'll be ready."

"Until then we have something special," she breathed. "A promise. The love between our fathers will continue through us. That is our inheritance."

She put her arm around my shoulder and I slipped mine around her waist. Side by side, we resumed our journey back to the world of men.

THE END

A MESSAGE FROM JULIAN

To everyone who has followed Dóta's adventures, a sincere thank-you from the bottom of my heart. It means so much to me. Throughout this journey, there have been plenty of times when I wanted to give up, but the enthusiasm of my readers keeps me going. If you would indulge me one more favor, I'd be very grateful if you could please leave an honest review, as it'll help readers find my books.

I was inspired to write *Tooth and Blade* when I encountered *Beowulf*, stepping into the world of heroes and demons, mead halls and monsters. Sharp-eyed readers will recognize many similarities between *Tooth and Blade* and the epic. I'd consider Grethor a blood relative of Grendel, though my story stands apart as an original creation. I've always loved stories told from the viewpoint of an outsider and that appealed to me much more than the idea of a straightforward adaptation. Though my education is much more in Greco-Roman history than that of medieval Scandinavia, I have done my best to capture the spirit of the age, language and culture, diving deep into the primary sources. In my choice of language, I tried to stick with words of Old

English, Germanic or Old Norse roots as much as possible, though I have often used words from Romance languages for the sake of clarity. You may notice that Dóta spins the tale using kennings, one of the favorite tools of a skald.

All the characters are made up. None of this is real. You'd think the presence of talking squirrels and such would be a dead giveaway, but you'd be surprised at some of the emails I get. Though I strive to be authentic in my depiction of the Norse world, I sought to give *Tooth and Blade* the timeless quality of myth rather than confine it to any specific region or century. It is enough to know the adventure takes place in a world of haunted meres, iron and magic.

While I've done my very best to fit in with Norse mythology as written by Snorri Sturluson, I have also invented a few things of my own. You won't find references to Módor, Dóta in any compendium of Norse myths. If you do consult such a compendium, you'll find the way Bifröst works just a wee bit different, as well as the layout of Yggdrasil and the backgrounds of Ratatoskr and the Norns. Gosh, it was so fun writing them all.

You might spot a few particular historical liberties. For example, Icelandic sagas indicate the Althing was typically held outdoors and attendees did indeed carry weapons. Yet I needed to sweep readers into the setting of Valdskali, the seat of power in Hrut's kingdom. Having Dóta disarmed and in a confined space with a lot of humans was the perfect way to take her out of her comfort zone, to show the best and worst of humanity.

On the portrayal of women, you may have noticed I had a lot of fun playing with the ambiguity surrounding the existence of shield maidens. While they are often referred to in sagas and legends, there is scant archaeological evidence for the existence of female warriors in the Viking world and references in historical sources are spotty. However, since *Tooth and Blade* belongs very much to an age of myth and legend, the shield maidens fit well into my story, whatever Anskar's thoughts on the matter. Given the crossover between depictions of Valkyries and shield maidens in sagas, it made sense for Dóta to see Princess Arína that way. And before anybody starts jumping up and down saying I invented the idea of a maiden king to further some kind of PC agenda, there are plenty of references in Old Norse and Icelandic literature. If you'd like a really good overview, check out *Women in Old Norse Literature, Bodies, Words, and Power* by Jóhanna Katrín Friðriksdóttir.

About the mushrooms... I went with the tradition that the poisonous hallucinogen *Amanita muscaria* induced the Berserker rage. While the wolfish Berserker warriors are well attested in medieval sources, there is considerable debate whether their rage was chemically induced by a psychotropic plant or fungus. And if it was, there are other suspects just as likely.

Finally, I shouldn't need to say this, but I will anyway. Don't try any of this at home. It's a work of fiction, not an instruction manual. Do not go around licking, tasting, or otherwise ingesting strange mushrooms. Do not try breathing the smoke of burning herbs or engaging in any form of violence. All of this is stupid and will inevitably lead to heartbreak, injury and death. Definitely, definitely, definitely don't try to usurp the throne of a small Scandinavian kingdom. As you've seen, it only ends in tragedy.

I do have some ideas for a sequel to *Tooth and Blade*. If the series takes off, I'll definitely pursue them. If you'd like to read it, please shout about the books to anybody who'll listen. Sign up for my newsletter if you want to be kept up to date.

I hope you'll join me for the journey.
Julian

Blog: jbarrauthor.com
Twitter: @jbarrauthor
Facebook: facebook.com/jbarrauthor

P.S. If you enjoyed *Tooth and Blade*, you might get a thrill from my epic fantasy trilogy based on Greek mythology, *Ashes of Olympus*. Read on for a preview of Book One in the series, *The Way Home...*

BONUS PREVIEW: THE WAY HOME

"A sharp, action-packed novel based on ancient myth." –
Tansy Rayner Roberts

> *The gods betray you.*
> *The winds are hunting.*
> *Nowhere is safe.*
> *The journey begins...*

The war of the gods has left Aeneas's country in flames.
Though he is little more than a youth, Aeneas must gather
the survivors and lead them to a new homeland across the
roaring waves. Confronted by twisted prophecies, Aeneas
faces the wrath of the immortals to find his own path.

First in a trilogy based on Virgil's epic poetry, *Ashes of
Olympus: The Way Home* is a tale of love and vengeance in an
age of bronze swords and ox-hide shields.

Available as an e-book and paperback. Read on for a
preview of the first chapters...

1

———

"AENEAS, for the love of the gods, open up!" cried Sergestos, pounding on the front door.

Aeneas ran to the door and wrenched it open. "Stop yelling, would you? My father will flay me if you wake him." He stopped short as he realized Sergestos's round face was covered in soot and reeked of smoke. The scholar wore a studded baldric over his tunic. "What's happened?"

"It's the Greeks, they're here."

Aeneas swore. "Let me get my gear. I'll be at the main gate in—"

Sergestos shook his head. "Aeneas, they're *here*. Inside the walls."

Aeneas staggered. The sea god had built the walls himself. They stood over forty cubits tall. No mortal power could break them.

"What? How can that be? They sailed home yesterday."

Sergestos shrugged. "Something to do with that horse. Point is, half the city's in flames."

Aeneas rushed upstairs to see for himself and Sergestos followed.

Fire.

All his life Aeneas had loved to look down upon the city, to gaze at the twinkling lanterns in the streets. Now thatched rooftops were alight, the flames glaring like eyes in the night. The fire was spreading from the outer city, where the peasants lived. The screaming echoed heavenward. He blinked sweat out of his eyes, straining to peer past the flames. Far off, the city gate gaped like an open wound. Column after column of Greek warriors passed through, hungry to pillage the defenseless Troy. They were making a beeline toward the palace, marching up the main road. The bronze of their helmets and armor glistened in the burning.

What in Hades was going on? Somebody should have rung the warning bell. This wasn't a battle. It was defeat, the end of everything. The thought twisted in his belly like a knife.

"Daddy?" Little Julos waddled out of his bedchamber at the foot of the stair, rubbing his eyes. His curls were tousled with sleep.

"Hey, little man," said Aeneas. "Where's Mummy?"

"I'm here," said Kreusa. "Has something happened?" She emerged from the bedchamber opposite Julos's, tying her hair back with one hand. Looking up, she saw the embers spiraling into the sky. "The city," she breathed.

Sergestos swallowed. "Gods help us, our training never prepared us for this. Troy has fallen."

Aeneas shook his head and jutted his jaw. "Not yet. Not if we save the king."

Sergestos glanced from Kreusa to Aeneas. "Right. See you shortly, then." He clapped Aeneas on the shoulder and bolted down the stairs past Julos and out the door.

Tightening her lips, Kreusa beckoned Aeneas downstairs and into their bedchamber. "Julos, wait in your bedchamber, please. I won't be long."

"But I'm—"

"It'll be fine, son," said Aeneas.

Kreusa passed Aeneas his sword belt, her hands steady.

He buckled it to his side, put on his leather jerkin. Aeneas glanced up at his polished helmet and breastplate mounted on the wall. Father had given them to him for his eighteenth birthday last year. No self-respecting warrior would go into a fight without full armor, but there was no time.

Father gave a snore from down the hall.

"I'll get him up," Kreusa said, reading Aeneas's mind. Julos padded into their bedchamber, slurping on his fingers and she scooped him into her arms. "Go on. We'll be fine." Kreusa looked him in the eye, resolute.

Aeneas had always loved Kreusa for her ability to take charge, right from their betrothal day. He reached for her and Julos.

Kreusa kissed him once, hard, on the mouth. Then she pushed him away gently. "There'll be time later. You need to go," she whispered. "Please, love. Just go. And if you run into enemy gods, stay out of their way." Kreusa turned, but it didn't hide the tear streaking down her cheek. She swept out of the chamber, holding their son tight. Julos peeked over her shoulder at Aeneas, eyes wide and green as his father's.

Aeneas stared after them for a moment, then shook himself. Kreusa was right, he'd wasted enough time already. He snatched up his gear on his way out, found the weight of his spear a familiar comfort. The leathery smell of his ox-hide shield reassured him it was ready to protect.

Taking a deep breath, he passed over his doorstep.

2

Aeneas tasted smoke upon the air and the fumes made his eyes water. He might as well have stepped into the flames of the Underworld. The fire was around the corner, the crackles edging ever closer. Even from a few blocks away he could hear the sound of marching footsteps. A child standing by Aeneas's house shrieked for his mother, a blanket tucked under his arm. An old woman clutching a bucket brushed past the boy and slopped water onto the cobblestones. People fled down the street with what they could carry. Sergestos stood fidgeting at the foot of the steps, the long plait that ran down his back swaying as he looked left and right. The scholar had already drawn his sword.

"Let's go," said Aeneas. He set off at a brisk pace up the street.

Sergestos jogged to keep up. "Slow down, Aeneas. I don't have long warrior legs like—"

They both froze, seeing a glint of bronze from the alleyway ahead. Aeneas tensed as he heard a soft laugh.

An armored figure swaggered from the darkness, his plumed helmet nodding. In his hand he held a wine sack.

Two warriors weaved out behind him, unsteady on their feet. One was a giant, the other slight. Their skin was pale, like that of all invaders from the western lands and they wore identical cloaks of blue. The strangers' round shields were painted with the image of a wild boar and Aeneas recognized it as a sigil from one of the Greek kingdoms.

The commoners in the street shrieked and scattered.

The commander of the Greeks leered. "Evening, young masters. This your street?" He spoke the enemy's liquid tongue, known to all peoples of the Middle Sea. He took a nip of wine and grinned at Aeneas. "Is your woman home? We'd love to pay her a visit." The Greek dropped the wine sack and red spilled over the cobblestones. His hand drifted toward his blade.

Aeneas didn't hesitate. He raised his spear, aimed and threw.

The drunkard raised his shield an instant too late. The spear tip lodged in his throat and the man crashed to the ground.

One Greek down, two remained.

Aeneas whirled to find the larger of the Greeks held Sergestos by the throat. Sergestos squirmed like a fish in a net, his face turning purple. The Greek's sword flashed as he raised it.

Aeneas tightened his grip on his sword hilt. "Hey, you!"

The big Greek's head snapped around and he dropped Sergestos.

Aeneas's sword hissed from its sheath. They stared at each other for a moment and then the Greek slashed at Aeneas with a snarl.

Aeneas deflected the blow with his shield, kept his eyes locked on those of his foe.

The Greek snorted and raised his blade above his head,

ready to cleave Aeneas in two. Seeing the opening, Aeneas struck. The tip of his blade darted in and out through a gap in the man's plate armor. Shock splashed across the Greek's face and then disbelief. He toppled forward, drew a last shuddering breath and collapsed on the cobbles.

The shorter one still lingered in the alleyway. He was a cadet no older than fifteen, barely old enough to have received the marriage torch. The youth held Aeneas's gaze for an instant, desperation reflected in his eyes. Then he turned and disappeared down the alleyway. No point chasing him.

Aeneas wiped his sword on his tunic and sheathed it, then pulled his spear from the first Greek's throat. He walked over to Sergestos, offered him a hand up.

Sergestos clambered to his feet, but his eyes remained fixed on the heavens. "Evening's first wanderer shines bright tonight. But so too does the red wanderer. Odd, I wouldn't have expected to see either through the smoke."

Aeneas raised an eyebrow. "Did you hit your head?"

Sergestos shook himself. "No. Well, yes. But I'm fine. Just..." He grimaced, glanced over at the bodies. "They wandered off from the main group?"

"I guess."

A shrewd expression fell upon Sergestos's face. He bent and started undoing the clasps on the Greek captain's cloak and then put it on himself. "What do you think? Do I look like a Greek?"

It wasn't a bad idea at all. But still...

"It's hardly honorable."

Sergestos gave a shaky laugh. "Is there any honor to be had tonight?" He plucked up the shield, testing its unfamiliar weight.

"Fair point." Aeneas swallowed, then crouched to undo

the clasps on the big Greek's cloak. He remembered Kreusa's warning. *"But if you sight enemy gods, keep your distance."*

"Got it. Let's keep moving."

A few Trojans were heading in the same direction, but nobody went near them as they passed through the streets. They might as well have been shadows.

The sound of footsteps marching in time came from around the corner. The soldiers wore crimson cloaks and their shields bore the sigil of a blood-red mountain lion. Aeneas's eyes widened. These were no drunken brawlers. This was a company of the Red Capes of Epiros. Sergestos made to pull back into the shadows.

Aeneas grabbed him by the shoulder. "Forget it, they've already spotted us. Anyway, we're Greeks, remember?"

At the head of the column marched a man wearing a Greek diadem. He gripped an axe in one hand and a burning torch in the other. Maybe it was a trick of the flickering light, but Aeneas thought there was something snakelike about his face. The king of Epiros looked as though he had been fed nothing but poisonous herbs all his life. Spikes of orange hair erupted all over his head.

A chill passed over Aeneas as the Epirote gave him a sidelong look.

"What are you staring at?" hissed the warlord and he glanced at the sigil on Aeneas's shield. "You're meant to be at the palace already. Ithakan sluggards." And he moved on without a second glance, heading uphill toward the palace. His troops followed, row after row marching.

Aeneas released the breath he didn't realize he'd been holding. "Back streets. Through the marketplace."

"Definitely."

They were about two blocks from the palace when the sharp smell of pinewood filled his nostrils.

In the dim light, Aeneas could just see the outline of the great wooden horse standing in the empty marketplace. It towered over them, a crude likeness. He exchanged a dark look with Sergestos. The Greek lords had clasped hands with King Priam just yesterday morning and the rulers exchanged gifts as tokens of good faith. Priam had given each of the Greek warlords dishes of gold and silver. The king of Ithaka had left this. A monument, he'd said, to honor the fallen. Aeneas edged closer, for he'd not had the chance to look at it properly. He stared upward, lip curling. On the underside of the horse, an open hatch swayed upon hinges carefully concealed. A rope ladder dangled. Within the beast Aeneas saw only darkness.

So that was how the mongrels had gotten in.

The hiss of arrows filled the air. Aeneas pulled Sergestos into a crouch. He raised his shield and Sergestos copied. Thud after thud came as arrows lodged in the layers of ox-hide and pinged from the shield's iron boss. Shafts splintered on the pavement.

Who was shooting at them? Aeneas risked a quick peek over the bronze rim of his shield, spotted Trojan archers on the temple rooftop against the orange mist. He ducked just in time to avoid losing an eye.

Sergestos leaned over to Aeneas, a skull-like grin plastered across his face. "Worst idea we've ever had?"

"Yeah and that's saying something. Any ideas?"

"Wait for them to run out of arrows?"

Aeneas gave a hollow laugh.

Sergestos's smile died on his lips. He pointed over Aeneas's shoulder, pale and quivering.

The god leaped down from the rooftop behind them. Ares had no skin; perhaps an immortal warrior had no need of it. He was all iron and sinew. His bare chest rippled and ropey crimson muscles pulsated. The man-shaped beast wore a cloak of tattered hides. In his paws he wielded a sword of sapphire flame. A war helmet masked his face, everything but the eyes. Sergestos quailed under his red glare.

Aeneas choked back a sob. Ares fought for the Trojans. He must have come to finish the work the bowmen had started.

He squeezed his eyes shut and thought of Kreusa and Julos.

Want to know what happens next?
The Way Home is available via the online store of your choice!

ACKNOWLEDGMENTS

Thanks go to friend and fellow author Chris Spensley for supporting my writing career and this story in particular right from day one. Mark Stay of the *Bestseller Experiment* provided useful notes and constant encouragement at all stages of the project. Thanks as ever to the BXP Team for their constant advice and enthusiasm. Many thanks to Matt Wolf for letting me pick his brain about Norse mythology and for designing such an exquisite cover for little more than a heartfelt thank-you. Yvette Hunt created some amazing illustrations to promote the project. And without Kelly, Noah and Tristan, none of this would be possible.